# The Surrender
# of Lady Jane

# The Surrender of Lady Jane

## MARISSA DAY

HEAT | NEW YORK

THE BERKLEY PUBLISHING GROUP
Published by the Penguin Group
Penguin Group (USA) Inc.
375 Hudson Street, New York, New York 10014, USA
Penguin Group (Canada), 90 Eglinton Avenue East, Suite 700, Toronto, Ontario M4P 2Y3, Canada
(a division of Pearson Penguin Canada Inc.)
Penguin Books Ltd., 80 Strand, London WC2R 0RL, England
Penguin Group Ireland, 25 St. Stephen's Green, Dublin 2, Ireland (a division of Penguin Books Ltd.)
Penguin Group (Australia), 250 Camberwell Road, Camberwell, Victoria 3124, Australia
(a division of Pearson Australia Group Pty. Ltd.)
Penguin Books India Pvt. Ltd., 11 Community Centre, Panchsheel Park, New Delhi—110 017, India
Penguin Group (NZ), 67 Apollo Drive, Rosedale, Auckland 0632, New Zealand
(a division of Pearson New Zealand Ltd.)
Penguin Books (South Africa) (Pty.) Ltd., 24 Sturdee Avenue, Rosebank, Johannesburg 2196,
South Africa

Penguin Books Ltd., Registered Offices: 80 Strand, London WC2R 0RL, England

This book is an original publication of The Berkley Publishing Group.

This is a work of fiction. Names, characters, places, and incidents either are the product of the author's imagination or are used fictitiously, and any resemblance to actual persons, living or dead, business establishments, events, or locales is entirely coincidental. The publisher does not have any control over and does not assume any responsibility for author or third-party websites or their content.

PRINTING HISTORY
Heat trade paperback edition / July 2011

Library of Congress Cataloging-in-Publication Data

Day, Marissa.
    The surrender of Lady Jane / Marissa Day. — Heat trade paperback ed.
        p. cm.
    ISBN 978-0-425-24125-7
    1. Magic—Fiction. I. Title.
    PS3576.E77S87 2011
    813'.6—dc22          2010039272

# One

*I'm here, Jane.* The urgent male voice sent a hot shiver of long-ing down Lady Jane's spine. *I'm waiting.*

Jane was dreaming. She knew she was dreaming, and in the dream she opened her eyes.

As she had every night for the past three weeks, Jane found herself standing in a dark corridor carpeted with deep plush. Some nights she had been clad in only a white silk robe. Some nights she was dressed in a fantastic concoction of velvet like a medieval lady. Tonight, she was dressed for dancing in pale blue silk with three tiers of silver lace and rosettes. She felt the weight of plumes decorating her hair. But what truly mattered was the voice. Calling to her. Longing for her.

*I'm here, Jane.*

Jane began to run.

Doors flashed past her shoulders. Hints of movement caught at the corners of her eyes, but she did not stop. *He* was waiting, and she must find him.

Breathless and flushed, she stopped before one of the identical closed doors, knowing, in the way of dreams, that it was the right one. She laid her gloved hand upon the surface, anticipation quickening her pulse. This was where the dream would change and become new. The only thing that would be the same after this was the waiting man, and the feelings he aroused in her.

Jane opened the door.

Warm candlelight filled a chamber as spacious as any royal apartment. The room was an oriental fantasy furnished with all manner of velvet couches and lounges, some big enough to accommodate four or five people at once. Silken hangings adorned the walls and green velvet draperies hid the windows.

A man stood in the center of the room. Like her, he was dressed for dancing. Tight, white knee breeches encased his muscled legs and he wore a gray silk waistcoat embroidered with silver over a spotless white linen shirt. His coat was a shimmering emerald green with more silver at the cuffs and throat.

But the beauty of his attire was nothing when compared with the beauty of the man. He was not too tall, only topping Jane by six inches or so. He wore his blond hair long and tied back in a sailor's queue. Neither was he too broad, but built in good proportion. Everything about his form spoke of active living. His face was magnificent, with high cheekbones and a strong jawline. Jane's breath caught in her throat as she met his bright green eyes. They slanted dramatically but were saved from being too feminine by his heavy brows.

"Sweet Jane." He opened his arms. "You are very welcome here."

Jane ran at once into her dream lover's embrace. His mouth fastened on hers in a strong kiss. His tongue pressed against her lips and she opened eagerly, ready for the strange, sweet sensation of his tongue stroking hers while his hands caressed her shoulders and her back, gliding down to the curve of her derriere, around her hips and up again to brush the sides of her breasts. Jane shivered and felt him smile against her mouth.

"Are you glad to be here, Jane?" he whispered as he drew his lips along the curve of her jaw.

"Very." She sighed. His mouth brushed her throat, as if seeking to learn its every line while his strong, capable hands caressed her waist and the curve of her belly through the layers of silk and muslin that clad her. For all he was a compactly formed man, he enfolded her completely in his embrace in a way her late husband never had. She liked that. She was no petite miss and had no wish to be treated as if she might break. Her mother had more than once despaired over Jane's curves, which were of the sort much more suited to pannier skirts and cinched waists than this time of high-waisted gowns and minimal foundation garments. But her dream lover appreciated the whole of her body. As he claimed her mouth again, he took her derriere in both hands.

"Such a beautiful ass," he murmured as he squeezed and kneaded, clearly relishing the softness of her flesh. He pressed her even closer to him, until her breasts rubbed his chest and her belly circled the ridge of his erection. Jane groaned with pleasure and tilted her hips against him. He smiled and took her hand, kissing the palm.

"Do you feel that?" He laid her hand against the outline of

his cock, drawing her palm up and down its length. "This is yours. This is what you do to me."

"I want you," she whispered hoarsely. "I want to give myself to you."

"Do you?" He smiled mischievously and leaned in to graze her lower lip with his teeth. "How would you give yourself to me?" He released her hand, turning her as he spoke, until he stood behind her, one strong arm wrapped around her waist to pin her against his hips. His cock was so hard and so strong that she could feel it pressing between the halves of her ass, despite the layers of her skirts and petticoats. His other hand closed possessively over her breast, making her gasp. "What would you do when you give yourself to me?"

She meant to answer, but he began to plump and pet her breast, and Jane found she could do nothing but groan. His fingers found her pebbled nipple and rolled it. It felt delicious and wicked, and all she could think was how much better these caresses would be without the barrier of their clothing between them.

"Tell me what you would do, Jane." His breath was hot against her ear, his body a wall behind her. She had no strength. He supported her entirely.

"I would lay myself bare for you. I would open my thighs . . ."

"These thighs?" Without ceasing to play with her breast, he ran his other hand down her hip, his fingers knotting into the fabric of her skirt. "These luscious, smooth thighs?" He drew her skirt up as he lovingly spoke each word. Cold air touched the heated skin of her legs, sending fresh shivers rippling through her.

"Yes," she said. "The whole of my body would be yours."

"Would you touch yourself for me?" Now his hand traveled up the soft skin of her thigh, caressing her, slowly, possessively, almost reaching her straining center, but not quite. "Would you let me see how beautiful you are when you play with your breasts and this sweet pussy?" He cupped his hot palm over her damp curls and she sighed with relief and pleasure. "Would you do that for me?"

"Whatever you would want."

"And if I should want to play games of desire?" His mouth was on her shoulder now, kissing soft, sensual trails down her bared skin. "If I should wish to hold you helpless to our pleasure while I worked my will upon you?" Skilled and infinitely wicked, his fingers played with her folds, sending flashes of desire through her body.

"Yes, anything."

"Anything, as long as I do not stop," He laughed, but he did not stop. He stroked her and cupped her. His knowing fingers found her damp slit and pressed into it, and she writhed with delight. He caressed and massaged her breasts roughly even while his arm made sure she remained tight against the length of his body so the halves of her ass rubbed hard against his cock.

"Yes, please." She did not think on what she said. She only thought of his hand on her breast and his fingers in her slit, for he had found the hot and swollen center of her pleasure and was rubbing it in earnest now.

"Such a sensitive little clit. So eager to be pleased," he crooned and the fire in her roared higher. Jane felt her whole self begin to slip away into the glorious current of pleasure.

"That's it, Jane. Come for me. I want you to come for me."

"I want you!"

"You shall have me soon, but you must obey your lover, and come for me now."

He thrust his fingers deeply into her, pressing hard, stroking fast until the sensation of that decadent friction became too much to contain. Pleasure broke from her in long, simmering pulses, rocking her buttocks against his cock and wringing wordless cries from her.

"That's it, Jane. That is so very good." His breath hitched in his throat as he cradled her body, made limp by the force of her satisfied desire. "Every moment brings you closer to me, my beautiful Jane. Soon I will hold you in truth, and then you will have all that you desire."

And he was gone.

Jane woke with a start, the aftermath of pleasure still coursing through her veins. But the essential vitality had vanished along with the dream and now she felt deflated. Jane lay curled in a truckle bed with a lumpy straw mattress, at the feet of her new and profoundly pregnant mistress, Her Royal Highness, Princess Victorie of Saxe-Coburg-Saalfeld, now Duchess of Kent, and wife of Prince Edward, Duke of Kent and Strathern. The sounds of the sea rippled through the open window along with the salt breeze. Slow hooves thudded on the dirt lane and a bird twittered tentatively. Calais was beginning to wake.

Sweet Jane was as far gone as her dream lover, and she was only Lady Jane DeWitte once more. Biting her lip against a groan of fatigue and disappointment, Jane curled her knees tighter to her chest. How much longer could these sweet, torturous dreams continue? Each night of the journey across the Germanies and France, her nameless lover had called to her in her sleep. Each night, his urgent voice had led her to a scene of sensuous luxury. There, his words and intoxicating caresses sent her hurtling over the crest of pleasure. But each time when she woke, she was only restless and bereft.

Because despite all she had been given, Jane wanted more. During the daytime, as the carriages bumped over the country roads, she had found plenty of time to imagine what that "more" might involve. She had yet to see her dream lover naked, had yet to bare herself fully to him. They had not performed the marital act. Widowed as she was, Jane was familiar with the feeling of a man inside her. But Lord Octavius had never touched her as her dream lover did. She had never before been aware there existed such a dizzying height where she could ride delicious waves of feeling. Surely, having her dream lover inside her would be similarly intense. That idea regularly robbed her of her breath, until she had to reach for her violet water to calm herself.

Women dreamt of men. Jane knew that. As a girl on the threshold of marriage, she'd often dreamt of being held, and being touched. But to have such dreams occupy so much of her waking thought now that she was full grown and much more experienced was ridiculous. No, it was insupportable, and possibly a sign she had somehow become unbalanced.

But even that did not frighten her as much as the possibility that this new plaguing restlessness of her body might drive her to risk her reputation and position by entering into a liaison with a man.

Tomorrow, the ducal party would all board the royal yacht to return to London for the birth of the child her mistress carried. That child might one day wear the crown of England. To have secured a place in the household of the royal family was no small feat for a woman without family or money. To have one in the household of the heir presumptive was nothing short of miraculous. Jane could not do anything to jeopardize her standing.

*The dreams will eventually end.* Jane knotted her fists in the inn's stiff bedsheet. *I will simply have to bear it until they do.* Jane squeezed her eyes shut, shuddering against the sense of loss that accompanied the thought.

*Mad.* The word whispered itself in her mind. *I am going mad.*

# Two

"Jane! My dear Jane!"

A familiar and very welcome voice cut through the glitter and elegance of Lady Darnley's ball. Jane turned to see Georgiana Martins—who had lately become Lady Hibbert-Jones—make her way through the crush of London's finest, all invited to welcome the Duke of Kent home.

"Georgiana! How good to see you!" Jane stretched out her hand, deeply relieved. The ducal party had only arrived in London that afternoon. Her maid, Tilly, had not even finished unpacking the trunks, and yet the duchess had insisted Jane be here.

"You are to pay particular attention to what the ladies say," the duchess had told her earnestly. "I know the prince regent would rather we had stayed in Saxe-Coburg. It is vital to know if the lords of England think the same. Their ladies can tell us that."

So, here Jane was, turned out in her finest ice blue satin with its gold netting and scallops. She smiled and made small talk, and was ready to fall asleep on her feet. She reached out to Georgiana as she would to a lifeline.

"You're looking very well," said Jane to her friend as they clasped hands. Georgiana's second marriage evidently agreed with her. Her brown eyes sparkled with good humor and she carried herself with pride and energy. Her gray gown, trimmed with freshwater pearls and ivory rosettes, set off her black hair very well.

"But you, my dear, look positively exhausted." Georgiana tucked her arm in Jane's and steered her closer to the wall and the blessed breeze allowed by the open French doors. "Tell me, was the journey very tedious?"

"The weather was awful." Jane flapped her fan and peered over its edge to locate the Duke of Kent. Plain-faced, portly, flushed with wine and exertion, he stood with a group of exquisitely tailored men who all laughed heartily at some bon mot. He appeared to be in a better humor than he had been upon their arrival at Kensington House. As soon as they'd walked in, he'd pronounced the place "dim and pokey, be-gahd!" This despite its silk-covered walls, painted ceilings and many beautiful windows.

"The duke insisted on driving the duchess the entire distance to Calais himself, in an open landau of all things," Jane murmured to Georgie. "It was . . . most difficult."

"And how does our new duchess?"

Jane thought on her mistress sitting in her wing-back chair behind the great curve of her belly. Much younger than her husband, the new Duchess of Kent was plump and sturdy rather than pretty. The journey of more than four hundred miles in the seventh month of her pregnancy had worn on her but had not damped her spirits in the least. She'd a ready answer for the duke as he barged about the parlor, complaining of Lord Darnley holding a welcome ball the very night of their arrival.

"Lord Darnley could not have foreseen the delay in our crossing," the duchess reminded him firmly in her idiosyncratic mixture of German and French. "Otherwise I'm sure he would have moved the date. But his lordship has done so much for us, we must not neglect what he does in our honor."

"If I tell you anything of the duchess, Georgiana, I am relying on you to spread the word," said Jane seriously. "It is the only subject anyone wishes to converse on, and I am worn out repeating myself."

"Jane!" Georgie hid her mock astonishment behind her ostrich plume fan. "What sort of gossipmonger do you take me for?"

"One of the best I know."

Georgiana stared at her for a moment of genuine astonishment and then laughed heartily. Jane joined in. It felt so good to relax with a friend after spending so many months abroad and alone, not to mention spending so many nights teased and plagued by her wicked dreams.

*Don't think on those right now.* Her mind had been wandering too much as it was. If she should start dwelling on imagined pleasures, she would quickly become useless.

"Of course I'll tell everyone whatever you like," Georgiana was saying. "They'll all be asking me anyway."

"And I need to hear all the news."

Georgiana eyed Jane shrewdly. "You do, or your patrons do?"

"Georgie . . ."

"All right, all right, I won't press. But I will tell you, Jane, it's going to be hard going. The regent wants nothing to do with either of them. Any of them."

"Yes, we'd heard." In fact, the prince regent had refused to advance a single penny to help his brother return to England. The duke, who was perpetually in debt, had been obliged to turn to friends to raise the needed cash, Lord Darnley among them. Jane opened and closed her fan restlessly, eyeing the glittering crowd. It was impossible not to notice how many gentlemen, and ladies, stood talking confidently to each other as their eyes sought out the various members of the ducal party; his highness, his private secretary Captain Conroy, herself.

"But the prince regent . . . can be persuaded, can't he? He has proved willing to change his mind on other matters." This in particular was a point the duchess asked her to sound out. The Prince of Wales could be as changeable as the spring weather, especially when he sensed the opportunity for love or money.

Georgiana paused as she considered her words. "All the little birds tell me the regent complains the Duke of Kent is claiming too much privilege too soon. After all, his child is not yet born, much less been declared heir apparent. He says he is insulted. I suspect much of this springs from his feelings over the death of the Princess Charlotte."

The reminder of that tragedy silenced them both for a moment. Jane had met the princess a few times, and formed a good impression. Compared to her luxury-loving father, the lone child of the Prince and Princess of Wales had seemed remarkably sensible. But Princess Charlotte had been both married and buried two years since, and her stillborn son with her.

Jane fingered her fan for a moment. She did not want to ask her next question. Her interest was purely mercenary, and it shamed her. "At the risk of sounding terribly indelicate, what is the state of . . ."

"Hymen's War Triumphant?"

"Georgiana!"

"Tush, Jane! It's only what the papers are all calling it. Truly, it is shocking." Georgiana sighed, and her bright manner faded to expose the sharp and observant woman underneath. "Twelve princes and princesses, who among them have brought forth near fifty children, but not one both alive and legitimate." She rolled her eyes heavenward looking for explanations. "The regent still hopes he might sire another legitimate child, but that will require a new, legitimate wife. My husband says parliament is not in the mood to grant a divorce, no matter how many Italians our Princess Caroline is caught with. Of course, any potential Princess of Wales will have to be willing to overlook the fact that the regent is already married to Mrs. Fitzherbert and is carrying on with Lady . . . let me see, I think it's Lady Jersey this week." She tapped her fan against her palm. "So that's the first in line. Second, the Duchess of York is past childbearing. This leaves the closest competition for your patrons as the Duke of Clarence and his new duchess."

"Have you seen her yet?" Jane asked.

"I have. I don't speak German so well as you, but she seems to me both healthy and pleasant. The greatest shock is that she and the Duke of Clarence appear devoted to one another. I would be most surprised if there was not an announcement from that quarter shortly."

Jane's fingers closed a little too tightly around her fan. The Duke of Kent lived beyond his means. Everyone knew it. If parliament could not be persuaded to extend him an additional income as father to England's heir, there might have to be accommodations made. The first of these would be the dismissal of some members of the household. At which point, Jane would find herself with nowhere to go.

"Perhaps that's for the best," murmured Jane, struggling for disinterest. "It cannot be a good thing for the future of the nation to rest on a single unborn child."

"I'm sure you're right." Georgiana's face and voice both hardened. "Look at us. We spend our days talking of fripperies and scandal. In the meantime, there are riots in the streets and the king runs mad. His sons think of nothing but how to get their hands on the public purse strings, his daughters have been made into a flock of nuns, and none of us knows what is coming next. Is it a wonder we dance all night? If we stopped to think, we would drop dead of terror."

Hearing the anger and the warning in her friend's voice, Jane laid a hand on Georgiana's arm. "I'm sorry, Georgie, I'm not good company right now and I'm spoiling your night."

"You are the best of company, Jane." Georgiana patted her hand. "You are only tired from your travels." They smiled, each understanding the other saw past their politesse, but each silently agreeing it would be best to move back to conversation more proper for a ballroom.

Just then, movement caught Jane's eye.

"Oh, no," Georgiana muttered. "It is our *dear* Mrs. Fortesque."
A woman with a square jaw and square brow overshadowed by a forest of dyed ostrich plumes strode straight toward them through the crowd. Claret crepe encased thin shoulders and an improbably full bosom.

"I'll distract her, Jane, you make your escape." Without waiting for Jane's answer, Georgiana fixed on a brilliant smile and sailed directly into Mrs. Fortesque's path. "Agnes! I was so hoping I'd find you here!"

Jane did not wait to hear what Mrs. Fortesque replied. She slid out the nearest French door onto the balcony and dodged sideways where she would not be immediately visible from either door or window. The fresh night air that enfolded her was chill, but exceedingly welcome. Jane closed her eyes and raised her chin, relishing the cool breeze as it swept across her skin, and tried not to wish herself elsewhere.

The dinner had been excellent. The music was delightful. The whole of fashionable London, dressed in their finest, swarmed a ballroom hung with French blue, said to be the prince regent's current favorite color. This was diplomatic of Lady Darnley, Jane thought. In a pinch, either of the Darnleys could argue they had chosen the color to remind the royal duke where their ultimate loyalties lay.

And this was only the beginning. Hyman's War Triumphant, indeed. Should the Duke of Kent's babe be born whole and healthy, the nobility would begin jockeying for position in earnest, and Jane as the Duchess's attendant and presumed confidant would be hauled into the thick of it, whether she wanted to be there or not.

Jane sighed and forced her eyes open. The gorgeously illuminated formal gardens spread out beyond the balcony. Couples strolled to and fro, enjoying the evening. As she watched, melancholy dug its claws into her. No such activity awaited her this night or any other. She was the eyes and ears of the duchess of Kent, and she was the sole survivor of a family that had fallen up to its hips in debt. Love and desire were nothing but the stuff of dreams for Lady Jane, and she must find a way to make her peace with that.

"A pleasant night, is it not?" inquired a man's deep voice.

Jane straightened at once, snapping open her fan to cover the shock on her face. She glanced wildly about, but saw no one.

"Down here, and I am sorry if I startled you."

Cautiously, Jane advanced to the balcony's carved stone rail. There, she looked down onto the shadowed figure of her dream lover.

# Three

He was little more than a silhouette, half in and half out of the balcony shadow, but after so many nights of intimate imaginings, Jane recognized him instantly. The man who stood below her like Romeo in an amateur theatrical was *her* man, her lover from her dreams.

She must have gone stark white, for he frowned and moved more fully into the candlelight that spilled over from the ballroom.

"I hope, madame, I have done nothing to offend. If I have, I assure you, it was in no way deliberate."

"Oh, no, sir, indeed you have not." Jane fluttered her fan and grasped desperately for her manners. The weak denial was clearly not enough to convince him. He frowned and trotted up the broad marble steps, moving with both grace and lightness of foot.

"Come, come, ma'am, you are in some distress. Do let me offer my assistance."

If any doubt had existed in Jane's mind as to the connection between this man and her dream lover, it was removed as soon as he reached the top step. Light from the windows fell across bright golden hair pulled back from finely sculpted features and tied in a black ribbon. But it was his eyes that removed all trace of doubt. She could now see them plainly, and they shone as green and compelling as they had in all her dreams.

He was fashionably dressed in a forest green coat embroidered dramatically in black. Similar black work decorated his fawn waistcoat. His breeches and stockings were pure white, and tight enough that she could clearly see the powerful line of his muscled legs.

*"Do you feel that?" He pressed her hand against the outline of his cock, drawing her palm up and down its length. "This is yours. This is what you do to me."*

"May I at least fetch you a glass of punch? Or escort you inside?" He held out his arm politely, but Jane's gaze drifted to his hands.

*His hands, so hard and strong, playing at her breasts, rolling and toying with her tight nipples, stroking her stomach, lifting her skirts to caress her thighs . . .*

The man lowered his arm, genuine consternation creasing his wide, pale forehead. "Perhaps you will permit me to introduce myself?" he suggested. "Sir Thomas Lynne, and I am quite at your service." He bowed, very correct and formal. Seeing this, Jane found at least some of her polite reflexes still functioned, and she bobbed a curtsey.

"Lady Jane DeWitte, and I do beg your pardon, Sir Thomas. I had thought I was alone."

Sir Thomas smiled and Jane's heart thudded against her ribs. Her breasts strained against the confines of her narrowly cut ball gown, as if reaching for his touch. *How would you give yourself to me, Jane?* his heated voice whispered from memory.

"Your servant, Lady Jane." Sir Thomas bowed once more. "May I join you?"

*No, no! I won't be able to bear it if you come closer.* Because if he came closer she would feel the warmth of him, and be able to see his eyes even more clearly.

*Collect yourself, Jane!* "Certainly, Sir Thomas." She made herself gesture toward one of the balcony's marble benches. "Shall we sit?"

He bowed again. "Thank you, ma'am."

Jane's knees felt weak as water. It took all her concentration to adjust her train so she could settle at the absolute end of the bench. She thought Sir Thomas would come sit down at once, but he stayed where he was, one foot on the balcony, one foot on the stair, watching her carefully. Jane snapped her fan open. She was too warm, despite the chill in the air. The strength of Sir Thomas's curious regard, combined with her too-vivid memories, brought out the heat of her blood.

"At the risk of being impertinent, Lady Jane," he said, tilting his head thoughtfully toward her. "I must ask; why do you look at me as if I frightened you?"

"I do no such thing."

"You do," Sir Thomas replied, meeting her eyes. "You are doing it now."

Jane's gaze darted to the crowded ballroom. But if she went back inside, she would have to face the flock of gossips. They would all see how flustered she was, and she would be very much remarked on. The only other escape from this balcony was the staircase at Sir Thomas's back. Jane imagined fleeing into the gardens, out the gates and into the streets, to somehow make her way back to Kensington House before it could be learned she had gone as mad as the king. The whole time, Sir Thomas kept a polite distance with his hands folded behind him, prepared, it seemed, to wait as long as necessary for her answer. Ragged clouds passed across the moon overhead. Candlelight, music and talk drifted out of the ballroom at her back, reminding Jane she was part of an ordinary gathering on an ordinary evening. Suddenly, she felt quite ashamed of her fancies. But what could she say to him? She fluttered her fan, trying to think of the most polite lie. Nothing came to her, however, and she found herself left with only the truth.

"I . . . I dare not tell you my reasons, sir," Jane dropped her gaze and folded her fan. "You will think I've entirely lost my wits."

"I will think nothing of the kind. Please, Lady Jane," Sir Thomas added softly. *Tell me what you would do, Jane . . .*

It was impossible. She could muster no defense against this man who was the very image of her secret desires.

"I . . . I have been dreaming of you." Jane trembled as she spoke the words. Now he would go and she would not have to look into those green eyes anymore to remember all the promises of her wicked dreams. Now he would go, and she would never see him again.

"You dream of me?" His dark and heavy brows arched.

"Every night these past three weeks."

Sir Thomas made no immediate reply. His face remained calm, as if they discussed nothing more important than the weather. "Are you sure these dreams are not just of a man with green eyes?" he asked. "They are unusual, I admit . . ."

Whatever else he might be, this Sir Thomas was gallant. His words offered her the chance to pass the whole of the conversation with some pleasantry so their talk could turn to less alarming subjects. But then she would forever wonder what would have happened had she found the courage to speak. In her heart, she understood that an eternity of not knowing would be far worse than any fear she might face here and now.

"No," she said. "Not just a man with green eyes. You."

Sir Thomas nodded. For a long moment he gazed out across the illuminated gardens. Jane sneaked a glance at his profile. His face was pale as if sculpted from marble, and as perfectly formed as man's could be. Yet he was no idle dandy, for under his perfectly cut coat his body was hard and muscled. Her hands itched to touch his shoulders, to caress the planes of that chest so well-clad in silk and linen. She knew her fingers to be clever. She could make quick work of laces and buttons and push that cloth aside and . . .

He turned toward her, one brow arched. A blush blossomed across Jane's cheeks. He saw. He knew she had been staring. For the first time, Sir Thomas's impeccable manners slipped ever so slightly and a smile that was both knowing and delightful spread across his elegant features. "And may I be so bold as to inquire what, besides myself, occupies these dreams?"

*Pleasure, pleasure from your hands, your body, your devilish words . . .* Jane's blush deepened.

"I see," Sir Thomas murmured.

"Please." Jane opened her fan once more and applied it in a futile attempt to cool her burning cheeks. "Let us say no more about it."

"We could do that," he agreed. "If you wanted."

A fresh shiver shot down Jane's back. "What do you mean?"

"I mean, do you want to say no more? Do you want me to go?" He gestured toward the stairs. "Or would you rather I stayed?"

Jane found herself quite unable to breathe. She thought about the violet water in her reticule. She thought about the retiring room, the gardens, the refreshment room, anywhere she might get away from this man. But she didn't move. "I could not say," she whispered.

"I think you could. What is more, if this were one of your dreams, I think you would." Sir Thomas lowered himself onto the bench beside her, still keeping a polite distance. He could not accidentally touch her from there. It would have to be deliberate. He would have to reach out his gloved hand, lace his fingers between hers, guide her hand where he wished it to be, where she wished it to be.

"But this is not a dream," she reminded him, and herself. *For if this were one of my dreams, I would kiss you here and now. I would beg you to hold me and to touch me in any way that pleased you. I would thrill to hear your voice urging me to bare myself for you.*

"No, it is the real world, and we walk in it, you and I." His green eyes seemed darker now, and unfathomably deep. She could drown in those eyes. "So think carefully of what you say next. Send me away, and I will make my bow and go. But be aware, it is your choice."

The finality in his words tore at her thoughts. He meant it. If he went now, she would never see him again, in daylight or dreaming. Jane felt weak, as if all the blood had drained from her heart.

There was no one to guide her, and no safe answer to give. There was only him, and her, and she could not trust either one. "What choice would you make?" Jane murmured.

"I?" Sir Thomas said, as if surprised she would ask so simple a question. "I would choose to remain with you. I would especially choose to hear more about these dreams in which I am so prominent a figure."

Jane knew she should end this madness and tell this bold man to leave her alone. She was not the usual widow, free to kick up her heels as she chose. She had no money, no land, nothing except the income from her position. Her entire inheritance, including her widow's portion, had gone to pay her father's debts. If her reputation did not remain spotless, she risked her living.

At the same time, it seemed unbearable that Sir Thomas should go.

"Madame?" Sir Thomas whispered, his voice tender and filled with concern. "Lady Jane?"

"Please stay." The words came out as a tremulous whisper. She meant them with all her heart, but her heart was still afraid.

Slowly, Sir Thomas reached across the distance between them and took her hand. His touch was as soft as his voice, and yet she could feel the warmth of him through the layers of their silken gloves. She looked into his astonishing green eyes and her heart constricted at what she saw; a quiet pleasure that mixed with a dark intensity. She knew that look from her dreams. It was desire.

"Thank you." Without taking his gaze from hers, Sir Thomas bent and touched his lips to her fingers. Jane clamped her mouth closed around a sigh.

"Now, Lady Jane," he lifted his head. A subtle change came over his manner, lending him an air of command that had so far been lacking. "Let us speak of these dreams."

Jane would not have believed she had any blushes left. But Sir Thomas's gaze lingered on her cheeks, letting her know she colored crimson once more, and he smiled. The expression brought a dangerous and breathtaking light to his eyes.

"Would I be right in thinking they are dreams of love?" he murmured.

*His fingers thrust into her slit, stroking her, demanding she surrender to the pleasure he brought. His cock pressed hard and rigid against her ass while she writhed and cried out . . .*

She dropped her gaze to her fan. Jane had no real experience with flirtation. She did not know how to speak of love to a man, much less to hint at the kinds of desires her dreams had brought. She had been married young to Lord Octavius De-Witte, at her father's urging. Octavius was a steady man, but he had not wanted a companion for his heart. She was to be housekeeper and hostess, and provide an heir if that could be managed. During the five years of their marriage, he praised her competence and level-headed management of the house. He'd given her anything she asked for, but never teased her, much less tempted.

Fingers traced feather soft down her cheek. Sir Thomas's touch was as instantly familiar as his person had been. It ignited sparks against her skin and sent them tumbling down to her breasts, her thighs and her tightening center.

"You are so beautiful," he whispered. "Any man seeing you would dream of love."

"But you are not the one who dreams, sir." The words emerged in a low and husky voice, quite unlike her own.

Sir Thomas let his fingertips linger a moment on her jawline. "And yet, Lady Jane, you do not tell me I am too bold."

Tell him he was too bold? Impossible. It was all Jane could do not to lean into his hand and rub her cheek against his warm palm. The cool night wind carried his scent to her, a mixture of leather, brandy and spices that worked its way into her blood and her brain, wreaking havoc upon what little reason remained to her.

"It is impossible." Tears pricked her eyes as she took his hand and lifted it away.

"No, it is not." His fingers curled around hers, preventing her from pulling her hand back.

"I have a position to maintain, sir. I am not free as others are." It was monstrously unfair. The whole court was at liberty. The wealthy widows—the wealthy *wives*—flaunted entire trains of lovers in every public setting. But depleted of money and family, utterly dependent on the good opinion of her mistress, Jane was condemned to remain as alone as any unmarried girl.

Sir Thomas pressed her hand gently, urging her to look at him. But Jane knew if she did, she would be utterly and finally lost. She kept her gaze fixed on the gardens and the winking torches that burned so brightly in the distance. The sound of women's laughter reached her and she winced to hear it.

"Listen to me, Jane." Sir Thomas pressed her hand once more. "If I have but one thing from you, all others will become possible."

"What might that be?" She'd meant those to be bitter, jesting words, but they sounded only of despair.

"Give me your assent," said Sir Thomas calmly. "Say yes, and I will be with you this night, and any other time you desire me."

She stared at him. He met her gaze and returned it, completely unperturbed.

"It is impossible," she repeated.

That only brought a smile from him. "More impossible than that you should dream of me before we ever met? More impossible than that you should desire the companionship of a stranger, even now?" She must have looked startled again because he nodded slowly, never taking his gaze from hers. "Yes, I know your feelings, Jane, because they are mine as well."

Her eyes, traitors to all propriety, traveled down to where their hands were clasped, tracing his form along the way. His breeches were tight, his coat was open, and she could clearly see the straining outline of his hard cock. She remembered her hand pressed against his erection. She remembered all the longing she'd felt to strip away the clothing from between them, to see him fully naked beneath her hands.

To touch him, to take him inside her.

"Say yes, Jane," Sir Thomas whispered. "And we will both have what we want so very much."

A slow pulsing began deep in her center, and she knew it

came from seeing his cock swollen for her, from holding his hand and from receiving the lightest of his touches. She would never have believed it possible to feel so much from so little, but there was no escaping this pure, intense desire that made her breasts swell and softened her pussy.

Alone at night, woken from her dreams to her cold, narrow bed, she had wept in her frustration at being denied. Now Sir Thomas offered her all she had ached and agonized for.

"What is your answer, Jane?" Sir Thomas asked.

"Yes," she said. "My answer is yes."

Sir Thomas let out a long, slow breath. He turned her hand over and kissed her palm, and she felt his tongue, quick and light, touch the silk. This time she closed her eyes. This time she sighed.

"Be patient but a little longer." Sir Thomas set her hand down against her thigh. His fingertips brushed her skirts softly as he stood to make his bow. "I promise, I will be with you again soon."

Jane could not move. She could not breathe. He saw her paralysis, and in return offered another of his breathtaking smiles. A fresh flash of desire shot straight to the core of her. Then, Sir Thomas turned and made his way slowly back down the balcony stairs, vanishing into the shadows.

# Four

Thomas Lynne sat back on the plush seat of his recently hired carriage and considered Lady Jane Markham DeWitte.

He'd glimpsed her at a distance months ago and been struck at once by her appearance. But that glimpse and the half-reality of dream and glamour had left him unprepared for her true beauty. Lady Jane was a magnificent creature. Old enough to be possessed of character, but young enough to be merry, she had a lovely face and a pair of sparkling brown eyes. Her gown of ice blue silk had draped across her form beautifully, showing her luscious curves to advantage. His cock pulsed at the memory of those curves; so soft and yet so strong. It had been all he could do not to reach for her breast as they sat together, to caress and play with it in the way he knew she liked. She would moan sweetly and throw her head back, begging for his touch with her whole body.

And he would give it to her. He would give her all she desired and so much more. In the dreams, she had been intoxicatingly responsive to his touch. How much finer would she be when they were at last together in the flesh?

His cock was stone hard now. Thomas cursed mildly, adjusting himself in an attempt to find a more comfortable position. He considered undoing his breeches and seeking a more active relief, but decided against it. He had only this single errand. After that, he would be able to call Jane to him, and sink his cock into her silken heat. Any discomfort he felt now would only enhance the pleasure of that moment.

Sir Thomas grinned out at the passing city. He stroked his cock slowly, but only once, a promise to himself of the delights to come.

The rain had begun again, a steady, drenching April shower that could very well keep on for all the next day. The carriage turned a corner and passed through an arch in a high brick wall that marked the entrance to Hyde Park. Instead of elegant houses and shops, the carriage now traveled a lane flanked by rolling meadows and ancient trees. One corner of this green expanse in the middle of sooty London had been carved out to make the grounds for Kensington House, the palace that held his lovely Jane securely behind walls of stone and cold iron gates. But Hyde Park itself held far more surprising things. If those who served England's royal family had known of them, they surely would have housed their hoped-for heir much farther away.

"Stop here!" Thomas thumped his cane on the top of the carriage.

The driver, who had been hired with the carriage, drew in

the reins to halt the healthy but dispirited horses. Donning his high hat and pulling the brim low, Sir Thomas climbed out onto the sodden gravel roadbed.

"Sir!" protested the man. "It's pouring!"

"And because it is, you may take the carriage directly home," Thomas told him. "I shall follow in my own time."

The man ogled Thomas in the light of the carriage lantern. For a moment, he plainly thought to protest. As he was being paid extra to be discreet, however, he shut his wide mouth. He wagged his head hard enough to shake his double chin, but he also touched up the horses and drove on.

Alone, Sir Thomas set off through the rain, whistling as cheerfully as if he strolled through a pleasant summer's afternoon. He carried no lantern, but the dark did not trouble him and his stride remained long and sure. An observer would have noted with surprise that despite the soaking ground, no mud spattered his gleaming hessian boots, his well-tailored overcoat or his perfect white knee breeches. No rain touched the sleeves of his great coat, or the brim of his hat.

Still whistling, Thomas made his way to a thick grove of oaks at the edge of the greensward. Once he stepped beneath the trees, the rain ceased. Here, the ground was perfectly dry. Fern and bluebells wafted their rich fragrance into warm and pleasant air. In the distance—much farther than might have been suggested by the size of the grove from the outside—burned a preternaturally clear and steady light. This light had nothing in common with mere daylight or ordinary flames. This was the silver of the full moon that somehow also granted the clarity of a summer morning.

Sir Thomas removed his hat. The silver light fell against his face like a caress.

"Welcome, my most loyal Sir Thomas Lynne! Come forward!" The voice was lovely beyond comprehension. Warm, rich and merry, it was nothing less than the sound of love. It went straight to the blood and the heart, opening both wide to the desire to hear the voice's owner speak again.

Thomas could now make out an opening between the ancient trees before him. It had not been there an eye-blink ago, and yet somehow it had always been there.

Sir Thomas bowed his head and stepped into the presence of the Queen of the Fae.

Outside, the cold English spring might lurk, but beneath the queen's silver light, perfect summer reigned. Roses bloomed in scarlet profusion and ivy twined the trunks of thorn and oak trees. Slender girls clad in simple Grecian tunics lounged on the emerald grass with their arms twined about each other and bare legs stretched out. They nibbled the fresh fruits from the wooden platters that lay between them. They might have been simple pastoral maidens of the sort seen in classical paintings, unless one dared to look at their eyes. Not one of the maidens had human eyes. Instead they were golden with slit pupils like cats, or round and solid black like birds. The human eyes belonged to the knights standing guard around the edges of the clearing. Each man had been selected for the perfection of his body, which were all on display. They wore nothing with their golden breastplates and helms except leather loincloths. But the silver tips of their spears were wickedly sharp, and Thomas knew from experience that all of them were deadly fighters. He should, for he had trained them.

In the center of this gathering Her Glorious Majesty, Tatiana, Queen of the Seelie Fae, sat on a throne of gold and starlight and smiled radiantly as Sir Thomas knelt at her feet.

Tonight, the queen had chosen to appear as a mature and voluptuous woman. Her golden hair tumbled freely about smooth shoulders clad in a delicate fabric that was both sparkling green and quite translucent. If he dared to glance up, Thomas could see all her abundant curves, the tight buds of her nipples and the dark triangle between her rounded thighs. His cock, already hard with thoughts of Jane, stiffened unbearably tight. It was an act of will to remain where he was, but Thomas held still none-theless. No matter how she displayed her changeable beauty, Her Glorious Majesty expected her knights to remain civilized and gallant until she commanded otherwise. If he gave way to this maddening desire even slightly, he would face his queen's disapproval.

"My true knight." Smiling, the queen leaned forward and touched Thomas's shoulder in blessing and welcome. "Tell me, is there news?"

"There is, Your Majesty." Thomas could not keep the trace of pride from his voice. "I have met Jane DeWitte and gained her assent to an assignation in the flesh."

"Excellent." The queen's hand cupped his chin, lifting it until he looked into her unearthly eyes of silver and violet. "But then it is only as I expected. What mortal woman could resist you, Thomas?"

"My queen flatters me," Thomas murmured. As he gazed into the queen's eyes, wonder took hold of him. He could see clearly all her beauty and her power. She was the center of all things here. Even the warm light of the grove flowed entirely from her. As the light cradled him, she cradled him, warming his skin and blood with her caress. She was all love, all desire. There was nothing in the world he needed so much as to be in her presence.

The queen's laugh rang through the grove and she broke her gaze, leaving Thomas suddenly bereft.

"Come, Sir Thomas, and sit beside me," Queen Tatiana commanded lightly. She clapped her white hands and two of her nymphs scampered to fetch a wooden chair for him. Thomas bowed as he stood and took the seat as best he was able, for his straining member did not permit for easy movement. The queen's sparkling gaze caressed his erection, but she only smiled as if it were a shared joke between them.

"So, Thomas," she said. "Is the hook well baited?"

"I would take an oath on it, Majesty. Lady Jane DeWitte's a bold wench, for all her downcast eyes and aloof manners. The dreams I have sent her have thoroughly roused her, even more so than I would have initially thought." Memory of Jane's blushes touched him, and Thomas felt himself smile. He had enjoyed their little flirtation. Seeing her yield to a woman's natural desire for love and warmth had been an unanticipated delight. He was looking forward to bringing her many others.

"You must not linger over your task, however pleasant you may find it," said the queen. Thomas bowed his head, startled and ashamed to find his thoughts had wandered. The queen's gaze touched his erection once more. Thomas fought to hold his tongue. He could not offer himself to her, however much he wanted to. It was for her majesty to choose when and how he would serve, and she had other uses for him tonight. "We have very little time left to us to put paid to the prophecy."

The prophecy. As the queen spoke those two words, a fresh wind laden with frost stirred in the summer grove, and the ones gathered there—both Fae and human—shivered.

Generations ago, the druids of Britain had sought after the hidden wisdom of the world. In this quest, they accidentally opened the gates to the realm of the Fae, and the Fae had poured through into the mortal realms. Tatiana had been queen of the day then, as well as the night. But then, Arthur rose from the ranks of men, and his mortal queen Guinevere with him. Both had sacrificed much for their power and knowledge, she even more than he, and together, the upstarts had driven back the armies of Oberon and Tatiana, allowing their Sorcerer Merlin to shut the gates the druids had opened.

Those gates did not close entirely, however. In time, another Fae army had forced its way through. It was Queen Elizabeth and her Sorcerer John Dee who beat back that second invasion.

Determined not to risk another defeat, Queen Tatiana had sought the wisdom of powers older and more terrible than she. Alone, she ventured to the daemon realms. In exchange for a price of blood and treasure, the daemons worked their own foul magics to grant her a prophecy. That prophecy warned that a third queen would arise from among the Britons. If allowed to ascend the throne, this third queen would chain the gate to fairyland shut forever. But if her rise could be prevented, the Isle of the Britons would stand defenseless, and the Fae might again claim its rich, green lands.

Armed with this knowledge, the queen determined that, this

time, the Fae should move by stealth. Instead of gathering an army, she patiently slipped her servants through the cracks between the worlds in ones and twos. Once established in the mortal realms, the Fae agents set about to two tasks. The first was to recruit human magic workers to their cause. The second was to spoil as much as they could the ruling family of Britain.

At the latter, they had succeeded beyond their wildest hopes. The old king was now both blind and mad. Jealousy and fear had driven him to lock up his daughters. As for his sons, a more foolish pack of mortal men did not exist. Each one of them had been induced to fall for the charms of women they could not or would not marry, and their indulgences had left the royal pricks scarcely able to even twitch for the women to which they did become legally espoused. The one daughter of the house who had lived to adulthood lay dead along with her stillborn child. As matters stood, the only legitimate child of the House of Hanover grew within the belly of the Duchess of Kent.

Queen Tatiana needed to know if the child was male or female. She needed to know what move to make next, and for that she needed access to Kensington House, which, like all the royal residences, was guarded with barriers of human magic and the deadly cold iron. It was to breech those wardings that Thomas had been sent to seduce one of the princess's waiting women.

"I live only to serve my queen." Thomas laid his hand over his heart. "All will be done as speedily as I can contrive."

"Good." The sharp edge of the Fae queen's gaze slid across Thomas's perception and he nearly winced with the pain of it. But in the next heartbeat, his queen smiled and all was unclouded summer again. "After all," she said merrily, "you would not wish me to think you preferred this lady's company over mine."

"Impossible, Majesty!" Thomas cried. "She is pleasant, I'll grant you. Teaching her the arts of love will be no hardship, but there is none I esteem above you, nor could there ever be."

"I do know it, my Thomas." Queen Tatiana reached out and ruffled his hair as if he was nothing more than a stripling boy. For a moment, Thomas's pride stung. She had often enjoyed his manhood, why did she feel the need to treat him so?

"Tumble the lady thoroughly." She laughed and her eyes sparkled so that Thomas forgot his fleeting discomfort. "Teach her all she is able to learn of pleasure. But one of my servants must be able to gain free entry to the house before the next full moon." The winter frost crept back into her regard. "That is all that matters."

"I swear, Majesty," said Sir Thomas evenly. "It will be done."

The queen gazed deeply into the eyes of her servant, and smiled.

# Five

Thankfully, the strains of his recent journey caused the Duke of Kent to leave Lord Darnley's house at the relatively early hour of one o'clock in the morning. Although fairly weighed down by exhaustion, Jane reported to her mistress's chamber. There she was informed by her attendant Frau Seibold that the duchess had retired and now slept soundly. Grateful beyond words, Jane crept to her adjoining room. Her maid, Tilly, waited there to help her off with her gown. As soon as they'd gotten Jane into her night attire, Jane dismissed Tilly to her own bed in the servant's quarters. She did not want any company tonight, or any witness to . . . to whatever might happen next. Assuming that anything did happen.

But as soon as Tilly bid her good-night and closed the door, Jane began berating herself. What a fool she was! How on earth could she expect Sir Thomas to be able to arrange an assignation for them? Even if he could somehow get a message to her before the morning, she could not leave the house. He must know that.

He had been playing with her, building upon her fantasies, thinking of ways to take advantage of this loose and unstable woman. And she had let him.

Although these thoughts ran riot through her, Jane made no move toward her narrow bed. Her mind might not believe what Sir Thomas said was possible, but her body did. Clad in night-dress, cap and dressing gown, her fire banked for the night, Jane's skin prickled from the room's chill. Her blood, however, burned hot from the memory of Sir Thomas's eyes upon her. Any attempt at sleep now would be useless. Besides, what if she did sleep? She would only dream again, and the desires those dreams raised would be worse than the regrets and uncertainties that tormented her now.

Jane rested her fingers on the windowsill and looked out at the night beyond her pale reflection. The sky was dark with clouds and rain pattered steadily against the roof and window-pane, muting all other sounds. The great house slept. Rain and dark blocked out any view of the gardens, let alone the wall or the gate. Jane felt as if she had already fallen into a dream where no one and nothing existed beyond her small room.

Jane laid her brow against the cold glass. *I must get over this,* she told herself. *I must forget this. Forget him.* She closed her eyes and drew in a long, shuddering breath.

*Jane.*

Jane's head snapped up.

*Jane.*

It was Sir Thomas's voice. She heard it plainly, just as she had in all her dreams. For a moment, Jane wondered if she was doz-ing. But no. She could feel the chill in the air distinctly, as well as the grain of painted wood under her hand. Scents of candle wax, smoke and perfume lingered from the day. Frau Seibold's inelegant snores reverberated through the connecting door.

*You can come to me now, Jane.*

Jane's heart fluttered against her ribs. This could not be happening, and yet she yearned with all her being that it might be. She remembered the light in Sir Thomas's brilliant green eyes as he bent to kiss her fingers, and her palm. She remembered the fire and passion of her dreams, of his hands caressing and possessing her body, and his hot, demanding mouth . . .

Jane steeled her nerves. She took her cap from her head and slid it under her pillow. Her heavy braid hung down to the small of her back. She considered loosening it to let her curls tumble free, but that would take time, and she felt certain time was short.

She held a taper to the remaining coals of her fire and used it to light a small oil lamp, turning down the wick until it barely flickered. The door hinges were well tended and made no noise as Jane slipped into the long corridor. Her unsteady lamp light fell faintly against the scarlet carpet and gold-trimmed doorways. Jane hesitated. In which direction should she go? It was one thing to imagine one heard a lover's call in one's mind. It was quite another to go chasing after it.

*This way, Jane.*

The words filled her with instinctive certainty. Jane started down the corridor toward the back stairs. She did not run. She wanted to, desperately. She had run in each of her dreams. But, as she reminded herself with each step, this was not a dream. If any other person came upon her roaming about in the dark, she would have enough to explain without being caught racing down the hallway like a giddy girl. So, she put one slippered foot decorously in front of the other in ladylike steps with her head erect, but eyes modestly lowered, holding her hems out of the way in her free hand so she could move with the dignity to which she had been trained.

The journey through the darkened palace took so long that her patience strained against her resolve. Indeed, it felt as if she passed through too many chambers. Some she recognized, like the princess Sophia's sitting room, or the cupola room with its great clock. Others, though, seemed strange and vague, as if they were stage sets rather than real places. Jane tried not to think about it. If she thought, she might stop before she reached her destination, and she did not want to stop. She told herself the palace was huge, and she had not even been in residence a full day yet. That was surely the reason it felt so large and strange.

At last, Jane came to a side corridor she had not previously noticed. Four doors were set in its walls, two on each side. Golden light slipped from under the farthest left-hand door. Jane's breath hitched in her throat, and she stepped into the corridor. It seemed the air stirred as she moved forward, bringing the scents of rain and growing things.

The left-hand door was unpainted wood, simply carved. Its gilded knob had been worked into the shape of a summer rose. Jane heard no sound from within. In fact, she heard no sound at all beyond the pounding of her heart. She stood on the brink and she knew it. No matter how much or how little happened afterward, once she entered the room beyond this plain-seeming door, something fundamental would change. Now was her very last chance to turn back.

Jane raised her hand, and softly knocked.

"Come in, Jane," said Sir Thomas from the other side.

Her heart in her mouth, Jane pushed the door open and stepped across the threshold.

And caught her breath.

The chamber was like no guest room she had yet seen in Kensington House. Her slippered feet sank into plush Turkish carpets. Figured emerald silk covered the walls and green velvet drapes fringed with silver covered the windows, muffling sound and rendering the light from the many candelabras lush and cool with reflected color. The room was mostly furnished with sofas and chaise longues of various heights and widths, just as the chamber in her dreams had been. Against the back wall, however, waited a massive bed, canopied and curtained in more splendid summer green. Elsewhere, deep pillows covered with damask and velvet had been scattered about. A black and gold Japanned sideboard and matching massive wardrobe flanked the bed.

In the middle of all this opulence stood Sir Thomas. He still wore the emerald coat he had on at the ball, but he had discarded his cravat and collar so that his white shirt hung invitingly open. A blush crept into Jane's cheeks as she became acutely aware of her nightdress.

"Welcome, Jane." Sir Thomas came forward and caught up her free hand. He bowed deeply as he kissed it. His mouth was soft and warm against the delicate skin on the back of her hand, and Jane found herself wishing he would never stop.

"I was afraid you might not come." He straightened to look into her eyes, but he did not release her hand. "That was foolish of me. I should have trusted you more."

Jane found she had difficulty drawing breath. Her blush deepened, and the heat from it seemed to flow directly to her fingertips clasped in his strong hand.

"But what is this?" she managed to say, gesturing about the decadently furnished room with her lamp.

"Ah, Jane," Thomas took the lamp from her and set it on a small mahogany table. "Let us for the moment say this is our place." Holding both her hands, Sir Thomas led her deeper into the chamber. "Here, you and I may meet without interference, or interruption. Please, sit." He lowered her onto one of the sofas. It was in the Grecian style, backless with curved arms at either end, made more for reclining than sitting upright.

"And this all came to be by magic, I suppose?" Jane joked to cover her uncertainty. "You are a fairy prince come to steal me away underhill for a hundred years?"

"And if I was?" Without looking away, Thomas raised her hand to his mouth once more and rubbed her fingertips against his sensuous lips. That small, bold caress robbed Jane of what little breath she had remaining, and her eyelids felt suddenly heavy. She wanted nothing more than to lean back against the sofa's conveniently curved and comfortably cushioned arm while he caressed her in this way and any other his invention could devise.

Years of practice at maintaining appearances came to her aid and Jane stiffened her spine. "Then I should say my prayers like a pious Christian maiden, and banish you back to fairyland."

"Oh, that would be a most cruel fate." Sir Thomas turned her hand over, and with his thumb began to make slow circles against her palm. This new, intimate motion poured a wealth of feeling into Jane, destroying her ability to concentrate on anything except that small place where his skin moved restlessly and rhythmically against hers. "How shall I convince you as to my true nature?" He wondered aloud and slid his hand up hers, stroking his fingertips against the sensitive underside of her wrist. "Ah, I have it. Have you heard that the good neighbors, as they themselves prefer to be called, have no hearts?"

"I . . . believe I have heard something of the kind." It was so hard to keep her voice steady as he caressed her wrist and played with her fingers, delicately touching each one like a connoisseur examining a piece of fine porcelain.

"Well, then." Sir Thomas lifted Jane's hand to his open shirt, guiding it under the linen so that her palm pressed against the bare skin of his chest. "Do you feel my heart, Jane?"

She nodded. She felt the heat of his skin, the crisp curls of hair, the rise and fall of his breath, and, yes, his steady heartbeat. How she ached to move her hand, to explore the landscape of his body, but he held her firmly. Then, he lifted her hand from his chest, and instead pressed it against his cock.

"And do you feel this?" he whispered.

She did. She felt how hard and thick he was, and how maddeningly separated from her by his silk knee breeches. But touching him even this much caused a riot of sensation in the exact center of her physical being, and she turned soft and liquid there. Jane's mouth began to water and she hardly knew why. Her breasts seemed to swell even while her stomach had clenched tight.

"I am no Fae, Jane." Thomas moved her palm up and down. "I am a man who wants to please you."

Jane abandoned resistance and closed her eyes, the better to concentrate on the sensation of stroking him. He controlled her hand entirely, but he guided her so she could feel the shape of his balls, his shaft, his blunt tip. The combination of freedom and restraint thrilled her in some unaccountable way and Jane groaned.

Thomas leaned close so his lips brushed her ear, but he kept her hand in place against his cock. His breath on her cheek and throat smelled of brandy and spices and she breathed deep. "Jane, I want to stretch you out beneath me where I can watch the whole of you as I work upon you with hands and mouth and cock. I want to hear you scream with delight and beg for more. And if you cannot hold yourself still to learn all I have to teach you, I will tie you down until you gain the discipline you need to obey me as master of your body's pleasure."

Although she felt she could scarcely draw breath, Jane made herself say, "I am to be a servant then? A light wench you may bid to come and go whenever you please?"

"Oh, you will come at my bidding." She could feel his grin as his mouth moved lightly down her throat to her shoulder. His teeth grazed the skin there and she shivered. "And I shall teach you all the ways that bidding is to be done. As for the rest . . ." He pulled away suddenly and Jane's eyes flew open. He was smiling at her, his expression a combination of mischief and desire that shot straight to her heart. "Say rather that I am your good teacher, and like any master of art brought to instruct a young lady, I expect attention and obedience."

"Shall you prove a very strict tutor?" She could not believe she was falling in so easily with his heated flirtation. Like his firm and controlling hold on her wrist, it touched some previously unimagined part of her, adding a savor to this sensual scene and deepening the fire in her veins.

"That very much depends on how unruly my pupil proves to be. If she is good and tractable, she will find herself amply rewarded." Thomas's fingers caressed her throat, and moved down to the top of her breasts. Jane's nipples tightened abruptly. "But I do warn you, Jane." His green eyes darkened and he laid his finger against her lips. "I will be a stern taskmaster in the matter of your pleasure, and I will not countenance argument. When I say to do a thing, it is to be done. Disobedience will be punished. Do you understand?"

"Yes." It felt good to move her lips against his finger. Jane found herself seized by a number of thoughts, all of them wicked, all of them weakening her, softening her, opening her further to her need and his oh-so-evident desire.

"Tell me what you are thinking, Jane."

Her first instinct was to shake her head, for she could not possibly confess to such indecency as filled her mind at that moment. But she pushed that aside. "I want your arms around me," she whispered. "I want my body, my . . . my breasts against you. I want your fingers in my mouth so I can suck on them, hard. I want to kiss you, I want you to kiss me. I want . . ." She hesitated.

"Say it."

"I want your cock. In my hands. Inside me."

"That is good, sweet Jane. Very good."

And all at once, she was in his arms, and he was kissing her. His tongue licked her lips sensuously, pressing at the seam of her mouth until she parted them so he could slip inside. His tongue slid along the edge of hers, a caress filled with heat and promise. It felt wonderful, and she opened to receive him more fully. She clung to him, wrapping her arms tight around his shoulders, and she writhed in his hard embrace to rub her aching breasts against his chest. In answer, Thomas laid her back against the plush, slanted arm of the sofa, without once breaking their deep kiss.

At last he lifted his mouth from hers. Jane gasped for breath and a tiny moan escaped her. Thomas swung himself about so he straddled the sofa. The spread of his legs displayed for her the outline of his magnificent erection. He lifted Jane's right leg and rested it against his powerfully muscled thigh to remove her slipper. Then, he ran his hand under the hem of her nightdress, up her bare calf, causing her to moan again. That only broadened his grin, and his hand rose higher, to the back of her knee, to her warm inner thigh. Unbidden, her hips strained upward.

"What do you want, Jane?" He stroked her thigh firmly. "You must say what you want."

"Higher," she croaked. "Please."

"Ah." He curled her leg around his hip, resting her heel at the split of his buttocks. "For that, Jane, you must give me something in return." He lifted her other leg and removed her other slipper. "Undo your ribbons. Show me your breasts."

With his touch gliding up her calf to her thigh, Jane found her hands had gone clumsy. She could barely find her bows and was ready to weep in frustration. Thomas did nothing to aid her, only continued his lazy, appreciative exploration of her legs. At last, she managed to undo the knots and pull the gathered fabric open, exposing the curving tops of her breasts to the candlelight and his gaze.

"All of them, Jane." He slid his heated palm up her inner thigh, almost to her drenched tangle of curls. Almost, but not quite. "Offer them to me."

Jane's hands trembled. She reached beneath the soft linen of her nightdress and slowly lifted out her right breast. The touch of her own hand against that so-sensitive flesh mixed with the heat of Thomas's gaze and the touch his hands and body between her legs. How would it be if she caressed herself, perhaps even fingered her own nipple? It would feel good, she knew it, especially with him watching her like he did now. But not as good as his knowing touch. She lifted out her other breast, and could not help but let her hand linger there. His eyes sparked when she did. He liked to see her touching herself. He'd said as much, and now she had proof of it. That knowledge added fuel to her inner fire.

She scooped her hands under her heavy breasts and lifted them up.

"Please," she said again.

"Oh yes," he breathed. "My good, sweet Jane."

With both hands he reached out and clasped her breasts firmly. He ran his thumbs across their burning tips, and smiled wickedly as she mewled. Slowly, agonizingly slowly, he bent forward and circled her aureole with just the tip of his tongue. Jane gasped and arched her back. In response, Thomas wrapped his lips around her pebbled nipple and sucked her deep into his hot mouth.

Dizzying pleasure washed through Jane. She sighed and moaned and struggled, her naked calves rubbing against his silk-clad hips. Her hips arched of their own accord, and she felt herself strain open. But Thomas seemed too busy pleasuring her breasts to notice. His mouth moved from one nipple to the other, as his hands plumped and squeezed mercilessly, maddeningly.

"Yes." She moaned. "Oh, Thomas, yes!"

"Ah-ah." He lifted his mouth from her breasts, leaving only his strong, blunt fingers to play with her, and that was nearly as maddening. "When we are like this, you must call me Master Thomas."

"Yes." She moaned again.

"Yes, what?" He pinched her left nipple and the startlingly sweet pain robbed her of the ability to speak.

"Yes, Master Thomas," she gasped finally.

"Very good, Jane." He squeezed her breasts tight together, kissing each nipple in turn. "So very, very good." He slid his mouth lower, planting hot, wet kisses on her ribs, licking the curve of her belly, moving lower, dragging the nightdress with him.

No, surely, he didn't mean to put his mouth . . .

As soon as she'd thought it, she felt his lips against her damp, sensitive folds. She cried out, startled, but he pressed his mouth more firmly against her, until Jane's surprise melted into fresh delight and she sighed. She felt him chuckle, and then she felt his tongue pressing into her slit. It was very strange. In fact, it tickled. Jane gasped and squirmed, laughing. But Thomas clasped her hips with both hands and held her firmly down. He began to lap and suck in earnest then, running his tongue up and down her slit, until he found the throbbing pearl that was the center of her pleasure; her clit, he had called it in the dreams. He pressed the tip of his tongue there, and searing delight tore through her. "Oh yes!" she cried, knotting her fingers in his hair. "Oh, Master! Yes!"

He was relentless. He held her hips tight as he tormented her clit with his hot, wicked tongue, then licked down again and plunged straight into her sheath. Jane wailed and strained against his hands trying desperately to urge him deeper.

But her lover, her tormentor, straightened up and she cried out in her disappointment. This only served to make him laugh.

"You want more, Jane, I take it?" he asked as he disentangled her from the nightdress entirely and cast it aside.

"Yes, yes," she panted. "More, please, more."

She moved to reach for him, but he pressed one hand flat against her mound of curls, and slipped one finger into her slit. He found her pearl, circled it with his finger. She couldn't speak. She could only feel, and it felt so good. Then, swiftly, his finger plunged into her sheath.

"So tight," he murmured. "How long has it been, Jane? How long has it been since you've had a cock in this hot, wet pussy?"

"Years." She moaned, and he slid a second finger inside her.

"My poor Jane. Alone in the dark with no one to care for your pleasure." His fingers began to thrust with a steady rhythm. "But it's good now, isn't it, Jane?"

"Oh, yes!" she cried as he thrust in.

He'd played with her thus before, in dreams, but those dreams created a mere shadow of the feelings that flooded her now. His mouth had primed her to pleasure. With each thrust of his fingers, her hips arched to grind against the hand holding her down. Her bare bottom caressed the plush sofa and her calves rubbed his silk-clad hips. So very many layers of sensation, all blending to a single glorious whole as his fingers glided in and out of her sheath.

"Harder!" She was beyond thought. There was only need. She felt as if something wild were trapped within her and it struggled to be free. Her hips bucked up into his hand, forcing his fingers deeper, for it was only his touch that would release this unbearable sensation inside her.

"So demanding." But he complied, thrusting deep into her, drawing out, and thrusting again. A third finger joined the other two, stretching her farther yet, and she moaned as he pressed so deeply his palm rubbed her folds. "So hot and hungry." His thumb dove into her slit, and found her sensitive nubbin once more. "And such an eager little clit." He pressed down and she cried out with the perfection of the feeling.

"You wanted it harder." His thumb rubbed her clit, sending raw fire through all her nerves as his fingers thrust again, and again. "Harder, you said. Harder."

"Yes," she cried, and the muscles of her sheath clamped down around his fingers. Even this felt nothing but good. "Oh yes, Master!"

"You're close now, Jane. Very close. I want you to beg me. I want you to say please."

"Please, yes, please."

"Please fuck me with your fingers," he instructed, his voice suddenly stern. "Please suck me hard."

"Yes. Yes. Please. Fuck me, Master Thomas. Suck me hard."

His mouth claimed her breast again. His tongue rolled and lapped at her nipple. His teeth nipped the very tip, even as he fingers pressed deep into her sheath once more.

A dam of emotion and sensation deep within Jane burst, allowing waves of burning pleasure to flood through her. Still, Thomas thrust his fingers into her. Still, he sucked and teased as her body, caught in the wild currents of delight, shuddered uncontrollably.

# Six

"There now." Thomas lifted his mouth from her breast and softly kissed Jane's lips. She could barely muster the strength to respond, but he did not seem to mind. His hand was still inside her, but his movements were much slower now, soothing rather than arousing.

"I didn't know," she whispered. Her strength was almost gone, but she managed to lift her fingers to touch Thomas's face and his beautiful mouth. "I didn't know," she said again.

"I understand, Jane." He smiled gently against her fingertips. "It pleases me immensely to know I am the only man who has made you come in this fashion." His fingers slipped from her sheath, which still pulsed with echoes of the intensive pleasure he'd given her. He drew his hand up her belly, leaving a trail of warm musk behind. Was it possible for her to feel more? But Thomas's warm, damp fingertips toyed with her nipple, circling the tip, and desire—slow, rich and infinitely pleasant—moved through her blood.

"And we haven't even . . ." She stopped, uncertain how far to go with this lovers game. "You didn't . . ." She looked at his breeches. Yes. He was still hard, and beautifully so.

"Why, you greedy little miss!" He sounded shocked, but she saw the burning mischief in his eyes. "Was all that not enough for you?"

She met his gaze and boldly shifted, arching her shoulders so her breasts pushed up toward him. "No, sir," she said. "It was not."

"Well, this time you must work for what you want." Thomas lifted her legs from around his hips, setting them on either side of the sofa so she sprawled lewdly open to his gaze. "I will not have you growing lazy."

Thomas leaned back against the sofa's curving arm and glowered at her. "You will undress me, Jane," he commanded. "And you will not stop until I am fully naked, no matter what I may do."

Jane pushed herself into a sitting position, and eyed Thomas. His pose was filled with masculine arrogance and the sense of mischief was entirely gone. She remembered what he said about obedience, and punishment. The tiniest wisp of nervousness crept into her mind.

"I gave you your instructions, Jane," Thomas growled. "I expect you to carry them out."

But Jane was a gentlewoman born and she rebelled at the idea of performing a servant's task. Even as she thought this, however, her gaze lingered on the undiminished ridge of his erection. The sight made her acutely aware of the emptiness of her sheath and of a fresh ache in her breasts that already longed for the resumption of his touch. There was only one way she could think to have what she wanted.

Jane dropped her gaze. "Yes, Master Thomas."

Grateful that she was familiar with the intricacies of male clothing, Jane decided to begin with his boots. She swung herself off the sofa and crouched at his right foot. Suddenly, absurdly, awkward in her nakedness, Jane's first idea was to strip Thomas of his garments as quickly as possible. The thought of him naked in front of her turned her bones to jelly, but the memory of how he had undone her with his hands and mouth gave her pause. Surely it was right she return some of that lingering, maddening pleasure. She ran her hands down the shining length of his hessian boot, savoring the smooth feel of the leather, and the strength of the leg it encased. As she did, Thomas reached out and stroked the top of her head, playing idly with the waving tresses that had come loose from her braid. It was distracting, and she was sure he meant it to be. After all, he had said "no matter what I do to you." That piece of her instructions had not been added for naught.

Her hands remembered the trick of how to grasp heel and toe and smoothly pull a tight-fitting boot off. She set it aside. She found the buttons and buckles on his knee breeches and undid them. Then, as slowly as she was able to force herself to go, she slipped her hands underneath the breeches leg to caress his calf and find the top of his silk stocking, which she drew slowly, carefully down. All the while his hand petted her head, but she sensed a restlessness in his touch, perhaps even a certain dawning urgency. Jane smiled.

Feeling daring, she stood. Thomas lifted his hand away and

looked up at her, eyebrows raised. She circled behind the sofa, drawing her fingers up his arm, and across his shoulders until she stood directly behind him. There, she undid the knot in the black ribbon that held his hair in its neat queue and pulled it free so his golden locks cascaded down and brushed his shoulders. She ran her fingers through his hair, delighting in the touch and scent of the silken strands before she glided around to his left side and set to work removing his other boot and stocking. He said nothing, made no move, just let her perform her task. This was oddly exciting, but definitely frustrating. She wanted more from him. She wanted a sign that her play pierced his facade of indifference.

A new idea came to her. Slowly, letting him see each move she made, Jane climbed up on the sofa and knelt between his thighs. She lifted his right arm, and brought his hand to her mouth, kissing his palm lingeringly, lapping quickly at it with the tip of her tongue, the maneuver he had taught her. Only then did she draw off his coat sleeve. He growled low in his throat, and the sound sent a bolt of heat shimmering down her spine.

She expected him to drop his hand then, but he instead clasped her breast firmly and Jane gasped. His eyes flashed with triumph as he began fondling and massaging. Jane sighed. She wanted nothing so much as to stop there, arching her back and closing her eyes to concentrate on his delightful attentions. But she had her instructions, and while she was sure his idea of punishment would prove . . . highly instructive, she felt it important that she prove to be an apt pupil for him now. Struggling to control her breathing and thoughts, Jane reached to draw Thomas's other arm free from his coat sleeve. He continued his heated, diverting attentions at her breast, toying with it as he had previously toyed with her hair. When she had removed his second sleeve, he leaned forward so she could draw the coat and waistcoat out from behind him, and so he could kiss her, deeply and warmly with his tongue teasing at her lips. He took hold of her other breast and rubbed his thumbs hard against her tight nipples. Pleasure swept away thought and Jane sighed into his open mouth.

Fortunately, what she desperately wanted to do then was also what she needed to do. She ran her hand along the taut, enticing length of his cock until she found the buttons on his fly and scrabbled to undo them. His hands, his tongue, were driving her frantic. She had to have him—naked before her, buried deep inside her, his cock thrusting hard and deep as his fingers had. All control gone, she shoved her hands into his open fly, grabbing fistfuls of linen to yank his shirttails free.

"Ah-ah, Jane." Sir Thomas pulled back, one of his large hands clamping around both her wrists. She stared at him, panting, unable to understand for a moment what was happening. He was so hot, so hard. She was ready. She was drenched, open, desperate. She could think of nothing but her need. Didn't he want her?

"You are doing so well, but I will not have you giving in to impatience." He clamped his other hand around her wrists. He was so strong, so overpowering. "Do you feel this?" He wrapped both her hands around his hot shaft. The touch of him, so hard and yet so velvet soft, drew a moan from her throat. He moved her hands on him again, stroking up and down with agonizing slowness. "I have been waiting a very long time to have this inside that sweet pussy of yours, and to feel you writhing underneath me while I drive into you. But I will not have this rushed, Jane. I will not forfeit one moment of the exquisite pleasure your body affords me. Do you understand?"

She wanted to move her hands faster, but he would not permit it. Slowly, slowly, he moved her up and down. Her breasts burned, her breath came in gasps. Her pussy strained open and clenched tight again, seeking him. She shifted, rubbing her thighs together, but this brought no relief.

"Do you understand, Jane?" Thomas demanded again.

"Yes," she managed to get the word out. "But oh, please . . . please . . ." She bit off the words and concentrated on her hands, on the heat of his most private and sensitive flesh, on how strong and vibrant he felt against her palms. With every ounce of self-control she possessed, she made herself move on him in the rhythm he set.

"That's better, Jane. Very good. Now, finish your task."

She ached. She burned. She was trembling in her need. But she loosened his cuffs and drew his shirt off. The sight of Thomas's chest, with its golden hair glinting in the candlelight, took her breath away. But he was not perfect. A white scar like a burst star puckered the flesh of his right shoulder. Another, long and jagged, stretched beneath his ribs. But she barely spared these a glance. Her attention was fully taken by his cock. Powerfully and magnificently erect against his flat belly, it was something to drive her mad, but she did not let herself hesitate. She laid her hands on his hips. He lifted them for her, allowing her to pull his breeches down. She leaned forward to finish the task and remove them completely. As she did, her cheek brushed his erection and she had to moan again. But at last his legs were free and he sprawled fully naked on the sofa.

"Very good, Jane." Thomas smiled indolently as his eyes raked her over. She was sure he saw how she shook and how flushed her skin had grown, but this only made his eyes shine that much brighter. "You please me very much. But you were careless and inattentive in your duties earlier. For that, you shall kiss my cock."

Jane stared at him. She had heard of women putting their mouths to men's cocks, but never imagined herself doing such a thing. Certainly her husband had never asked such a thing of her. But now that the idea had been put before her she wanted very much to try it. Her tongue actually darted out and licked her lips.

She straddled the couch again and ran her hands up his thighs, around his hips, and underneath to grip his ass. She bent forward and inhaled his scent of sweat and musk. Not sure what to do, she touched her lips to his hot shaft. That light contact held a shocking intensity and she sighed as she ran her mouth up and down his length, seeking to explore both his cock and the new feelings this intimate, wicked kiss awoke in her blood. His heart beat underneath his skin, under her mouth, she could feel it. He was so hot, so strong. She licked his smooth, damp tip, tasting his salt. That too was good. She slid closer, rubbing her damp folds against the velvet sofa even as she tightened her fingers on his hard ass.

"Swallow it, Jane," he ordered. "Suck on it."

Yes. Yes. That was exactly what she wanted. Jane opened her mouth and took him inside. His shaft filled her mouth. She wanted this, wanted him inside her in all ways he could be.

"Ah!" Thomas's gasp lit a fresh fire in her. Power. She had power, to give him pleasure, to undo him as he undid her. And oh, he felt so good filling her mouth. She could lick him all she wished to now, running her tongue up and down, as his hands stroked her back and the sides of her breasts.

"That's it, Jane." He knotted his fingers into her hair. "Suck it hard!"

The blunt tip stroked the roof of her mouth and that felt unexpectedly delightful. She wanted more. She wanted him to fuck her mouth as his fingers had fucked her pussy. Of its own volition, her head began to move up and down, a rhythm that caused her tight, heavy breasts to swing and rocked her pussy against the plush sofa, bringing her fresh, searing pleasure as her folds stroked against the velvet. She wanted it faster, she wanted it harder. She dug her fingers into his ass, urging him forward, begging him with mouth and hands to give her all of him.

Then, with a wordless cry, he pushed her back, so she fell against the other arm of the sofa. She stared at him as he reared over her, his long, thick cock swollen and shining from her attentions.

"Oh, you greedy thing!" he gasped. "Shameless, greedy wanton!"

He was on top of her, sparing her none of his weight, but she wanted no sparing. His mouth fastened on hers and his tongue delved into her. She felt his cock press into her folds and she arched underneath him. He reared back, his hands planted against the sofa arm on either side of her head. He poised there, the tip of his cock resting against her entrance, his eyes staring into hers. She saw wildness and darkness, delight and sorrow all swirled together with a world of memories and emotion she could not understand. But all that was lost as he plunged into her so far she felt his tight balls against her folds.

Jane cried out in delight and relief. Finally, *finally.* He filled her absolutely, thrust into her mindlessly. All games were over and done. There was no control, no finesse. Her legs wrapped around his hips, pulling him tight. Her heels dug into his thighs. Jane distantly heard herself calling his name, urging him on, but in truth, she was intent only on the sensations of their fucking; of his cock in her sheath, of his thighs working between hers, his balls rubbing, pressing, grinding against her folds as he strained to reach deeper. She was weeping for the pleasure as she fought to clasp him inside her, hold him still at the point of his deepest thrust where the pleasure burned brightest.

"Come for me, Jane!" he roared. "Come now!"

"Ah!" Pleasure's burning waves engulfed her. Her hips bucked, utterly beyond her control. She wanted no control, no end to this moment. She was drowned, lost, and he was crying out again, thrusting faster and harder, and he was coming too, coming hard, calling her name as his release merged into hers, rolling them both deep into a tide of pure joy.

## Seven

Jane scarcely knew how she got back to her own room. Thomas bundled her into her nightdress and robe with so many teasing caresses that she begged for him to take her, just once more. He'd silenced her with a firm kiss.

"Soon, Jane." His mouth brushed her ear, imparting flashes of desire with each whispered word. "You will have me again soon."

With the heat of that promise singing in her veins, Jane stumbled through the sleeping house and to her own room. She cast her night robe over the back of a chair and crawled beneath the blankets. Her skin and hair were as damp as if she'd lain in the dew. She shivered from the early morning chill, but much more from what she had just done. She knew she needed to think about her actions. There were important considerations beyond the pleasure they had brought her. She had much to plan, and to decide, but she couldn't. She could only burrow under her covers and sleep.

\* \* \*

"Lady Jane? It's nine o'clock, madame."

Jane sat up, pushing wayward strands of hair out of her eyes and blinking hard. Tilly was opening the curtains to let the rain-washed sunlight sweep into the room.

Memories of Sir Thomas and of their wicked tryst flooded back to Jane. She remembered the passion and delight and all the wanton abandonment she'd experienced under his hands, but try as she might, she couldn't remember exactly where she had been, or how she had gotten from that other room to this.

*It was a dream.* Jane frowned. *It must have been just another dream.*

"It's a glorious morning, madame," announced Tilly as she picked up Jane's night robe and shook it out. "Cleared up a treat after all that rain. It'll be cold though. Perhaps the green muslin for today?"

"Green, yes," Jane murmured. The room had been hung with green. Thomas had worn a green coat. But it wasn't possible she'd met Sir Thomas here in Kensington House, much less done . . . all those things with a man in the flesh.

"Very good, madame." Tilly folded the robe across her arm. As she did, a scrap of black cloth fell out of the pocket and drifted to the floor. Jane reached for it reflexively, and a sudden dizziness washed over. It was a black ribbon. The black ribbon. The one she had removed from Sir Thomas's hair while she undressed him. Before she took his cock into her mouth at his command and sucked on it so hungrily.

*It was real.* Jane's hand closed around the ribbon. *It is real.*

"Where'd that come from?" Tilly frowned. "I'm sorry, madame. I thought the girl had tidied up in here."

"It's of no importance, Tilly." Jane said, forcing her gaze away from the ribbon. "The green muslin will do very nicely, thank you. I'll need my cream shawl as well, since you say it is cold, and the gloves that match. Also, please be sure my satin bonnet with the roses is brushed up. The duchess may have errands for me today."

"Very good, madame." Tilly bustled off to put away the night clothes and bring out the day apparel. Jane opened the cover of the book at her bedside, and slipped the ribbon inside.

As she sat in front of the dressing table with Tilly brushing her hair, Jane searched her face for any change. Surely the abandonment of every propriety to blatant sensuality must leave some outward sign. But no, that was still Jane Markham DeWitte in the mirror. Jane of the undistinguished brown eyes and reasonably good chestnut hair, the oval face with its skin still clear despite being almost thirty, except for the single obstinate freckle beside her nose.

It was only inside she had changed. For already her mind was drifting to the book and the concealed ribbon, and beyond these, to Sir Thomas and his secret room. Oh, she was Old Jane enough to want to know how any of this had been possible, and she would question him closely as soon as the opportunity presented itself. But more than knowledge, she wanted to be in that room again, where she could receive his touch and his kiss, and play more of the games of desire and pleasure he devised.

*Soon, Jane. You will have me again soon.*

Jane shivered once. Then, she mustered enough personal

discipline to set those hot, nighttime thoughts aside. The day had begun. She had duties that would not wait on her fantasies. Her patrons seldom woke before eleven, but Jane, as the duchess's lady, had to be dressed, breakfasted, and ready to wait on her mistress as she made her toilet.

Jane found herself to be surprisingly refreshed, as if she had slept a full night rather than just an hour or two after a . . . series of exertions. She also had a tremendous appetite. Consequently, she was very glad when Tilly pronounced her fit to be seen so she could take herself across to the private dining room. As might be expected, the Kensington House staff was very efficient, and a piping-hot breakfast had been laid out on the sideboard. Jane helped herself to a chop, toast and marmalade and a cup of strong coffee. She then took a seat at the otherwise unoccupied table and prepared to enjoy her meal.

But as she tucked in, the door opened again. Jane looked up to see the man who entered, and muffled a small sigh.

"Captain Conroy," she said, keeping her voice studiously polite.

"Good morning, Lady Jane." Also studiously polite, Captain Conroy, the duke's personal secretary bowed. "May I join you?"

"Certainly," she replied because she had no choice. It would not be reasonable to refuse another member of the duke's household a seat at the breakfast table.

"Thank you."

Although she tried to keep her attention on her own breakfast, Jane could not help sneaking glances at the captain as he helped himself to the food. Conroy was a tall man with a long, handsome face. His dark hair was richly curled, but had also begun to recede. He kept his sideburns full, perhaps to make up for this fact. This morning he wore a sober burgundy coat over a waistcoat striped blue and white. The excellent cut of his clothes, the heavy gold chain across his middle and the diamond ring on his right hand spoke of his rank and prosperity. Jonathan Conroy handled all the Duke of Kent's affairs, which, considering the duke's ever-growing mountain of debt, took both persistence and delicacy.

The captain had traveled with them all the way to Saxe-Coburg and back, and in all that time he'd never been anything less than polite and correct to her. Despite this, Jane could not find it in her to actually like Captain Conroy. He had a way of watching everyone and everything as if calculating its worth that got into the back of her mind and left her profoundly uneasy.

"So, how does this morning find you, Lady Jane?" Conroy settled himself across the table from her with his plate of kippers and coddled eggs.

Jane did not consider John Conroy attractive, as she knew some ladies did, but even she had to admit he had a pleasant voice. The combination of his Welsh and Irish ancestries gave his words depth and musicality.

"Very well, thank you." Jane nibbled at the corner of her toast. She now regretted taking so much food. It would make a quick retreat more difficult.

"And how did you like Lady Darnley's rout? A dreadful crush, I thought." Conroy's eyes sparkled with all the suppressed glee of the unrepentant gossip. Jane found her dislike deepening by a fraction of an inch.

She sipped her coffee to buy time while she framed a diplomatic and empty answer. "Lady Darnley's parties are always excellent. I think the duke enjoyed himself."

"I believe you are correct. Did you hear anything of interest?"

Jane's shoulders stiffened. Conroy stirred two lumps of sugar into his cup, tasted it, and added a third, but all the time, he managed to still eye her keenly. Was he looking for a sign that he had flustered her? Nonsense. Why would he do so?

She sliced off another portion of her chop. "I don't know what you mean, sir." He was very quick on the uptake, was Captain Conroy. This should inform him she was no fishwife to chatter with anyone who came within earshot.

Conroy, however, did not seem prepared to take the hint. "Come, come." He set his cup down on its saucer with a clink. "Our mistress asked you to bring her the news did she not?"

Jane frowned, feeling somewhat caught out. She had been so consumed by her tryst with Sir Thomas, she had nearly forgotten the reason she was sent to Lady Darnley's ball to begin with. That was inexcusable for a confidential companion to one of the royal family.

"Surely you cannot expect me to tell you before I speak to Her Grace," she replied coolly. "Much less require me to speak when I have not been given permission."

"Very good, Lady Jane." Conroy raised his coffee cup to her in salute, quite ignoring her frown. "Your discretion does you credit."

"Do you mean to test me, sir?"

"I pray you, take no offense. It is only that I have been in the duke's service for a long time, and the situation at court is so very . . . changeable these days. You can understand, I'm sure, how important it is that we who serve be kept abreast of any turn of event that might affect our households."

Jane studied Conroy's face. His countenance was open and his blue eyes seemingly free of guile. Perhaps she had been mistaken. She had been so concerned of late with keeping her own position secure, she might have succumbed to one of the most common diseases of the courtier—suspicion of other courtiers.

"I do understand, Captain," she said. "And I will be happy to speak with you on any subject, after I have spoken with Her Grace."

"Again, your discretion is greatly to your credit, but, Lady Jane, strictly between ourselves . . ." He glanced meaningfully toward the door before he leaned forward, planting his elbow on the table. "Is it not the case that sometimes those born to the highest positions lack, shall we say, a certain practicality? It is no fault of theirs, of course. Their attention is occupied by weightier matters. It is for us to apply our efforts toward smoothing their paths, and anticipating their needs." He smiled again. "And naturally, nothing must disturb Her Grace at this time. Any agitation could prove injurious to her health."

Now she felt the full weight of his smooth and plausible charm. Felt it, and dismissed it. Jane laid down her knife and fork and met his frank gaze with all the steel she could muster. "What do you want from me, Captain Conroy?"

"Lady Jane, from your tone it might be thought you suspect me of some intrigue! I want only to serve the duke to the best of my abilities. Now that he is married, this includes guarding and guiding his wife as best I may." Conroy swirled his coffee, watching the currents his agitation created. "We both know how very treacherous the court may be."

"A noble sentiment," Jane replied flatly. "But it does not answer my question."

"Very well." Conroy set his cup down and pushed his chair back. He eyed the door again, but now all his semblance of coy intimacy had vanished. "What do I want? I want to cultivate your friendship, Lady Jane, as is proper for two people who serve in the same house. I want to talk with you about what you learned last night, and anything else you know that could affect the standing of the duke and duchess. Together, we can sort through what we know and decide how we may best serve."

"We decide? Not they?"

"We," he repeated firmly. "For in looking after the well-being of the duke and duchess, we see to our own, and that well-being may require more forethought than our patrons have been proven to possess."

Jane could not tell which troubled her more: that Captain Conroy spoke so frankly, or that she knew how much truth lay in his words. The Duke of Kent was a match for any of his royal brothers when it came to drinking, gambling and wenching. His favorite mistress of the past decade now lived in Paris and drew a comfortable pension despite the fact that his creditors went begging. The duke had said publicly that the only reason he set her aside was for the chance to father the next heir to the throne. What he did not say was that fulfillment of this paternal ambition was sure to bring an increase in his income from parliament, but everyone knew it was in his mind.

Conroy was a man of intelligence, and ambition, but also a

man dependent on his superior for his living. Jane could easily see how a man responsible for managing the duke's affairs might come to see his duties extend to managing the duke himself. After all, what had she been doing these past weeks but fretting over the safety of her own income?

Conroy was waiting for her answer, and Jane still had no idea what answer to give. She saw the reasons for what he said, perhaps she even agreed with them in part, but she still did not like this man, especially now that she could see how triumph mixed with the expectation in his demeanor.

But the door opened and Tilly stepped into the room, saving Jane from having to make any answer.

"If you please, madame." Tilly curtsied. "Her Grace is asking for you."

"Thank you, Tilly." Jane got to her feet. "You will excuse me, Captain Conroy?"

"Of course." Conroy also stood. "We can resume this conversation at another time."

*And we will.* The words hung unsaid in the air. An unquiet sensation filled Jane's mind, and she had to work not to scurry from the room.

The Duchess of Kent sat at the window in her heavily ruffled dressing gown, her dark hair piled under a neat white cap, a china cup and saucer in her hands. The smell of warm chocolate mingled with the scent of Frau Seibold's strengthening tonics and medicinal salves.

"Ah, Lady Jane, good, good." The duchess greeted Jane in her expansive German. "Please, you will sit?" She gestured Jane to an embroidered chair. "So, what you heard at the great party of Lady Darnley you will tell me. And, my Jane, you do not spare my feelings. I need to know how the great lords and ladies of England think of me."

Captain Conroy's words about the lack of practicality among their masters came forcefully back to Jane. But as she looked into the duchess's dark eyes she had the distinct sensation of a sharp intelligence waiting beneath that pretty, mature, rounded face. It reminded her the Duchess of Kent was the sort of woman who was consistently underestimated.

Choosing her words carefully—for she was certainly about to reach the limits of her German fluency—Jane told the duchess about how all the royal dukes had now rushed into marriage. She detailed the rumor of a feud between the duke and the prince regent, as well as the lingering sorrow over the death of Princess Charlotte, and the simmering dislike among the people in general of the Prince of Wales.

The duchess listened without once interrupting. Although she sipped at her chocolate, her attention never wavered from Jane's words. When at last Jane ran out of breath and observations, the duchess nodded once. Then her face broke out in a pleasant smile.

"Now, Lady Jane, I have for you today some work," she said. "For I find I have no acceptable clothing. Yes, I am in my confinement, but there are still the levees of the queen, and the . . . the drawing rooms, yes? And of course, I must be at home to certain persons. I cannot make do with nothing in the English style to wear. It is bad enough that I trip so badly over the language, despite your most patient instruction. So you will go to the fashionable districts and you will inspect the dressmakers and modistes, yes? View their stock, and speak to the principals? Those you find most satisfactory, you will make appointments for them to come here."

"Certainly, ma'am."

"You will make it known I will have a long list of requirements. A very, very long list."

"Naturally, your highness." Jane imagined the sober London merchants with their eyes aglow at the thought of outfitting the new Duchess of Kent. She also imagined how very ready they would be to extend her credit, notwithstanding the duke's already spectacular debts. Patronage came in many forms, and rumors of an open purse could buy all kinds of favors, low and high. Looking at the duchess, Jane was quite certain she knew exactly what she was doing.

"And do take your time. Enjoy your return to your home. A call or two to a friend may prove pleasant and informative, yes?"

"Thank you, ma'am."

So, there it was. If last night had not been proof enough, this sealed it. Jane's place in her highness's establishment was as newsmonger-in-chief. Well, it made sense. Born and raised in the petty courts of Germany, the duchess surely understood the importance of staying one step ahead of the gossips. While money might be the ultimate power, it was talk that shaped reputation and so much in the world of courts and the *haut ton* rested on reputation.

A soft scratching sounded on the door. Frau Seibold opened it to admit Fraulein Lehzen, another of the ladies who had come with the party from Saxe-Coburg. She was as stiff and precisely turned out as a china figurine, but far less brittle. Jane always got the feeling Lehzen could come through a hurricane without a stitch or a hair out of place.

"Good morning, your grace." Lehzen curtsied. "Princess Feodora asks if she may come into her mama now?" Princess Feodora, the duchess's twelve-year-old daughter by her first husband, had come to England with her mother.

The duchess smiled fondly, showing the dimples in her cheeks and chin.

"You will go now, yes?" said the duchess to Jane. "I must dress, and then I have told my Feodora we will spend the morning together." She patted her proudly curving stomach. "My good girl, she so looks forward to meeting the new little one."

"Certainly, ma'am." Jane made her curtsy. She nodded cordially to Fraulein Lehzen, but Jane did not miss the other woman's sharp glance as she turned. It was a look meant to discern secrets, and reminded her uncomfortably of the looks John Conroy had treated her to from across the breakfast table.

*You all wish to know what secrets I hold.* The vision of Sir Thomas's face, his green eyes alight with desire, rose before her mind's eye. *I must hope to Heaven you never find out.*

# *Eight*

Tilly, it turned out, had been correct. Despite the sun, the morning remained chill. Jane donned her stout shoes and best blue coat along with her rose bonnet and cream shawl. Thus armored against the weather, she climbed into the duchess's carriage with Tilly, feeling well prepared to take the measure of the city's dressmakers.

Leaving Kensington House for the crowded, workaday London streets was a relief to Jane. Her errand would also, blessedly, allow her time to gather her wits. So much had happened in the short space of time since Lady Darnley's ball, Jane desperately needed a moment to take stock.

To this end, Jane stopped the carriage as they approached Oxford Street and announced her intention to walk. She did not miss the fact that her maid seemed less than enthusiastic about the prospect.

"It's quite all right, Tilly." Jane allowed the footman to help her out onto the cobbles. "You can follow with Jacob and the carriage."

"Are you certain, madame?" Her desire for comfort and her sense of propriety clearly both plucked at Tilly's elbows.

"I will be perfectly fine," Jane surveyed the passing crowd, enjoying the sensation of being back on familiar ground. As charming as the people and environs of Saxe-Coburg had been, she'd been nothing but a servant and a stranger there. She was much accustomed to being alone, so she had faced her condition stoically. But to step into this bustling familiarity was like stepping into the sunshine. She might even see a friend.

And very soon, she did.

"Look, there is Mrs. Beauchamp," Jane said to Tilly. "I haven't seen her for an age." Without waiting for Tilly's response, Jane sailed into the crowd.

Mrs. Beauchamp was a diminutive lady, bent down both by age and old sorrows so that she had to lean heavily on her stick. She was not a close acquaintance, but she was of long standing, having been a friend of Jane's mother well before Jane came to town. Georgie said Mrs. Beauchamp had been exiled from both court and her family over some past indiscretion, possibly even involving one of the royal dukes, who had in their youths all displayed a pronounced taste for mature women. That she had for a time sung on stage did not aid her reputation.

Despite such adventures, Mrs. Beauchamp remained alert and active. She quickly noted Jane's approach, and gave her a nod and a bright smile of greeting.

"My dear Lady Jane! So good to see you again!" As she spoke, Mrs. Beauchamp touched the coat sleeve of the much younger man beside her. He turned, and Jane stopped dead in her tracks.

For the man in the perfectly ordinary blue coat and beaver

hat standing in the perfectly ordinary street was Sir Thomas Lynne.

"I had heard you were back, of course, but I'm surprised to see you out so soon," Mrs. Beauchamp gazed up at Jane. Time had dimmed those eyes, leaving them weak and watery. "You're looking very well, child, very well. Now, Lady Jane DeWitte, you must allow me to present my godson, Sir Thomas Lynne."

"Your godson?" repeated Jane stupidly. This was the second time he had come on her unawares, and the second time her mind was unable to accept his presence. Sir Thomas Lynne was a creature of candlelight, fantasy and secret desire. Such a wicked dream did not walk in daylight, let alone reveal himself to be the godson to an ancient, even partly respectable, dame.

"How very nice to see you again, Lady Jane." Sir Thomas tipped his hat and bowed, all polite and correct, just as he had been at the ball the previous evening.

Mrs. Beauchamp squinted from one of them to the other. "Are you two acquainted?"

"Only slightly." Jane could barely hear her own words over the pounding of her heart. Hopefully, Mrs. Beauchamp would take her high color as the natural result of a brisk walk. Sir Thomas, of course, appeared perfectly at ease. Except for his eyes. His eyes were alive with fire and secrets. Their secrets.

For a moment, Jane thought she might swoon right here in the public street.

"Oh yes, now I remember," said Mrs. Beauchamp. "Thomas did say you'd met at Lady Darnley's, and of course you both only just returned to London. Thomas is just back from the Jamaicas, as I'm sure he told you."

"No. He did not mention it," Jane murmured. When had there been time? They had been so much occupied otherwise. "How did you find the islands, Sir Thomas?"

"I'm afraid I did not much care for them. I was very glad to return to England." Thomas's smile softened, but she could tell he was thinking of their night, of how he commanded her and how she obeyed. Jane desperately wanted to glance at his trouser front, to see if he was hard from those thoughts. Of course she could do no such thing. Not here. Not now. But oh, how she wanted to.

"He's staying with me while he's in town," began Mrs. Beauchamp chattily. Then, a thought seemed to strike her. "You must come for a visit, Jane, if Her Grace can spare you. I must hear all about your time in Saxe-Coburg. Have I your promise?"

Jane forced herself to turn to Mrs. Beauchamp. Another moment of Sir Thomas's green eyes and she would be lost to all propriety. "Of course," she said to the invitation. "If I can."

"I'll be so glad for a chance to talk with you properly, Jane, and it has been very good to see you. I think often of your poor mama and . . . well . . . Are you stopping here?" She gestured toward the glove maker's shop beside them.

"Oh, no. I need to visit Madame Levant for Her Grace." *I need to get away. I meant to think. When am I to have time to think?*

"Well, I'm going to be a bit. Takes me forever to make up my mind these days." Another idea struck Mrs. Beauchamp and she touched Sir Thomas's arm. "Thomas, I'm sure you don't want to be sitting around with a dithering old woman . . ."

"Not at all, godmother!" Thomas announced immediately, and with credibly sincere indignation.

*The Surrender of Lady Jane*

But Mrs. Beauchamp dismissed his words with a wave. "Why don't you escort Lady Jane to Madame Levant?"

Sir Thomas bowed toward Jane with a silent inquiry in his arched brows.

"I would not wish to take you out of your way, Sir Thomas." Thankfully, Jane's voice remained steady despite the fact her heart pounded fit to burst.

"It would be no trouble, I assure you," he answered. If any hint of mischief showed in his manner, it was visible only to Jane's imagination.

Exasperation surged through Jane, along with a healthy dose of fear. Her emotions were entirely disordered from the simple exchange of a few words with her . . . her lover. If she had to walk any distance with him, she'd surely faint, or run mad, or any of a dozen equally unacceptable things.

Jane opened her mouth to refuse, but when she saw little Mrs. Beauchamp looking so pleased with herself, Jane found she hadn't the heart. "Very well then," she said. "Thank you."

Sir Thomas bowed, and turned one last time to his godmother. "Are you sure you'll be all right . . . ?"

"Dear boy." Mrs. Beauchamp patted his hand. "I've Chloe, and Dennis is right there with the carriage. I will be fine." Suiting actions to words, she gestured to her maid, a plump woman of middle years, who immediately opened the shop door to allow the old lady entrance, and leaving Jane face-to-face with Thomas.

Thomas bent at the waist, courteously holding out his arm. Jane swallowed and laid her fingers lightly on his sleeve. He looked down at her timid hand, his face a study in disappointment. Jane bit her tongue and, after a swift glance to make sure

77

Tilly and the carriage were still where they should be, she set off as rapidly down the street as the crowds and her skirts would permit.

"Are you in such a hurry to leave me, Jane?" Thomas asked lightly as he fell into step beside her. With his long legs encased in his gleaming hessian boots, he had no trouble keeping the pace she set.

"Please, sir, remember where we are." Jane glanced behind her again. Tilly had brought some mending with her and was stitching away studiously as the carriage bumped slowly down the cobbles. If she was not truly oblivious to her mistress's new companion, she put up a convincing show.

Unfortunately, Jane's frosty tone quite failed to disconcert Sir Thomas. "We are on a crowded street in the middle of Mayfair," he replied calmly. "Where absolutely no one is paying attention to us. I could say any number of things to you now, and they would be none the wiser."

A flush touched Jane's cheeks and her steps faltered. "I'm not certain I can do this."

"Do what? Walk with me? Speak with me as a friend?"

"We are not friends," she snapped.

"No," Sir Thomas admitted, and Jane was sure she heard a trace of regret in the word. "We are both more and less than that, aren't we?"

"Much more. And much less."

"Jane." As he spoke her name, she heard something new, a kind of tentativeness that had not been there before. "Are you ashamed?"

"No!" The word came out more quickly and with more force

than she had expected. "At least . . . I don't believe so. I'm not certain what I feel."

"I understand." She couldn't hear him properly with all the traffic noise and the shouting street vendors, and it was vital that she hear him properly. Something was going on inside this man, something raw and real beneath the well-cultivated surface.

"You understand?" she prompted.

"Oh, yes. What we have shared is very powerful, and it can be confusing." He wasn't looking at her. He was far away in memory and what he found there had wiped the mischief and humor from him. Suddenly, Jane thought, he looked tired.

"Do you . . . do you find it so very difficult, Jane, to walk with me like this?"

Sir Thomas cast the question out like a lifeline from whatever sad place his thoughts had gone, trusting her to catch it and hold on. It was an unexpected moment of vulnerability. She had longed for a way out of this entanglement, and this could well be it. With a few seemingly careless words, she could put some distance between them.

But Jane looked up into Thomas's tired, distracted face, and found she couldn't do it. He looked . . . lonesome was the only word for it, and her heart went out instantly to that loneliness. She could not have stopped it, even had she wished to. She knew too many long days in dim, empty rooms, mourning yet another death, while her father locked himself in his study with his papers and his letters that detailed, she now knew, his mounting losses in the stock market. She had hoped to find some relief from her isolation in her marriage, even if it was only as the companion of a man's age. But Lord Octavius had spent his time in his clubs, leaving her to the house and her own devices. He had never been unkind to her, but she had realized soon after their wedding he was not a man with whom she could ever share her mind, let alone her heart.

Jane curled her fingers more firmly around Thomas's arm. "I . . . could become used to walking with you in time, I think."

The tiny lines around Thomas's eyes softened, and the tension in his jawline eased.

"You are a very special woman, Jane." Sir Thomas pulled his arm in, bringing her minutely closer to him. "I would like to know you better."

"As my tutor?"

"As your friend, if you will permit."

His soft words touched Jane with a sensation that was nearly physical. Whatever else remained unsaid between them, this was the truth. She was sure of it. This mysterious man who had been so ready to give her pleasure, now offered her something far more rare, and she yearned to accept.

At the same time, memory furrowed Jane's brow.

"Jane? Have I said something wrong?"

"No, no," she replied hurriedly. "I just . . . another man today said something similar to me. But then it was rather less well meant."

"I confess a great curiosity to know what man this was."

"Captain Conroy, the duke's secretary. There is something in his manner that makes me . . . uneasy."

Sir Thomas watched the foot traffic in front of them for a long moment before venturing an answer. "You have good instincts, Jane. You should trust them."

"Hmm. Most men dismiss feminine intuition."

"Do you consider me most men?"

"Never that. But then I know nothing about you."

He looked down at her, his face perfectly sober, but the by now familiar mischievous glow had returned to his eyes. Jane felt her cheeks burn as if touched by the sun.

"Please, Thomas," she murmured.

He smiled and the results were devastating. Jane wished she'd thought to bring a fan. "I do so love to hear that word from you," he said softly. Jane was certain she could feel his words brushing her cheeks, feathering across them like gentle, familiar fingertips. "Say it again."

"Please." She was very aware of how her lips felt shaping the word. She wanted to touch him, taste him, and for a wild moment, she didn't care who might see.

"So very sweet," Thomas whispered.

Jane squared her shoulders and lifted her chin. This really was a bit much. They were in her place now, not his, and he needed to learn they would not always be playing his games. "You are changing the subject, sir," she said loftily. "I say I know nothing about you."

Sir Thomas smiled. "Your persistence is one of your most excellent qualities, Lady Jane. Alas, there is not much to tell. I am the younger son. My father made his money in ships, and I followed him in the business. I've worked for the crown and for myself at various times, and mostly profited by the effort."

"You do not seem old enough to have done so much."

"You would be surprised." His attention threatened to drift back to his memory, but he shook himself quickly. "Now, it is your turn, for I also know nothing about you."

"I have not much to tell either. I am the eldest daughter. My mother had insisted I be well and widely educated. I think she knew my father's high living would catch up with us eventually. He died two years ago, leaving behind a mountain of debt. It was Mother's acquaintances and my husband's that enabled me to get my place with the Duke of Kent." Jane remembered the hours spent laboring over the letters, all her pride put into her pocket. She did not want to sound desperate, even as the bailiffs were carrying the furniture out of her husband's house. Even when she'd had to beg them to allow her to keep her writing desk. "It was thought, you see, that the new duchess should have at least one English lady in her train. I speak German, and could teach her English and perhaps help her . . ."

"Cultivate English manners?"

"Just so." She waited, but Thomas kept his thoughtful silence. He saw she had not told him everything. She had only a moment to distract him from probing further. "Aren't you going to ask the question?"

"Which question?"

"How do I find the duchess? It is the one thing everyone wants to know."

"I am not everyone."

"No," Jane agreed, but now her impatience began to show. "Nor just anyone, nor most men. And nothing you have said explains the greatest mystery."

"You want to know about the dreams."

"Yes, I do. And how you called me to . . . to that room."

"Naturally." He stopped in front of a bay window filled with the latest silks and brocades from Paris, and decorated in flowing gold script. "But you see, here we are at Madame Levant's."

If she had not been the one setting the pace, Jane would have sworn Thomas had timed this. It was all too neat. "I will not be put off, Sir Thomas."

"I know that, Lady Jane," he said, his eyes sparkling. "You may be sure I will satisfy you."

"You . . ."

"You do not wish to be seen standing in the street talking with a man, I think. But you may be assured," he bowed over her hand, "you shall have all you want, and very soon too."

Jane moved to protest, but Thomas slipped nonchalantly away into the traffic at a pace that meant she would have had to run to catch up with him, which would have caused enough of a scene to make even the busy shoppers around her take note.

But he had said, "You shall have all you want." He'd said he would satisfy her. Desire curled tightly in Jane's center and she turned toward Madame Levant's door. She had to distract herself before thoughts of Sir Thomas's style of satisfaction could congregate too closely.

He would surely call to her tonight. There would be time enough then to find answers to both her questions, and her need.

If only that time did not seem so far off.

# Nine

"Welcome back, Sir Thomas." Red Fiora, who was now called Fiora Beauchamp, smiled a little too eagerly as Thomas entered the small, second parlor of her Mayfair house. "Did you meet with success?"

"I believe I did." Thomas took a seat in a wing-backed chair while his hostess rang for a cold collation to be sent up. "Lady Jane's thrown off balance, which for our purposes is good." He smiled, remembering how hastily Jane had darted into modiste's shop and close the door behind her. As if a flimsy construction of wood and glass could truly separate her from him.

God's legs, but Jane had been lovely today. The bonnet with its cheerful roses had been a perfect frame for her oval face. While they walked, a single chestnut curl had escaped its confinement and slanted across her brow. He'd been seized by the desire to reach over and tuck it back into place, and draw his fingers across her soft skin in the bargain. She'd like that, he was sure. She enjoyed the little touches that were intimations of affection at least as much as she did his erotic caresses. He'd been oddly aroused by seeing her all buttoned up to her chin in her demure blue coat as well. It had worked on his imagination, that coat, constantly reminding him of the lush and perfect curves it concealed, which, in its turn, lead him to consider the many ways he had yet to pleasure her.

Thomas realized he'd said nothing for at least a minute and that Fiora still looked at him expectantly. "I also think she's that much closer to trusting me," he went on.

"That's good. No, that's excellent." Fiora's sallow, wrinkled cheeks flushed. If Thomas looked closely, he could still see the young woman he had known in the Fae realms. Traces of that other life lurked in her watery blue eyes and he could even spy some red beneath the gray of her hair. "You must let me know at once what I can do to help."

"You already help me. With you I have address and identity, and both are unassailable. If I am to gain entry to Kensington House by day as well as night, this is exactly what I need."

After her banishment from the Fae court, Fiora had been thrown onto the mercy of the daylight realms. Fortunately, the lovely voice that had brought her to the queen's notice allowed her to make her way as a singer on the stage, eventually snaring her the son of a wealthy merchant. Money lavishly spent had helped people forget the stains of her past, in the mortal world at least.

"But I can do more," insisted Fiora, her voice growing shrill with urgency. "I will do more . . ."

"Fiora," Thomas stopped her. "Be calm. I will tell Her Majesty you repent and are her true servant. I swear it."

"I am glad to be of use to Her Majesty." Fiora looked so wretched, huddled on her sofa in her old woman's cap and shawl. Sir Thomas remembered her dancing before the queen and the court. She'd been infinitely delicate and graceful then, with her red hair floating free about her bare shoulders. She'd had laughter like golden bells, and her singing could stun an entire gathering of Fae to silence.

Now, she lifted her rheumy blue gaze to him, and spoke so softly he could barely hear.

"Does she . . . Is my name ever spoken?"

"You are not forgotten." This was as close to the truth as Thomas cared to venture. The queen, of course, never forgot her anger. As for the rest of the court, their memories were sharply and purposefully truncated. They all knew it did little good to recall the ones Her Majesty had banished.

"Or else why would you be here?" Fiora finished for him in an attempt at lightness. "But, has she said . . . if all goes well . . . has she said if I might return?"

"If all goes well, you will not need to return. All this"—Thomas waved his hand toward the windows, and the city beyond—"will become our queen's dominion."

"Yes. Yes." Fiora drew in a deep breath. "We must fix our minds on that."

Before either one of them could speak further, the door opened and the servants entered with the food. Fiora dismissed them as soon as they laid it out on the table and set about fixing Thomas a plate of cold meats and breads, becoming once more the polite human hostess serving her guest. She handed him the pile of sandwiches and he thanked her.

"So tell me," Fiora went on, opening the silver tea caddy and measuring careful spoonfuls into the pot. Coffee stood ready at hand as well, but Thomas suspected she wanted to keep both mind and hands busy. "How do you find our Lady Jane? Is she as much the ice queen as she is reported around the regent's court?"

Thomas stared at her as if she had begun speaking Swahili. Who could see intense, passionate Jane as icy?

"Not that I would blame her," continued Fiora, helping herself to a piece of bread and a paper-thin slice of ham. "Lord Octavius was at least three times her age when she married him, and probably a terrible lover. They never did produce a child, that's for certain, so he may not have been very capable. A woman in a cold bed cannot help but grow cold herself . . ."

Thomas abruptly found himself on his feet.

"What is the matter?" Fiora exclaimed.

"We should change the subject." Thomas stalked over to the window before his discomfort could show in his face. Something was not right. Something that nagged at the back of his mind, but as he reached for it, it vanished, leaving only impatience and the beginnings of a headache.

But Fiora persisted. "What have I said?"

"Nothing." Thomas made himself modulate his voice. *What is the matter with me?* "I'd simply prefer it if you spoke of Jane DeWitte respectfully."

Fiora sat silent for a long moment. When she did speak again, she was clearly treading quite carefully. "Sir Thomas, it is difficult to return . . . to this world after a long absence. I know. All the motion and constant change can be overwhelming to the senses. Are you sure you are quite well?"

"Yes, yes." But he wasn't. Anger simmered just beneath the surface of his mind, but he could find no reason for it. Fiora's words about Jane . . . they were careless, but nothing to merit this . . . this surge of hard emotion. He stared out at the vans and carriages rattling past on the street. London had changed out of all recognition since he'd lived here as a boy. Then, the city was little more than a ramshackle wooden town clustered about the knees of its stone tower. Now, it was a sprawling metropolis, filled to the brim with the riot and roistering of life. When he'd arrived, he'd been stunned by the unrelenting noise, energy and chaos. Walking abroad its streets filled him with the excitement of discovery that he hadn't realized he'd missed. He'd even considered a run down to the Thames to see the ships, although moving water was inimical to magic, and it was risky for one of the queen's servants to walk too near the great river. He was ready to take that risk, for he wanted to lose himself in this city, explore it entirely and experience its myriad facets.

But at this moment he found himself wondering about the one particular facet that was Jane DeWitte. He wondered where she was and if she thought of him now. He felt almost certain she did. Perhaps this was what disordered his thoughts? Perhaps the bond he had begun to build of their mutual desire was already strong enough for her to reach out, all unwitting, and touch him. He had already seen she possessed a remarkable strength of character, as well as passion that matched her physical beauty. It was not impossible that her mind could already be in tune with their bond. He could reach out to her now, brush her thoughts, let her sense that he was there and thinking of her . . .

"Take care, Thomas Lynne."

Thomas swung around. Fiora had not moved from her place on the sofa, but the withered little woman had straightened and hardened. The blue eyes he had thought dim a moment before glittered keenly. "One might suspect you were beginning to feel something for the woman."

"Of course not." Thomas waved his hand dismissively. "I am Her Majesty's servant."

"As was I."

Thomas's guts clenched. Yes, she had been, once. But years ago, Fiora had broken the strictest law of the Fae court by daring to fall in love with one of the queen's chosen knights. Worse, the foolish man had loved her in return. Of course they'd both tried to hide their affair, and of course they'd been found out. In the Fae realms, even the wind reported to Their Glorious Majesties.

Queen Tatiana had been transcendent in her fury. Sexual congress was permitted among the mortals admitted to the Fae court, but never love. They pledged their hearts to her, and her alone.

Fiora was the lucky one. She'd only been banished back to the mortal world. But, the false knight, her lover . . . Thomas clenched his jaw. That man had been sent to much harsher kingdoms to pay his traitor's debt.

Thomas forced himself to consider his walk with Jane. Had he ever truly been in danger of such betrayal? No, surely not. For one thing, it was far too soon. Love, genuine love, took time. It must. Love required intimacy and respect, and above all trust. He had enjoyed Jane's smiles and her company, but he would have enjoyed as much with any beautiful woman, especially if he had taken her as a lover. It was the memory of their passion that made him wish Oxford Street had stretched on for miles, and that the inconvenient Madame Levant had set her shop at the far end.

*We are not friends.*

The echo of Jane's voice came swiftly back to him. He'd felt those words like a blow. No, it wasn't the words that hit him. It was his wish for them not to be true.

Which was reasonless. What did he care for her friendship? She was nothing but the exploitable weakness of a house to which his queen required entry. Magic worked by the shaping of intent. An invitation carried with intent, backed with genuine desire and need, became a powerful force. He'd fuck Lady Jane for as long as it took to embed desire of him in the depths of her body. Desire would bring as much trust as he needed, and she would invite him into the house. She'd desire him to be with her, and the strength of that desire would make a grappling hook to pull him through the wards around Kensington House. Each time he passed through, he would make a crack, a small leak in the hull created by those wards. Soon that leak would grow large enough to let the Fae queen's tide flood in.

For that mission, he only needed to inflame Jane's desire. Her friendship was neither here nor there.

*She'll hate me soon enough as it is.*

He pictured Jane's face drawn tight in anger, and his breath caught in his throat. She would not understand that what he did was for the good of her and her people. Their Glorious Majesties would bring the peace of their immortal reign to the isle of Britain, saving it from the fools and fops that now circled the throne. In their single, unchanging rule, there would be no more intrigues over power and money; no wars of succession or religion.

Thomas remembered his mother kneeling in church when he was a boy, tight-lipped and white with fear, her eyes fixed rigidly on the Host, which the priest elevated. They were not there because they believed in the priest and his sonorous Latin chant, but because Queen Mary burned men and women for not paying sufficient attention in church. A few short years later, Thomas knelt beside his mother in a different church. This time the priest spoke the liturgy in English, and his mother added her own in fervent whispers, praying that the new, virgin queen not turn to the stake to settle matters of religious dissent.

Pain throbbed hard in Thomas's temples. He had forgotten or missed something important. But it was like steering into a fog. He could see nothing clearly.

*God's legs, Thomas Lynne, you were sent here because you have self-control and Her Fae Majesty can trust you. One walk in the daylight with Lady Jane and you're dizzy as a schoolboy with his first whore.*

No, not whore. Jane was no whore, and it struck Thomas in that moment he would have killed any man who made such a comparison.

Thomas felt the blood drain from his cheeks. He turned to look at Fiora. He needed to look at her. He had to be reminded of the fate waiting for him if he permitted his imperfect, mortal heart to fasten onto an imperfect, mortal woman, even one so alluring as Jane DeWitte.

"Tell me how you miss it," Thomas said, ashamed to hear the tremor in his voice.

"Every day, every moment," Fiora answered instantly. "When the queen's regard is withdrawn . . . it becomes winter in your heart and you know it will never be summer again. When I feel the ache and have to creep along on legs that refuse to straighten, but still remember how very beautiful I was when I danced for Her Majesty . . . A dozen times I have almost ended this sham of a life. Only the thought that I might still find a way to return to our queen's favor has kept me alive." A tear crept down Fiora's sunken cheek and she dashed it away. "There. Look at these." She held up her damp fingertips. "Tears. When did we ever see tears in the Fae realms? Truly, I am become an old woman." She stood, brushing out her skirts. "I'll go write that invitation I promised Lady Jane. We'll bring her here for a so very civilized afternoon at home, and you can tie the knot that much tighter."

Thomas nodded, for he found he did not trust his voice. Fiora hobbled to the door, but paused on the threshold.

"I cannot die out here, Thomas," Her voice trembled. "It is too cold. I will do anything to prove I am still Her Majesty's true servant."

With that, she left him, presumably to go to the library and take up her pen. Thomas remained where he was, alone now with the untouched food and his troubled thoughts.

Fiora didn't understand. The point was not to bind Lady Jane, but to lead her to want to be bound. She must come freely or not at all.

Thomas pictured Jane crouched naked before him, bowing her head to his cock. The joyful, unabashed play of her mouth had caught him completely off guard, especially as he suspected she had never performed this act before. She'd made him lose control and he had fucked her wildly, caring for nothing except to hear her scream and find his release in the depths of her heat and her pleasure. She would have to be punished for that. The thought made his cock twitch, and Thomas smiled. Yes, he would bind her, punish and pleasure her, and she would beg for it. She could scream his name and demand his touch.

That was what he wanted from her, that passion, that pure, physical joy. Their walk together in the late April sunshine, the banter and conversation, the way she'd brought herself closer to him when they spoke of friendship, and the sudden yearning that had flooded him with that small tightening of her hand on his arm . . . these were nothing but sentimental echoes of a world he had willingly cast off. For all that, it might be best if he stayed away from her tonight. Yes. That would work well with the plan. He had set before Jane a feast of pleasure. A night without would increase her craving for it.

It would also give him time to right his balance. He should have taken longer to get used to being among mortals again before he ever went to Jane. He had to remember that until the Fae took this place back from the ironmongers and fools, this mortal world could be nothing more than enemy territory to him.

Even while Jane DeWitte walked in it.

# Ten

"A message for Lady Jane." The footman held out the silver tray bearing a neatly sealed letter and a visiting card.

Jane glanced at the duchess for permission and received a nod and a languorous wave. She was, Jane suspected, grateful for the interruption. They had been in the parlor for over an hour, laboring with conversational English and the results of Jane's latest shopping tour. The weather outside had turned foul with a cold, heavy rain and the drapes had been drawn shut. Despite the fire roaring in the wide hearth, the room remained chill. The windows, which Jane had so admired upon their arrival, were proving dishearteningly drafty. Frau Seibold had piled the duchess with so many quilts and blankets she was near invisible beneath the heap of fabric.

"Thank you," said Jane to the footman as she picked up the letter and the card. The letter was addressed in a thin, crooked hand she did not immediately recognize. But the card . . . Jane's throat closed around her breath. The plain card with its flowing black script read:

## *Sir Thomas Lynne*

"Did . . . did the gentleman say if he expected a reply?" The words emerged as little more than a hoarse croak. Yearning filled her, intense and immediate. He had not called her last night, and she'd tossed and turned, desperately afraid she'd done something to drive him away. As she read his name now, Jane wanted nothing so much in the world than to have him beside her, to see his smile and touch his hand.

"A gentleman?" The duchess straightened up, dislodging some quilts and shawls. Frau Seibold swooped down on her, and the duchess waved her off impatiently. "For you, Jane?"

With an extreme effort of will, Jane assumed a casual air. "An acquaintance, ma'am. The godson of my mother's friend, Mrs. Beauchamp. I met her the other day while running my errands, and she said she would be sending me an invitation to visit one afternoon." Jane held up the letter.

"But it is not an encounter with your mother's friend that makes you blush so." Jane's hand flew to her cheek, and the duchess chuckled. "I see Captain Conroy was right."

*Conroy?* "Ma'am?"

"He told me that you had been speaking with a man." The duchess beamed and switched to her labored English. "Does the gentleman wait?" she asked the footman. "You tell him come in, Simmons, and for more coffee send."

The footman bowed and departed.

Thomas. Jane's heart pounded against her ribs. Thomas was in the house and in a moment he would be in the room. Her heart constricted with a joyful pain for a moment before reason reasserted itself. This could not be. She could not let the duchess see how she looked at this man. Her countenance already betrayed enough. Her mind was an absolute riot, but even so, one question rose up clear of the storm.

How in Heaven's name did Conroy know who she'd met in the street?

"Your grace, really, this is not necessary. I can . . ."

But the duchess simply continued to smile. "Probably it is not. But I am dull this morning," she said, once more lapsing into German. "And make no progress with lessons. I would meet this man with his invitation for you."

The words were mild, but Jane recognized the undertone of assumption and command. She subsided, and concentrated on keeping her hands still so she didn't crumple the unopened letter. The duchess snapped and fussed at Frau Seibold to remove all the quilts and Frau Seibold murmured about the vile English weather and drafts and the imperative of minding Her Grace's health, and compromised on one quilt and two shawls.

*I can do this,* Jane told herself. *I have a lifetime's experience in this exact thing.*

No, not this exact thing. She was an expert at hiding true feeling, and discreetly judging the niceties of any gathering so she could comport herself with the dignity and discretion demanded by her rank and place. But never before had this discretion included meeting her secret lover.

Especially after a sleepless night of waiting for a call to her heart and mind that had not come.

"Sir Thomas Lynne."

Simmons stood aside to let Thomas enter. He was dressed

plainly in dove gray and cream, with his hair tied neatly into its customary queue. He flicked the barest glance at Jane before making his formal bow to the Duchess of Kent.

*Where were you last night? Why did you not call to me?*

"Do please come in, Sir Thomas," said the duchess. "It is good to meet you. You will sit?"

"Thank you, your grace." Thomas settled into the embroidered chair the duchess indicated.

Jane cast around frantically for a safe topic from which to launch conversation. "Sir Thomas is lately returned from the Jamaicas, ma'am."

"So? A most difficult climate for the Englishman, I think."

"One becomes used to it, in time, ma'am, but few of us come to truly enjoy it."

"It is different for those who are born there."

"Very," he replied, with an undertone that Jane suspected hid a wealth of opinion on a subject best not broached.

Fortunately at that moment Simmons and a small army of under-footmen appeared with coffee, cups and a selection of buns and fruits Jane was fairly certain Frau Seibold had added, lest the duchess begin to feel faint.

"You will pour, Jane," said Her Grace. "What do you in London, Sir Thomas?" she asked.

"I'm afraid I am resolved to pursue a life of leisure and enjoyment, ma'am."

"And the pretty women as well, yes?"

"I had not thought to pursue the general population, ma'am, but perhaps one or two."

Jane blushed and passed the duchess her coffee, which she

had mixed with a generous portion of milk, having previously been scolded by Frau Seibold, who did not consider undiluted coffee healthy for a breeding woman.

Thomas was very carefully not looking at her. She could feel him not looking at her. She must not look at him, not for more than a heartbeat. A single heartbeat to try to see beneath his facade and discover if anything was wrong. If he was angry with her, or had already tired of her.

"So." The duchess beamed proudly. She turned to Jane and spoke in rapid German. "You ask him should I lock up my Jane? I cannot permit any man to steal you from me just yet."

Before Jane could open her mouth to attempt to lie about the duchess's little speech, Sir Thomas smiled. *"Nein, nein, Ihre Hoheit, ich würde überhaupt nicht bitten, daß Sie ohne Frau Jane zurechtkommen."* *No, no, madame, I would not dream of asking you to do without Lady Jane.*

Jane froze, with the cup and saucer she was passing exactly halfway between the two of them. He reached for it, his laughter shining in his eyes. *"Danke schön, Frau Jane."*

The duchess cocked her head in approval. *"Sie sprechen wunderschönes Deutsch, Herr Thomas. Wo haben Sie studiert?"* *You speak wonderful German, Sir Thomas. Where did you study?*

"I lived a long time near Munich," he continued in the same language, the words flowing from him as naturally as English.

"You are a well-traveled man."

"My business has taken me many places."

"And what is that business?" inquired the duchess.

This time Thomas considered his words. "It has been many things at many times. Some I chose, some were chosen for me."

"Jane!" cried Her Grace merrily. "You have found a man of mystery."

"I hope, ma'am, you don't find me rude . . ."

"No, no. You are discreet. A trait to be valued. Perhaps you do work for the crown, so? It is best in these cases you do not say."

"Thank you, ma'am." Thomas bowed his head. Jane found herself lost in a sea of emotion. She was absurdly piqued that she had not known Thomas spoke German, or that he had lived near Munich. That was the sort of thing one ought to know about a man who aroused so much emotion with a glance and a smile. Jane longed to be alone with him, to ask about last night and to find out when they might be together again. But she had to find a way to bear this longing with disinterest, because what had become very clear as she lay in the dark in her narrow bed, waiting and worrying, was that her passion for Thomas was not at all safe. It already drove her to distraction. What would it do if she indulged in it for much longer?

At the same time, she was relieved beyond measure to see how well Thomas conducted himself in front of the royal duchess. His manners were polished without being stiff, and if he partook of the general curiosity in her condition, he was not indulging in it here.

The duchess moved to set her coffee cup aside. "Well, now, you will excuse me, for I am tired." She smiled archly at Jane. "Lady Jane will show you your way, Sir Thomas. Jane, you will then come back. I need you to read to me while I rest."

"Certainly, ma'am." Jane got to her feet and made her curtsey. "This way, Sir Thomas." Sir Thomas bowed to the duchess and followed Jane out. She could feel him behind her as she walked down the corridor. This was torture. The corridor was too narrow for them to walk abreast. She could not even see him, only sense his presence behind her, so close and yet infinitely distant. Without her even thinking of it, her footsteps lagged, to try to bring him a little closer.

The corridor was empty. She could have spoken to him in relative safety, but she had so many things she wanted to say the words felt piled up inside her skull.

Thankfully, Thomas spoke first. "I'm sorry, Jane," he murmured. "I promise, I only came to deliver my godmother's invitation. I certainly didn't expect to be invited in."

"No, I suppose not . . ."

"Will you come then?"

"What?" She had to get her thoughts under control. But control was impossible when all her body wanted was to melt into his arms, and beg him to caress her.

This man she knew nothing about. *Nothing.* She repeated the word firmly to herself. It made no difference. Because underlying the passion was the memory of his sadness, his loneliness that she had seen while they walked together. To add to that, she now had the sight of him as a gentleman, polite, dignified and proper. These small glimpses of the man were, combining with the passion, settling into emotion and memory, and, most treacherously, into her heart. She had never known real passion before, let alone been in love with a man. She did not know how to fight against it.

They had reached the broad stairs and Jane started down. Now there was room enough for Thomas to come beside her, and he did. She could see his profile. He looked worried, perhaps even anxious.

"So will you come to visit with my godmother?" said Sir Thomas.

"Given how you impressed Her Grace, I think she will allow it."

"Jane . . ."

He was going to say something about last night, about his absence, Jane was certain, but it was too late. The page waited by the door and a shadow approached across the marble floor of the foyer. That shadow was followed swiftly by Captain Conroy.

Jane swallowed hard as she stepped off the last stair. Conroy nodded as he passed, leafing through papers as he walked. He was clearly on business. This might be a coincidence. Jane did not believe that for more than a single, hopeful heartbeat.

But Thomas's eyes flickered sideways, and Jane was sure he made good notice of Captain Conroy.

Jane kept her own gaze steady. She could not afford to betray anything where others might see. "Sir Thomas's hat and gloves, please, Foster. It was good of you to come, Sir Thomas. You may tell Mrs. Beauchamp she'll have my reply shortly."

"She's very much looking forward to seeing you again. And now, I'll bid you good morning, Lady Jane. Please thank Her Grace for her courtesy." Thomas took Jane's hand and bowed over it. Very, very softly she heard him say. "Tonight."

The footman opened the door, the page brought gloves, hat and cane. Jane stood still as a statue while Thomas took his leave. The only part of her that seemed capable of movement was her heart dancing in her breast.

It could not be as easy as this. Was this how all women conducted their affairs? They simply called on their years of training in the detailed art of maintaining appearances and passed their lovers without batting an eye where others could see.

It could not be so simple. There was nothing simple about the emotions swelling her heart. The urges and longings and needs filling her body and blood were certainly not simple. Neither was the man who roused so much conflict and desire within her.

She turned, and from the corner of her eye, she saw Captain Conroy, standing in the shadows. He meant her to see him, of course. She did not permit herself to pause, but climbed the stairs without looking back and turned her steps once more to the duchess's rooms. But all the while, she felt eyes at her back, right between her shoulder blades. It hurt that she could not tell whether those eyes belonged to Conroy or Thomas.

She retreated into the duchess's parlor, but there was no relief to be found there.

"He is a very handsome man," her grace said as soon as Jane had closed the door. Frau Seibold was still layering the covers back over her mistress and she glanced at Jane sourly as the duchess pushed herself up and dislodged her careful work.

"I assure you, ma'am . . ." began Jane.

"Now, now, Jane, no need for blushes." The duchess waved her back to her chair. "We are both grown women. We know a pair of fine eyes when we see them. Now, what is that invitation?"

The letter still lay on the table beside Thomas's card, right where Jane had left it. "It is to supper one afternoon with Mrs. Beauchamp."

"Very good. You should go." Again the tone of quiet command, and the assumption of assent that belonged to members of the royalty.

"Thank you, ma'am." This was good. It was what she wanted, wasn't it? But there had been something under Thomas's manner when he'd asked her. Something strained. Had he thought she might refuse? Or was there something else? What else could there be? "If you're sure it won't be an inconvenience . . ."

"No, no. I am well looked after." She cast a baleful glance at Frau Seibold, who raised her chin and finished tucking in the black shawl. "But my other ladies, they are not English, nor of the . . . what is the phrase . . . the *haut ton*? As you are. You are not only my eyes and ears, but my public face, is it not so? So, if people see you are treated well, if they see you act well, they will gain the good impression. Captain Conroy and I are quite in agreement on this point."

So. Captain Conroy had already succeeded in his aim. He had enough of the duchess's confidence that she was taking his advice on how to gain favor in the ballrooms and drawing rooms where opinion was formed.

"He is devoted to my husband, Captain Conroy." The duchess beamed as she shifted beneath her burden of quilts and shawls. "And a most intelligent man."

"Most intelligent." *Has he gulled you, ma'am, or have you decided he is useful?*

"And also possessed of a pair of fine eyes?" said the duchess archly.

Now it was Jane's turn to lift her chin. "There are those who think so."

"Ah, Jane, I tease. You have other eyes to admire. It is I shut

up in here who must take my enjoyment where it can be found."
She stroked her belly underneath its pile of coverings. "Heigh-ho,
little one, you must get yourself born soon, so your mama can go
see this new country of ours."

Jane picked up the copy of the novel *Evelina* from the side
table and opened it. "Shall I begin, ma'am?"

A n hour later the duchess was soundly asleep, and Jane escaped the parlor, where Frau Seibold was adding yet more
coal to the fire. Jane intended to go to the gardens for some fresh
air, to think, to breathe, and to try to wrap her mind around the
new subtleties of her situation.

She was not, however, in the least surprised to find Captain
Conroy waiting in the corridor. Jane drew her skirts aside so she
would not accidentally brush him as she passed.

"Nothing to say to me, Lady Jane?" Conroy inquired.

She told herself she should be careful. But she was so tired
and so confused. Too much had happened in too short of a time.
She'd had no rest from her circumstances, or her feelings, and
he seemed so arch and confident as he looked down his long
nose at her.

"You were perhaps expecting my thanks for gaining me a
little favor from the duchess?"

Conroy bowed, smiling slightly.

Jane took two steps forward. Conroy believed she could be
influenced. He thought he had found the means to control her.
He was wrong. She had nothing left in the world but her integ-
rity, and there was no one who would take that from her.

"Captain Conroy," Jane said, her voice low and steady. "Let me be very clear. I have asked for nothing from you, and I do not intend to do so. What I earn, I earn on my own merit, not your say-so."

"Lady Jane, one might almost think I had offered you a bribe."

"I would never accuse you of anything so direct," she replied, and sailed down the corridor.

With each step her anger increased, with each step an inescapable realization coalesced within her mind.

Captain Conroy had known she'd spoken with Sir Thomas. That meant Captain Conroy had either followed her, or he had a spy to do it for him. That spy could be anyone, but the most likely candidate was Tilly. Tilly had been in the carriage the whole time and had seen the entire meeting. If Conroy had Tilly on his payrolls, there was no telling what other members of the Kensington House staff now reported to him in return for an extra share of the Duke of Kent's income.

No wonder Conroy smiled.

## Eleven

When Jane was finally free to return to her room in the early hours of the morning, she was still simmering with anger. Tilly bustled and chattered, friendly and efficient as ever. Jane could barely bring herself to look at the girl, let alone speak to her with any kind of courtesy. She suspected Tilly was as grateful as she was when Jane was finally wrapped in her night attire and able to dismiss her to bed.

Or to report to Captain Conroy.

Jane sat heavily on the edge of her bed, clasping her hands together. She had been very careful at Mr. Hume's party. She had spoken with no one but Georgiana and a handful of other female acquaintances. The whole time, Conroy had circulated around the edges of the room with his knife-edged smile and arched brows.

Jane wanted nothing so much as to fling his words back in his face, but that would label her this man's enemy, and she had nothing with which to fight him. He was the old and trusted servant; she was the newcomer, brought in on the grounds that she might prove useful. She had no doubt Conroy, who commanded the attention of both the duke and the duchess, could have her dismissed, if not at once, then soon. And then what? Yet, if she stayed, he would surely do everything he could to wind his chain more tightly about her.

It was brutally unfair. She had done nothing, nothing at all. At least, not where anyone could see. For a wild moment she thought Conroy might have witnessed her creeping through the dark along the corridors of Kensington House. But no. She'd been alert every moment for a stray footstep or sound.

*I was, wasn't I?*

Jane bowed her head into her hand. Loneliness washed through her and with it came a wish that Thomas was here now. Not to arouse her, but just to be with her, talking easily as they had when they walked down Oxford Street. She'd enjoyed the solid feeling of him beside her. She liked the way he talked, the way they joked. She'd never felt such comfort with any man.

And yet, if she stopped for a moment to consider the reality of her very peculiar situation, she had never had less reason for that comfort. What was she doing now, for example? She was returned from another ball where she'd spent another night alternating between answering endless questions about the duchess and "how she did," and trying to ferret out as much of the gossip as she could. But was she collapsed in bed asleep? No. She sat up, waiting for his mysterious, inexplicable call to another wicked tryst.

*Tonight*, he'd said. That had been hours ago, and she still felt the heat and promise of that single word; the promise of a man who, as she herself had pointed out, was not her friend.

That thought got Jane to her feet. She was tired of this powerlessness. Why did she need to wait? She had been to the room. She could find the way again. Why not go now? The house was sound asleep, including the duchess. Games of obedience with a lover were one thing, but this was different. This was trust of an entirely different magnitude. This was her life.

Jane lit her lamp, found her slippers and closed her robe. She bit her lip as she opened the door. She was not entirely sure what she hoped to accomplish. Perhaps she needed to overbalance him, as he had done to her. Perhaps she felt the need to do anything but sit and wait for something else to happen to her.

But in her heart she knew what sent her into the darkness was the simple need to see Thomas again, and to know that she was not alone.

In the back of her mind she felt sure there would be a price for this, and not the kind Thomas swore to exact during lovemaking. Something else was happening here.

Jane was almost to the back stairs when she saw the light reflected on the walls. Someone coming up the steps, and it was too late for her to turn around. Before she could make any decisions, a tall, thin woman emerged from the stairwell, a tray braced against her hip. She stopped when she saw Jane, startled.

They both held their lamps up, like clowns performing in a mirror farce.

Jane spoke first. "Fraulein Lehzen."

"Lady Jane," Lehzen replied. Unlike the duchess, Lehzen's English was fluent, although heavily accented. "It is very late. Why are you not asleep?"

"A cramp in my leg. I stood too long this evening. I was hoping a walk would ease it. And you?"

Lehzen gestured minutely with her chin to her tray. "Princess Feodora cannot sleep. I fetch her tisane and the warm compress."

"I will not keep you then." Jane stepped aside giving the other woman room to pass.

Lehzen nodded her thanks. "I hope your walk has the effect desired."

"Thank you."

Jane moved past the woman, and started down the stairs. She could have turned back. Perhaps she should have. If Tilly could be Conroy's creature, so could Lehzen. But if she turned around immediately and went to her room, she would excite even more suspicion than if she kept going as if nothing was wrong.

Afraid to go forward, but afraid to go back, Jane made her way hesitantly down the narrow stairs.

Which way had she gone? Jane crossed the cupola room. The great clock's ticking echoed the frantic rhythm of her heart. Had it been left after this, or right? She could not have missed the corridor. Truly, she could not. Kensington House was big, but not that big. Surely . . .

*Jane? Are you looking for me?*

Thomas's voice sounded as clear as a bell in her mind. Jane whirled around, half expecting to see him behind her. But instead she saw the short hall with its four closed doors. She must have passed it in the dark. Jane hurried forward to the door and turned the golden rose knob without bothering to knock. It opened onto the opulent summer green chamber.

And there was Thomas, clad only in shirtsleeves and breeches, waiting for her.

Jane ran forward and threw her arms around his shoulders. His body stiffened, startled, but he slowly settled his arms around her to return her embrace.

"Jane, what is this?"

"Oh, I'm sorry." She pressed her forehead against his shoulder. "I'm being so foolish!"

"Nonsense." He took the lamp from her hand and set it on the nearest table. "I'm glad you're eager to see me, but, Jane"—he ran his hands over her shoulders—"you're trembling . . ."

"It's nothing. I . . . I was agitated and I should have waited I know, and please, I'm not asking for a . . . punishment, I . . ."

"No, no. Don't worry about that. Here, sit down." A comfortable armchair and footstool she had not noticed before waited in front of the fire. He gestured for her to take the chair, and settled himself on the edge of the plush stool. "Tell me what's happened."

So she told him, about Conroy and Tilly and even about Fraulein Lehzen. She spoke of her certainty that Conroy was paying the household to spy, and that he meant to bring her under his power.

All the while Thomas held her hand, never interrupting, simply waiting for her to finish.

"You don't know what it's like at court," she said. "The prince regent has driven away all the honest men. The only people left are the ones who are trapped, like me, or who want something, like Conroy. I had thought I could steer clear of his kind, but I've gotten close to something really valuable . . ."

"And so they seek you out?"

Jane nodded, relieved to see how grave he looked. He understood that the situation was indeed serious. But as Thomas drew his hand away from hers, fresh fear touched her. Had she said too much? Did he resent her bringing the outside world into what was meant to be a place of games and pleasure?

Thomas got to his feet and faced the fire for a long moment, one hand on the mantle. "I have the strongest urge to find this man Conroy and teach him some respect."

All Jane's breath left her in a rush. "What?"

"What is he about, treating you this way?" Thomas swung toward her; anger glittered in his eyes. She saw again how strong his form was, and what hard fists he possessed. "You are a lady. It is boundless insolence to try to make you party to his schemes so he can enrich himself off his fool of a master. The man should be whipped through the streets!"

"He's only using them. It's what we all do."

Thomas loomed over her for a moment, but then bent swiftly and cupped his hands about her face, holding her still so she had to look at him. "Jane, do not let me ever hear you compare your honest service to that man's extortion."

He kissed her then, a kiss filled with rough and desperate reassurance. She melted at once in his hands. He was angry for her, not at her. What happened to her mattered to him. He wanted to help. Whatever feeling brightened between them, it was not simply a matter of sexual pleasure.

Although it was that too. He was on one knee in front of her now, pulling her to the edge of the chair, caressing her back, brushing the sides of her breasts. She moaned against his mouth.

After a day of uncertainty and petty schemes, she wanted exactly this comfort.

"Oh, Jane." Thomas murmured as he pulled away. She gazed into his eyes, and felt her fires rise. Thomas smiled and all his dark mischief showed plainly in his handsome face. Heat burst into Jane's blood.

*Yes, yes,* she thought. *Please. Make the rest of the world go away, just for a little while.* Explanations could wait. Now, she needed to feel that he cared, that he needed her.

Slowly, Thomas released her and stood. He planted one booted foot on the stool and rested his arm against his thigh so he could look down on her, and let her take a long look at him. She felt a tiny, fragile thing, quite helpless against his strength. Her mouth went dry and her heart fluttered.

"You made me lose control the other night, Jane," Thomas said sternly.

"I . . . ?" She feigned surprise.

"Yes, my pretty wanton. With that pert mouth on my cock, so very eager and greedy." He reached down and ran his thumb across her lower lip. A shiver of desire danced across her skin. "You liked it, didn't you? You liked sucking on my cock."

Jane lowered her eyes in a mock show of humility. "I did like sucking your cock, Master Thomas. But I thought . . . I thought only to please you."

"Very aptly spoken." He strode to the fireplace and folded his hands behind his back, slapping the back of one into the palm of the other in a steady rhythm. She watched his profile closely, thought she saw a moment of indecision, but it was gone so quickly she could not be sure. "I have told you time and again, I expect discipline from you," he said firmly. "I will have you understand I know more of pleasure than you, and it is I who will decide how it is meted out."

"Yes, Master Thomas," she whispered.

"So, another lesson is in order, do you not agree?"

"Yes, sir." All the muscles at her center tightened. She was flushed and hot, and just a little bit frightened. What would he demand of her this time?

"Very good." He dropped himself into a nearby chair, his legs splayed wide, his posture both indolent and utterly confident. "Then undress for me. Now."

# Twelve

ane's heart hammered as she rose to her feet. The game had begun, and she wanted to play her best. So she curtsied low with her eyes demurely downcast. She undid the sash and hooks of her robe, found the ribbons for the nightdress underneath and loosened the knots. Then she shrugged both garments from her shoulders, letting them pool at her feet so she could step out of their confining drapery.

She stood before Thomas in just her chemise. His eyes traveled up and down her body, lingering at her breasts. Her nipples tightened under his heated gaze. The corner of his mouth curled up into a lustful and appreciative smile. The candlelight showed the outline of his swelling cock under his buckskins, and Jane felt her mouth watering again. Her pussy was already soft, and she felt the formation of its hot, greedy tears as she anticipated his touch. Feeling greatly daring Jane walked toward him, loosening the ribbons on her chemise as she went. She slipped down one muslin sleeve, then the other. The sheer undergarment slid to the floor, the fabric caressing her body deliciously as it fell.

She stood before him, entirely naked. His gaze swept her body as the falling chemise had, touching her everywhere, lingering on her pussy until she thought she would scream from desire.

"Open my buttons, Jane," he said at last. "Take out my cock."

Trembling, she knelt and quickly undid the buttons on his fly. He was going to order her to suck him, she was sure of it. It had felt so good to have him filling her mouth, to run her tongue around his taut velvet skin and hear him groan. Now she would have that power and pleasure again. Excitement coiled tight inside her.

She ran her hand under his balls as she lifted him free, savoring how tight they were already. She licked her lip deliberately, ready to take him, waiting only for his command.

"Now back away."

Her eyes flew to his. "But . . ."

"Do as you are told."

Confused, Jane stood and retreated three small, uncertain steps. Thomas nodded. "That's right, Jane. Remember, you are in need of your lesson. You will go to the cabinet and open it. Inside, there is a red velvet rope. Bring it to me."

There was no mistaking the cabinet he meant. She had noted it on her first visit. It was a huge, japanned wardrobe, its gleaming black surface decorated with a design of flying cranes and golden fans. Jane turned the slick handles to open both doors, and stopped, stunned.

Inside was a collection of objects such as she had never seen.

Ropes of silk and velvet hung on hooks, some knotted, some plain. A coiled, velvet whip hung next to a complex arrangement of silver chains. One shelf was filled with lengths of colored satin folded beside circlets of fur and velveteen. On other shelves, intricately carved wooden boxes and beautiful perfume bottles waited with elongated objects of glass, jade and ivory, some of which looked startlingly like penises.

"I'm waiting, Jane," growled Thomas.

Jane swallowed against the nervousness that quivered at the base of her throat. After a moment's searching, she found a coil of red velvet rope hanging at the back of the cabinet. She reached for it and turned. Thomas's eyes glowed hungrily, almost predatorily, in the firelight. The fingers of one hand ran idly up and down his gorgeously exposed cock. A sigh escaped Jane. She wanted that to be her hand fondling him. She wanted to kneel at his feet where she could give him pleasure and receive his touch.

"You like it, don't you, Jane." He stroked himself roughly once. "You like a hard cock."

"Yes, sir." Her fingers tightened around the velvet rope.

"You like looking at it, but you like touching it more."

"Yes."

"What else do you like? Say it."

"I like your cock in my mouth." She squeezed the rope, twisted it, wished desperately she had his cock in her hands instead. "And in my pussy."

"Are you wet, Jane?"

"Yes, sir. Very."

"That's good. Now." He held out his free hand. "Bring me the rope and go lie down on the bed."

She could barely make herself move, even to go closer to him. It was torment to watch him touching himself and yet to be unable to touch him. Her nipples hardened to the point of pain, and her heart hammered against her ribs. Her thighs rubbed together with each step, and all she could think about was how his hand would feel between her legs, sliding upward to press against the drenched folds of her pussy.

She laid the rope across Thomas's palm and turned. She couldn't breathe. She could barely see straight. His heated gaze was like a caress against her back. What was he doing? What was he thinking?

As she drew closer to the bed, Jane could see the headboard's design of swans, lilies and swirling water was actually pierced through in several places. The green silk coverlet felt cool and sensuously smooth under her buttocks as she sat down.

"In the center," Thomas ordered.

Rebellion sparked. He meant to make her crawl, or slide awkwardly. She would do neither. If he was going to make her watch him, she would repay the favor. Jane swung her legs up until she lay flat on her back, threw her arms over her head and rolled to the center of the luxurious emerald sea.

"Very pretty," he murmured.

She glanced sideways. Oh, yes, he was stroking himself, harder now. He liked what he saw.

"I am so glad you approve, sir." She smiled at him, and shimmied a little.

"Mischief, mischief." Thomas stood and swiftly rid himself of his clothes. But all that time, his hungry gaze remained focused on her, pinning her in place on the soft bed. Proud and powerful in his nakedness, he loomed over her, his eyes on fire, his heavy cock rock-hard and ready for her, and the velvet rope coiled in his fist. Jane looked up at him, ready to beg or do any other thing he asked, if only he would touch her.

Thomas lifted the rope and laid one loop between her breasts. "You must learn to trust me, Jane." He drew the velvet across her straining nipples. She gasped in surprise at how good the caress of the soft fabric felt, which only made Thomas smile. "I do not simply command your pleasure. I desire it, and I will have it, every aspect of it. Each order I give is to discover that pleasure. Each punishment is to teach you to trust in our . . . in your pleasure."

Slowly, so she could see each motion, he lifted the rope from her and began uncoiling it. Jane's heart thumped once. What was he doing?

"Spread your arms."

The nervousness that had been confined to her throat spread through body, but, strangely, it in no way dampened the burn of her desire. Jane stretched her arms out to either side, and waited.

Swiftly, Thomas slipped a length of velvet rope around her wrist, then secured the other end to the pierced headboard.

"What . . . ?"

"You are unruly and undisciplined, miss," he announced as he circled the bed. "It is time someone taught you to behave properly." He looped a second segment of velvet around her other wrist and secured it similarly.

"But . . ."

"But what?" he snapped.

"I won't be able to touch you."

"No. Not until I give my consent." He stood back and his shining eyes raked her. "It is so very pleasant, to see my sweet Jane lying helpless in my bed. I've half a mind to leave you like this, while I sit on the sofa and tell you the many games I have planned. Perhaps I'll touch myself and make you watch." He stroked his shaft thoughtfully and Jane could not suppress a moan. "Oh, how you would beg to be allowed to make me come with that pretty mouth."

"Yes," groaned Jane. His words were building new tension within her. She imagined him stroking himself, harder and faster, imagined watching his desire take him to the peak of pleasure. She'd ache, she'd burn, but oh, how sweet it would be.

"And after I've spilled myself, I might make you suck me until I grew hard again and ready to take you however I fancied."

"Yes." She shifted her hips, straining against the ropes to reach him. "Anything."

"Another time, perhaps." Thomas smiled wickedly. "Tonight I have other delights in mind."

Thomas turned and walked out of her field of vision. Jane let her head flop down onto the silken pillow with a groan of frustration, which only earned her a chuckle. It was as well she was tied, or she might have been tempted to slap him for that. But that would probably have just earned her yet another punishment, and really it was all too much.

The mattress sank and Jane turned her head. Thomas sat on the edge of the bed and lifted up one of the delicate glass bottles she had seen in the black and gold cabinet.

"Sandalwood oil," he told her as he swirled the amber-colored liquid above the candle flame. "Highly prized for the making of perfumes, and very precious." He undid the stopper and released a warm and spicy scent into the room.

He tipped the bottle over her, pouring out shimmering liquid across her breasts and nipples, down her belly and onto each outstretched arm. Jane gasped and shrugged her shoulders, uncertain whether she liked this new tickling sensation or not. But before she could protest, Thomas set the bottle down, and slung his leg over her, capturing her thighs between his. He wrapped his broad hands firmly around her ribcage, and began to rub the oil into her skin.

This was nothing like his other caresses. There was nothing teasing or demanding in this touch, and yet a pleasant languor spread through her body.

"Mmmm . . ." Jane's eyelids slowly fluttered closed.

He stroked her skin firmly, kneading her muscles in a way that was quite new and strange to her. The oil warmed as he rubbed it into her skin. Where it touched, Jane imagined she shimmered golden with the precious substance. She floated adrift in a world where there was only the cloud of spiced scent and the mellow pleasure of his touch. She was beyond thought or worry or mischief. Even when he cupped her pussy to rub the sandalwood oil there, even when he stroked her forehead and temples, his oiled fingers sliding sensuously across her skin, she only sighed softly. She forgot the ropes that held her, forgot the spikes of need that had pierced her only moments before. This was a constant, perfect sweetness. She could lie here forever, with him massaging her in just this way and be content.

"So beautiful," Thomas breathed. "Never has there been a woman so beautiful."

Jane's eyelids drifted open, and what she saw caught her breath. His face had relaxed, and though she had never thought of him as old, he looked much younger somehow, as if some part of him long held closed had been opened. Instead of mischief, there was wonder in his green eyes. No, not wonder. Awe.

"Only with you," she breathed. "Only for you."

"Oh, by all that's holy, Jane . . ." Thomas leaned forward, stretching his body fully against hers and kissed her. It was a slow kiss, lingering, thorough and fully in the moment, just like his touch had been. Jane kissed him back, delighting in the play of her tongue against his, the weight of his chest against her heavy breasts, and best of all, his cock stroking against her belly. The mellow contentment began to ebb from her limbs, replaced by desire's more urgent compulsions. She felt it in Thomas too, not just in his hot, hard cock, but in his increasing heartbeat, in the press of his mouth as he strove to thrust more deeply into her. She moved to wrap her arms around him, but the ropes she had forgotten for so long brought her up short.

"Let me go," she whispered as he moved to kiss her throat. "Please. Let me hold you."

He pulled back just enough that she could see his face. Emotion flickered through his eyes, and Jane swore she saw longing there, and that it was followed swiftly by fear. But like the indecision she thought she'd seen before, this also swiftly vanished, replaced by his sly, mischief.

*Replaced or hidden?*

"Oh, no, sweet Jane," Thomas drawled, running his thumb across her swollen, sensitized mouth and then sliding his fingers smoothly down her oiled skin to her tightly furled nipple. His balls rubbed the oiled folds of her weeping pussy as he moved over her. "You shall not touch me yet. No matter how you beg."

An unreasoning and unexpected bolt of anger shot through her. "I do not intend to beg."

"No?" He sat back, and his thighs squeezed hers, compressing her pussy delightfully while at the same time reminding her how completely trapped she was. "We'll see about that."

He pressed his hands against her hips and stroked them. The oil made her skin like silk and his hard palms slipped easily across her. His thumb found the very tip of her slit and pressed there. Jane gasped as pleasure struck, hard and immediate. Thomas grinned, an expression of pure wickedness, as he began moving his thumb in a tiny circle, stroking her clit swiftly and lightly.

"Oh," Jane moaned. Her back arched, her breasts strained, but he did not touch them. He simply continued his swift stirring of that single exquisitely sensitive point. Jane's hips arched, and her legs strained to open so he could slide his fingers farther inside her, but his thighs clamped hers tight and he was far too strong for her to shift. She was trapped, held helpless to his will, and his will was all to torment her with this touch that was so small, and yet so powerful.

"Is it good then, Jane?" He slid his other hand under her ass and squeezed. "My unruly, greedy Jane."

Her hands knotted around the ropes. The velvet rubbed against her palms, a new sensuous friction to mingle with the silk and the oil and Thomas's wicked, merciless stroking of her clit, and now his hand fondling her ass.

"Tell me, Jane. Tell me you want it."

She clamped her mouth shut. She had said she would not beg and she would not. But oh, it felt so good. Her clit had swollen, she was sure. It was throbbing now, and the pleasure of his attentions radiated throughout her body.

"Nothing to say?" His hand underneath her slid up, and she felt his fingers probing the split between her buttocks. How could that possibly feel good? But it did. She liked the pressure there. It pushed her eager clit more firmly against his thumb. She strained, but she didn't know what her body sought, until she felt his one finger probing her anus.

She gasped again. He couldn't. *She* couldn't . . .

"Trust me, Jane," he murmured, pressing harder with both hands, his fingers pressing against her clit, and against her anus. "Let me show you how very good it can feel."

His fingers were still thoroughly oiled. His attention to her clit and her folds was so sweet and she wanted so badly to strain open, and his other finger, his other . . .

His other finger was inside her.

"There now," he whispered. "Isn't that good?"

It was good. Held firmly between his hands and his thighs, helpless to do anything but feel, it was very good. He increased his movements; thumb circling, finger moving in and out, fucking her backside with small precise motions, matching the rhythm of her blood where it pounded in her clit. The caresses and the pressure swirled together to fill her with intense delight.

"Beg me, Jane. Beg for it and you'll come. I'll make you come so hard, but you must beg me."

She couldn't stand it. She'd die of his touch. His strength was nothing. The rope was nothing. It was his knowing, wicked touch calling forth this inescapable pleasure that mastered her.

"Please," she moaned, writhing her hips against his hands, stirring her own clit, stirring the finger snug inside her ass. "Oh, please, I want to come! Make me come!"

"Yes." His fingers plunged deep into her pussy. With both hands he fucked her, front and back, his palm grinding against her throbbing, swollen clit.

Her orgasm exploded and Jane cried out in welcome. Her body rocked wildly, but he still held her trapped, the uncontrollable motion of her hips making her fuck his hands even harder to prolong her ecstasies.

Gradually, the tumult eased. Tension and trembling faded, and Jane's body settled deeply into the nest of rumpled silk.

"There, Jane, there," Thomas whispered, withdrawing his fingers from her, and caressing her slowly, possessively. "You see what rewards come with obedience?"

"Yes," she whispered.

He leaned down until his chest brushed her breasts. "Yes, what?"

She did not resist. The force of the pleasure he imparted had robbed her of all her strength. "Yes, Master Thomas."

"That's right." He kissed her, teasingly. "Your only master. Isn't that so, Jane?"

"Yes. Only you."

"Very good. Very, very good." He rolled aside. She only stirred a little as he parted her legs and settled himself between them.

"Shall I fuck you, Jane?" He took himself in his hand and slid the tip of his cock into her slit, stroking her slowly back and forth. Oh, she couldn't endure more, and yet it felt so very good.

"Please."

Smiling, he slid inside her. It was a comfortable, easy fit and Jane sighed with contentment.

"Yes, it feels good, doesn't it? You're so very wet and ready for my cock."

He took his weight on his knees and grasped her breasts, thumbing her nipples, and Jane almost swooned. Her breasts had so ached for his touch while he played with her pussy, now the sensation of it was overwhelming. She moaned and arched her back, knotting her fingers into the rope as she strained to press herself against him.

"And still you want more." He rolled her nipples in his oiled fingertips in time with the easy glide of his cock in her sheath.

"Never enough," she panted. "Oh, God, it will never be enough."

"No." His voice thickened, mischief gone, gentleness gone. In its place waited all the awe and longing she had only glimpsed before. "No, never."

His thrusts increased, urgency overtaking sport and Jane rocked her hips, meeting him thrust for thrust, urging him on, driving him on. He pinched her nipples, adding bright pinpricks of pain to season the pleasure and she cried out for more. He thrust deeper and he groaned, his hands sliding swiftly down her body, to cup her ass, to lift her to him, and to slip his finger inside her anus again.

"Ah!" How could anything in the world feel so wicked and yet so good? Caught between his cock and his hand, she was screaming, begging, pleading, and he only answered by fucking her harder, which was what she wanted most of all. He was master and yet she commanded him. Faster and harder, passion raising them up closer, higher, further into the blinding light of purest pleasure until there was nothing else in the whole world.

# Thirteen

"You promised you would answer my questions," said Jane as she stroked Thomas's chest.

Thomas looked down at the woman curled against his side. He had his arm around her creamy white shoulders and his fingers toyed with her chestnut hair where it tumbled around her breasts in magnificent disarray. The candlelight brought out sparks of red and gold in the luxurious tresses and he felt he could stare at them, at her, for hours. A wave of tenderness swept through him. By Heaven, she was beautiful like this; wrapped in cool green silk, her face and eyes still flushed with the glow of their mutual ecstasy. He had barely formed the thought when a warning tolled in the back of his mind.

*It's only your cock,* he told himself sternly. *It found beauty in her sheath, and wants to return.*

"If you say I promised answers, I'm sure I did," Thomas replied lightly. "But which questions are these?"

"The dreams," she prompted exasperatedly. "This room. How any of this is possible. How *you* are possible."

"Ah, yes." Jane had surrendered so completely to their erotic play, Thomas had hoped that she'd lost the urge to question how such pleasures came to be. He thought about kissing her again, about rolling her under and drowning her once more in desire, but he saw the steel flash in her eyes.

*I should have known better.* Lady Jane DeWitte was not one to be distracted for long.

"Magic," he said.

"I'll not be made light of, sir!" Jane snapped, lifting his arm from off her shoulders and flinging it aside.

"Never in life!" he cried, although he could not keep the laugh from his voice. "But you said it yourself our first night, Jane. "

Jane considered for a long moment, her eyes searching his face carefully. He would have to be more wary of those eyes. Jane saw far too much.

"Is there another explanation you would have me give? I can lie if you wish." *I have lied so much to you, one more should make no difference to either of us.*

"I do not know," she admitted. "But . . . magic?"

Thomas sat up a little higher on the pillows. "Magic is real. It is a part of the natural world, like lightning, or the force of gravity."

"But the ability to create dreams or speak to someone else in their sleep is not natural."

"It is. What you're not used to is that there are certain aspects of the natural order that can be influenced by intent. Think of sewing."

"Sewing?"

"Yes. A stitch is formed by the needle, the thread and the skill of the hand, which is in itself shaped by the intent of the person whose hand it is. When we speak of magic, we speak of a natural force, which is like the thread, harnessed by creation of a sympathetic circumstance, which is the needle, and the will or intent of the magician, which is the hand. Be the needle so fine or the thread so tightly twisted, it is ultimately the skill and attentiveness of the tailor that makes the coat a coat rather than a jumble of cloth bits."

"That's a very tidy explanation. You've given it before?"

"That's how it was explained to me. I also did not believe in magic when I first encountered it."

"So when I said you were a fairy prince . . ." she began, but Thomas stopped her with a hand on her arm.

"No, Jane. Never call me that. I've told you, I'm as human as you are."

"Then what am I to call you? Wizard? Sorcerer?"

"These also exist, but I cannot claim such a close command of magic. I have only been granted a few gifts."

"Such as the gift to create dreams?"

"Dreams are doorways. They lead into the hearts and thoughts of the dreamers. Magic, if properly controlled, can open doors."

As soon as the words left his mouth, Thomas realized he'd made a mistake. Jane pulled back farther in an attitude of suspicion that ran far too deep for comfort. "So you opened my mind, and put in it these images of desire?"

Thomas drew her swiftly to him, kissing her brow. "No, Jane. It was you who opened your mind to me."

"What? How?"

Thomas smiled. "The night before you left with the Duke of Kent's retinue for Saxe-Coburg, you attended a ball at Carleton House."

Jane nodded, rolling her eyes at the memory. "It was a nightmare. I couldn't believe the drunkenness, and the Duke of Clarence, those crude stories . . . I was miserable."

"I noticed."

Jane pulled back once more, but in surprise this time, not in fear, so Thomas let her go. "You were there?"

"I was, and like you, I wished myself elsewhere."

Carleton House, being a royal residence, was warded against magic. But the prince regent's constant remodeling and expansions had created cracks in some of those wards, not large, but sufficient to allow Thomas to slip in as far as the gardens. But even from there he'd seen how unruly the gathering had become. He'd known pirate crews where the men conducted themselves better than the silk-clad sots that the prince regent surrounded himself with.

Jane brushed restlessly at the sheets, slowly taking in the realization that the two of them had been in near proximity before Lady Darnley's. What he could not tell her was he had come there looking for her, or someone like her; a woman who could gain him entry to the household. A pang of regret touched him. He had known this time would come. What he had not counted on was how very reluctant he would feel spinning further lies for Jane. Of course telling her the whole truth was impossible, but she seemed to have awakened his conscience along with his desires, and that was very troubling indeed.

"I saw you strolling across the lawn," he told her, hoping that telling her at least some truth would help smother his discomfort. "I thought you were meeting someone."

"I was escaping the heat."

He nodded. "Again, I could not blame you. But what I remember was when you turned toward the house and I saw how lovely, and how sad, you looked . . ."

No, it had been more than that. Jane DeWitte had been a vision in the moonlight; proud and beautifully formed. Thomas had been in the presence of glamour-made perfection for centuries, but the sight of this mortal woman froze him in place. He hadn't even needed to resort to his magics to understand her. When she'd looked up at the house, the loneliness in her showed plain as day. He'd felt a powerful urge to go to her, to find out what was wrong, to tease and joke with her, or to do whatever else he could to bring a smile to that lovely visage.

It had been a long moment before he had been able to gather enough composure to ease open his perceptions and catch hold of the thoughts drifting from her. Those escaping thoughts told him she was leaving with the Duke of Kent's party. Thomas had been unable to believe his luck. The woman he wanted was also the woman he needed.

Thomas turned that phrase over in his mind uneasily. Because since that day, it had only become more true. He had only been with Jane in the flesh a few times now, but they had walked together in dreams for over a month. In those dreams, lush with sensuality and filled with seduction, he had found a merry woman, a spirited woman, an intelligent, graceful, proud woman. He had spent hours detailing in his mind what he would do when he held her in truth, and twice now she had destroyed his plans because desire for her had driven him beyond all control. His need to experience the fullness of her body and her passions had overridden his mission, which was to enslave her desires to him. And tonight . . . he'd meant to spank her, perhaps make her wear his chains, but she had been so tired and afraid when she came to him, he was seized by the need to bring her ease. It had been gratifying to feel her relax underneath him, to rub the tension and worry from her. It was power and trust of an entirely new kind, and he'd relished it more even than he had issuing her orders.

*What's happening to me?*

"You might have introduced yourself at Carleton House." Jane pursed her lips in an admirable imitation of a pout.

Thomas traced her jawline with his thumb. She smelled of sandalwood and love. "I could have made the introduction, but you were so stern, and so beautiful. Perhaps I was shy."

"You? Now you are teasing me."

"A little." He drew his fingers down her exposed shoulder and smiled when she shivered. "But when I asked about you, I learned you were leaving in the morning, and no one knew how long you'd be gone. It seemed hopeless to attempt an acquaintance. After that though, I couldn't leave off thinking of you. I felt a connection a . . . destiny is a grand word, but yes, a destiny." A grand word. A dangerous word, because no one ever understood what their destiny meant until it was upon them. "When you deal in magic, you learn not to ignore such feelings. Then, I dreamt of you, and I knew the connection was real."

"You dreamt of me?" Jane's eyes narrowed suspiciously.

Thomas found himself both surprised and impressed. She was dealing with this new knowledge with levelheaded tenacity. True, surrounded by his glamour, belief would come more easily than at other times, but he had still expected her to balk at what he said, perhaps even dismiss it out of hand. But no, Jane De-Witte knew the truth when she heard it.

This understanding sent an unfamiliar chill through him, carrying with it the fear of all the things he had not said.

"I dreamt of you running down a long corridor with an unlit candle in your hand," he told her, leaving out how he had followed her to the inn where the ducal party had rested before boarding their ship at Dover. "You were frightened and angry, and searching for someone. You kept calling and calling, but you got no answer."

"Oh." Jane pressed back onto the pillows, as if trying to make herself smaller.

He cocked his head toward her. "You know this dream."

"It is a nightmare I've had since my father died. No, that is not true. I've had it since I found out about his debts. In the dream I'm lost and I can't find the way out. I'm sure my father knows the way but he will not answer when I call, and the corridor gets smaller and smaller until it becomes a cell and I'm trapped in the dark . . ."

"I know," he said gravely. He shared her fear and outrage, and the horror of the walls pressing in. "I wanted to comfort you." That was a gross understatement. He'd wanted to fly to her rooms, to hold her close and wake her gently to kinder thoughts. It was not right that this lovely woman should be so tormented as well as so alone.

He had not thought much of the strength of his response then. But sharing dreams, like sharing thoughts, was an intimate magic and that tenderness, that concern lingered in him still. He found himself wondering if the nightmare had receded for her. And if it had, he wanted to know that he had been the cause.

"I hadn't even thought of the connection," Jane said. "Both begin in corridors . . . but the moods of the dream are so different."

"I reached out in the only way I could," Thomas told her. "I used my magic to reshape your nightmare." This was the truth, as far as it went. Thomas wished he could wipe away the sick feeling that invaded him. He was doing his duty, nothing more. The truth would not only hurt her, it would ruin his queen's plan. Why did it seem so difficult to skirt around it now?

"Should I apologize, Jane?" He smoothed her hair across her shoulders and lower, allowing his fingers a tantalizing brush against the curving tops of her breasts. "It was not right of me to do so much without permission, but you were so afraid, and there was nothing else I could do."

Jane lay silent for a long time, but she did not pull away, so he held his peace, and only continued to stroke her gently, soothingly.

"No, you do not need to apologize," she told him at last. "I am not sorry." Jane lifted her eyes to his, and what he saw there stopped his heart.

Trust. Entire and absolute.

Thomas bent and kissed her. He could do nothing else. Her lips parted easily for him and she sighed with contentment as his tongue moved inside to probe and to tease. He felt her nipples tighten underneath the silken sheet she'd wrapped around herself. She was a marvel of responsiveness, this woman. He knew instinctively that if he reached down and pressed his fingers into her slit, he would find her pussy was already damp. His cock twitched and swelled, seeking the warmth between her thighs as she pressed closer, her tongue urging him onward. Did she understand how very demanding she was, even in her surrender? He wanted to answer each and every demand, beginning this very moment.

"Oh, my dear, sweet Jane," he breathed against her cheek. "We cannot. The sun is almost up. I must send you back to your own bed."

"I know." But neither of them moved away from the other. "It is very strange to feel so much in such a short time."

He made himself smile playfully at her. "Passion has its own magics, my dear, and one of them is the enhancement of emotion. Now." He frowned at her in mock sternness. "Remember obedience. I tell you, you must dress."

She sighed. "Yes, Master Thomas."

Thomas had to stifle a curse. Just hearing those words sent a fresh pulse of blood to his hardening cock. Jane climbed from the bed, displaying her gloriously naked back and ass. It took every ounce of control to refrain from grabbing her shapely waist and tossing her back onto the bed where he could pin her down once more and fuck her until she screamed his name.

And if he did not stop thinking like this, he was going to be in real pain soon.

*You will accomplish nothing if she's caught sneaking through the corridors,* he reminded himself as he reached for his small clothes and breeches.

Jane slid back into her chemise. Thomas found her discarded nightdress and bowed as he held it out for her. Assuming a haughty air, she lifted her arms so he could draw the garment over her head.

"Get some rest," he told her as he kissed her in farewell. "You'll need your strength."

He saw by the flash in her eyes she understood him. Within a heartbeat, however, her face softened. "Thomas . . . do you think we should? At least until we can find out which members of the household Conroy has spying for him . . ."

His heart constricted. "You think I should not come to you anymore?"

"It is not what I want."

"I understand, Jane. But you must also understand, I am not leaving you alone with that man after you."

She smiled, an expression of tenderness that nestled warm in his heart and mind. "It is just for a little while." She reached up to brush her fingertips across his mouth. "I meant what I said," she murmured.

"What was that, my dear?"

"There is only you. You are the only one who could bring such . . . such response from me or with whom I have ever acted with such freedom." Her lips brushed his and she backed away. "Thank you."

She whisked from the room and closed the door behind her, leaving Thomas quite alone.

# Fourteen

The next week passed quickly for Jane. But the nights dragged into eternity.

It had been decided that the duchess needed to hold a formal reception at Kensington House. "Our friends expect it, my dear," said the duke as they sat together playing piquet after supper. It was the first night no party was being given in honor of their return, and despite his complaints of the constant noise and crush, it was clear the duke was bored. "Several of them have asked when we shall be hosting."

Jane sat by the fire, struggling halfheartedly with some fancy work on a christening gown she knew very well would never be used. Each stitch reminded her of Thomas and his explanation of magic, which only served to remind her of the contentment of lying wrapped in silk beside him where she could feel his warmth and savor every aspect of his face and form.

"They wish to inspect the royal belly for themselves," Her

Grace replied testily. "But, my lord, there is not time to do the thing properly."

"But there must be something. We cannot appear mean, or as if we were hiding you. You know what kind of talk that will breed."

They did. Georgie had written Jane that rumors were abroad that the child was not actually the duke's. They were absurd rumors, but it was not the rumors that were the trouble. The trouble was that the rumors were coming from the prince regent.

"I understand," the duchess laid down the ten of diamonds. "Very well. We shall hold a . . . a drawing room to content them."

"You were the first to point out how important appearances are."

"There are consequences to being right." The duchess sighed and selected another card. "Don't worry, my lord. With my Lady Jane and your Captain Conroy, we shall accomplish all things." She beamed at Jane, who managed a smile in reply.

"Capital. I leave it all to you then." The duke displayed his confidence in his wife and staff by taking the trick and tallying up his points.

The result of this decision was that Jane's days became immediately and entirely absorbed in planning. She drew up the guest lists, discussed shifting estimates of staffing requirements with the housekeeper and butler, and wrote out the most important and personal invitations. She also found herself sitting across tables from Captain Conroy for hours at a stretch, going over yet more lists of provisions, musicians and all proposed expenditures, while the duchess directed matters from a soft chair with her feet up and Frau Seibold hovering at her shoulders.

At first, Jane tried to watch Conroy to see if he lingered with one member of the staff more than any other. But that only served to make her head hurt. She began imagining dozens of contradictory meanings in the charming smiles he bestowed on everyone from the duchess to the parlor maid.

If the days were difficult, the nights were torture. Though Jane fell exhausted into her bed, sleep always eluded her. Some nights she remained awake until dawn, clutching the black ribbon she kept inside the book beside her table. Her mind strained to hear Thomas's call, even though she knew it would not come. Her body demanded his touch and gave her no peace, even if she resorted to rubbing herself until a kind of release came. No such solitary activity could slake her thirst, for when it was over and the meaningless spasms eased, she was still empty and alone.

She had penned a short answer to Mrs. Beauchamp's invitation, explaining she was required to assist with preparations for the duchess's drawing room, and regretting she could not possibly visit until after that time. She'd sealed the message with her head turned sideways so there was no risk of a tear falling onto the page. She detested the drama of her feelings. The intensity was beyond all reason, but it remained real nonetheless. Whatever her mind might have to say on the subject, her heart and body were united. She needed Thomas, and she herself had told him to stay away.

But there was nothing she could do about it. Conroy watched her every day, and Tilly watched her, and Lehzen watched her, and Heaven only knew who else. Even behind her closed door, Jane knew they waited and they watched, and she could do nothing at all.

*Or could I?* Jane wondered as she spelled out yet another

invitation in her best copperplate hand, readying it for the duchess's signature. *Is this really the only living for me?*

Once it took hold, that question grew roots, and the roots deepened. April faded into May. Preparations around the duchess reached fever pitch. The modistes and milliners came and went. Her Grace dithered over swatches of fabrics, lengths of antique lace, dozens of kinds of buttons and endless varieties of ribbon. Jane fetched her iced coffee and cakes, adjusted her pillows, rubbed her shoulders and back, and still the question grew in her mind. The weather turned bad again, all rain and gray skies to glower down at the swelling blooms in the gardens. Frau Seibold pulled the drapes and built up the fire until Jane thought she'd faint from the heat.

At last, though, it came time for the invitations to be delivered. Frau Seibold, however, declared the English spring was still too cold for Her Grace so close to her time. Therefore, as the duchess's lady, it was Jane's duty to take round the cards that could not be sent by the ordinary servants. Jane felt ready to press Frau Seibold's blue-veined hand in thanks. Tilly would go out with her, of course, but at least she would have some fresh air and a change of scene.

Perhaps, if she was careful, she could have more than that. Thomas had his magics and mysteries, but she had a few tricks she'd learned at the elbow of her good friend Lady Hibbert-Jones, to whom she penned a letter asking for assistance. It was not the first time such letters had passed between herself and Georgiana. After Jane became Lord Octavius DeWitte's wife, Georgiana had provided protective coloration for more than one escapade. Georgie would not let her down now.

The morning of the outing dawned clear and pleasant. The buds had broken on the trees, and the green leaves had emerged. Snowdrops were replaced by daffodils, crocus and primrose in all their spring finery. Soon the violets and bluebells would join them. Even a round of drawing rooms and weak coffee and prying questions seemed worth it to Jane if it meant a chance to breathe just some of that blossom-scented air.

And Thomas would be waiting for her. Georgie would have sent the second letter Jane had enclosed in the first. Georgie would not fail her.

Jane stood in the foyer, waiting for Tilly to bring her coat and bonnet, anticipation making her as jumpy as a child waiting for an outing. But the sound of stiff-soled shoes against the marble brought reality down hard. Before she even turned, Jane knew who she would see.

"Ah, Lady Jane," Captain Conroy smiled down at her. "I was hoping to catch you before you left. I have a letter that needs to be posted. Will you take it for me?" He held out the white square.

It was a request both ridiculous and demeaning, as if he did not have a dozen servants and under-secretaries available as soon as he touched the bell pull.

"Really, Captain. One of the servants . . ."

But he smiled again. "There's no need for this to be difficult, is there, Lady Jane? Have we not worked well together this past week?" His brows arched. "I had thought I might need to speak with the duke and duchess about you, but, well . . ." He coughed as if the matter was too delicate to mention. "Now I see that was overly hasty. I trust you'll forgive me?"

*He's testing me. Trying to find out if I've thought the better of trying to keep free of him.* Jane was still struggling to formulate the best reply as Tilly descended the staircase, carrying Jane's dotted Swiss pelisse and her lace bonnet trimmed with Clarence blue. Up above somewhere, Lehzen prowled, and Conroy had just threatened her position.

Once again, Jane made herself put her pride in her pocket. "There is nothing to forgive," she said pleasantly to the captain, and the words tasted of bile.

"Then you'll take the letter?" Conroy held the paper out.

"Of course." She took the paper. But it was not just paper that touched her fingers. There was something else. She could feel the slight lump against her glove.

Jane turned the paper in her fingers. And saw the scrap of black cloth. No, not just black cloth, a black ribbon.

Thomas's black ribbon.

Jane turned white as a sheet, and struggled for control, but control was not possible.

"Oh, I'm sorry." Conroy grasped the end of the ribbon between thumb and forefinger and drew it from her weakened grip before she could move. "Careless of me." While Jane stared, he tucked the ribbon in his pocket.

*He knows. He knows.* The words drummed against Jane's skull to the rhythm of her frantically beating heart.

She looked up at Captain Conroy, and it seemed a long way up. He smiled down with triumphant benevolence shining in his fine, dark eyes.

Jane stiffened her shoulders and stilled her hands. She could do nothing about the color of her cheeks, but she would not give this man any further satisfactions. "Are there any other errands you would have me perform while I'm out? I have only Her Grace's business to occupy me, after all." The remark was petty and bitter, but it was all she had.

It was all ashes though, because it set the seal on Conroy's triumph. "Not at this time, Lady Jane. Thank you."

They nodded to each other, and Jane let Tilly help her into her pelisse and bonnet. She would not shake. She would keep breathing. She would walk out to the carriage and climb in as if there was not the least thing wrong. Tilly would tuck the rug over her skirts, and sit across, smiling.

There was nothing she could do. Nothing at all. Conroy had her ribbon, and if he didn't know the name of Jane's lover, he knew her lover existed. He could go to the duke at any time.

Jane stared out at the gardens in their careless spring finery. The landau emerged from the gates at the end of Kensington House's garden and set a good pace through the park beyond. The day was as fine as it had appeared. Sunlight and a balmy wind touched her skin, but did nothing to lighten Jane's fury. The curious—whether on horse, on foot or in their own carriages—turned at the sight of the duke's coat of arms on the carriage door, and craned their necks to see who the carriage held.

*More eyes to watch. More gossips to talk,* thought Jane bitterly.

The first three deliveries went smoothly. Jane had found the ladies at home, and had drunk coffee with each of them, staying the requisite fifteen minutes before moving on. She had feared the ritual and meaningless talk would aggravate her temper, which had already been pushed past its limits. But, surprisingly, putting on her polite lady's mask had settled her.

She needed to be settled, because it was time to deal with Tilly. Georgie could be trusted to play her part in Jane's plan, but she was far less certain of how Tilly would react, especially after Conroy's trick with the ribbon. Everything could still go wrong in this moment.

"Tilly," Jane said in the tone she reserved for making small talk with those she could not afford to offend. "I've been thinking. We've neither of us has had a moment to ourselves lately, and it will only become busier, what with the drawing room, and the baby due at any time. So there's no need to rush ourselves today, is there?" Jane pulled five shillings and the captain's letter from her reticule. "Captain Conroy has this letter that needs posting. Why don't you take it? You can get yourself a little something as well, if you would like. I have some shopping for myself to do. We can meet at Mr. Drummond's warehouse at three o'clock and take round the rest of the invitations after that."

Tilly looked down at the letter, and weighed the shillings in her other palm. "I'm not sure . . ."

"It is for Captain Conroy, Tilly. I wouldn't ask you if it wasn't important." She made herself smile conspiratorially. "And, as I say, there's no real reason for us to hurry back to that stuffy house, is there?"

Tilly's thumb caressed the scattering of coins in her blackgloved palm and Jane watched the thoughts flickering across her face. Tilly didn't know Conroy had already shown Jane the ribbon. She thought she was getting away with something, and she liked that thought.

"Well, I suppose, since there's no hurry . . ."

Jane covered her relief by signaling Jeffries to stop. "None at all."

"Thank you, madame." Tilly stowed the coins and letter in her bag. "I will meet you at three o'clock."

Tilly hopped from the carriage and bustled down the street without looking back. Jane watched her go with something of an ache inside. Just two weeks ago, Tilly had been reluctant to let her walk outside the carriage; Now for a few coins, she was perfectly ready to abandon Jane entirely. Had she ever treated the girl badly? She didn't think so. Tilly probably just felt caged in the life of a servant, but had nowhere else to go and nothing else to be. Conroy's intrigue's offered her profit and adventure. Could she reasonably be expected to turn that down?

The only good thing was that Tilly was less likely to give Captain Conroy an accurate account of the drive now that she had taken Jane's money. If Tilly was at all intelligent, she would take what she could get from both of sides, for as long as she could.

*And so it begins.* Jane gave Jeffries Georgiana's address and sat back, watching the streets. Jane had known she could not live so near the court and escape intrigue forever, but somehow she'd never expected her first game to be played with her own maid.

*Why does it have to be this way? Why is living in this glass house my only choice?*

She knew the answer, of course. It had come back to her each and every time she asked the question over the previous week. She had no choice because no matter how destitute she might be, she remained a lady. She had been born an Honorable, and now lived as a baron's widow. Standards must be upheld, as her mother had so often told her. Appearances must be maintained. Her father had repeated this on the day of her wedding to Lord Octavius, and Lord Octavius had sighed it every time she presented him the accounts from the latest dinner party he had asked her to organize. All of them had made it clear it was up to Jane to help maintain appearances for all of them.

*But they are all dead.* A pang of disloyalty touched her as she thought this, but that pang was not as strong as the question that followed.

*Who am I maintaining appearances for now?*

# Fifteen

Georgiana and Lord Hibbert-Jones both had a love for the modern. Their house in the fashionable district just off Grosvenor's square was entirely new, with clean sweeping lines. Probably, Jane thought, with a bit of envy, all of its sparkling windows closed properly.

"You'll take in my card, please, Jeffries." Jane pulled one of her visiting cards from its case and bent down a corner to show that she had brought it personally. "And ask if Lady Hibbert-Jones is at home."

"Yes, ma'am." Jeffries touched his hat and took the card, but just as he climbed down from the carriage, the front door opened and Georgie emerged with her own maid in tow.

"Why, Jane!" Georgie did an excellent job of looking startled as she hurried to the carriage. "How lovely! I'm so sorry, I was just on my way out . . ."

"Oh, you mustn't let me delay you," replied Jane. From under her bonnet's concealing brim, Georgie tipped her a wink, and

Jane's heart soared. "I'm taking round invitations to the drawing room for her grace. I just wanted to give you yours." She pulled the neat gilt-edged card from the pile in the box beside her and handed it across.

"Thank you, Jane. You may give Her Grace my assurance that I will attend." Georgie paused for just the right number of heartbeats. "I've an idea. Why don't you ride with me a ways? I'm going to call on Lady Price. I'm sure she's also on the guest list, isn't she?"

"That would be splendid, Georgie." Taking up the box of invitations, Jane stepped from the carriage. "Jeffries, I'll be riding with Lady Hibbert-Jones. You'll take the carriage and meet us at Durham's warehouse at three?" She pressed a shilling into his hand. *I am quite the lady bountiful today.* "And you might want a mug of cider. It's turned quite warm."

"Very good, ma'am," said Jeffries calmly as he tucked away the coin in his vest. "And thank you."

The second gift did its work as well as the first. Jeffries didn't look back at all as he touched up the horses and eased the landau into traffic. Georgie handed the invitation to her maid and sent the girl back inside the house. Once the door closed, Jane seized Georgie's hand.

"He's just round the corner," said Georgie without Jane even needing to open her mouth. "There's a little park there. Mostly nurses and children at this time of day. No one we know."

"Thank you, Georgie," said Jane fervently.

Georgiana nodded, but her face was entirely sober. "Are you going to tell me who he is? Aside from a guest of Mrs. Beauchamp's?"

Jane looked at her friend's kind, clever, entirely trustworthy countenance and found she did not have it in her to lie, or even tell a partial truth. "Please, no questions, not yet. I'll tell you everything as soon as I can."

Georgie squeezed her hand tightly. "Is he good to you?"

"Yes, Georgie. I promise he is."

Georgie smiled and took the box of invitation from Jane's hands. That smile was a little sad, but still genuine. "Then I'll take you to him."

The park around the corner was a small green space bordered by a low fence, flower beds and benches. As Georgie had said, its tidy lawn was filled with nurses pushing infants or sitting together for a gossip while boys chased balls and hoops across the lawn and girls compared dolls or pushed them in miniature prams.

Thomas stood at the gate.

Jane felt her veins fill with warm honey, which turned swiftly into pure fire. With every fiber of her being, she wanted to throw herself into his arms and kiss him. No, she wanted to devour him, here, in broad daylight, where all the world could see. She wanted his mouth on her, everywhere. She wanted to be next to him, skin to skin, to be laid down by him at once and have his cock inside her, immediately, without hesitation, games or ceremony.

All this filled her to bursting, and she had to content herself with a bland, polite smile.

"Good afternoon, Sir Thomas," she said. "Georgiana, this is Sir Thomas Lynne. Sir Thomas, may I present my very good friend, Lady Hibbert-Jones."

"Your servant, madame." Thomas bowed over Georgie's hand.

Georgiana did not answer him at once. Instead, she treated him to one of her coolest, most penetrating stares. Jane had seen Georgie accurately size up the character of senior diplomats, experienced politicians and at least one popular Drury Lane leading man with that stare.

"How do you do, Sir Thomas?" she said with frosty politeness. Then she turned to Jane. "I'll pick you up in the barouche in one half hour."

Jane kissed her swiftly on the cheek. "Thank you, Georgie."

Georgie nodded, and with a last appraising glance at Thomas, she strode down the street toward her house.

"I think I am glad to know you have such a friend," said Thomas as he watched her go, a small, thoughtful smile on his lips. Then Thomas turned to Jane and looked into her eyes.

"Oh, Jane," he whispered. "I've missed you more than I would have thought possible." His hand lifted. He meant to touch her face, Jane was sure. It would be a swift, intimate, indecorous touch and she quivered in anticipation. But at the last moment, he seemed to remember where they were, and only held out his arm. "Shall we walk?"

Jane laid her hand on his sleeve. They moved beneath the trees and down the little park's well-tended path. The warmth of their contact flowed into her body, redoubling all her longings. The world around them seemed filled with phantoms. Only Thomas was real.

"There's something I need to tell you, Thomas."

"Oh?" He arched his brows just a fraction, but Jane felt the undercurrent of tension through him.

Slowly, softly, she told him how she had kept his ribbon, and how it had been both given to her and taken from her that morning.

Thomas said nothing immediately. His arm had gone solid as a rock beneath her hand, and she suspected he longed to make a fist. Was he picturing Conroy's face?

They reached the end of the little park and Thomas turned them as smoothly as if they were partners in a dance so they could walk the other way.

"I've spent a great deal of time lately thinking on your situation," said Thomas. "Tell me, would you say Captain Conroy is an exact and cautious man?"

Jane thought of Conroy holding up her lists for scrutiny, and how he reworked all her figures, patiently writing out the numbers with his silver pencil on the notepad that was his constant companion. "Very."

"Vain as well?"

"Quite." Beau Brummel at the height of his powers would have gazed in envy on the captain's spotless, perfectly tied cravat.

"I thought as much." As he spoke those words, Thomas's face changed utterly. He shed the polite gentleman like a swimmer shedding water. A new danger looked out of his eyes and traveled down to the set of his shoulders. This was not the danger of the wicked lover Jane knew, but something far more serious. It occurred to her that Thomas might have killed men. It occurred to her that he might be very good at killing men.

"I've met men like Conroy before," said this new and profoundly dangerous Sir Thomas. "He's the kind that keeps an exact account of how much he pays his spies."

"That's a terrible risk."

"You'd think so and so would I, but not a man like Conroy. Firstly, because such a man is so fastidious he needs to know where each farthing is going. Secondly, because it suits his vanity to look over the lists of those in his power."

Jane caught his gist at once. "If we could find his account book . . ."

"I presume he has an office in Kensington House?" Thomas smiled. "And a private apartment, of course?"

"Yes. It would be difficult to find a pretext to search them . . ." The picture of Conroy opening the door to discover her bent over his desk assailed her, and a shameful cowardice rippled through Jane.

"Difficult for you," Thomas acknowledged. "Rather less so for me."

"You?"

He nodded.

"But how do we get you into Kensington House— Oh, stupid of me. The drawing room. I make sure you have an invitation . . ."

"And once I am inside, I make the search."

"But where would you even start?"

"I'll know when I see the study." Jane opened her mouth, and Thomas brushed his fingertips against her hand. "You're about to ask me how I can be so sure. That is because it wasn't service to the crown that makes me discreet about my voyages, at least not entirely. Do you understand?"

She hadn't a moment before, but now she did. Her mind added up the sailor's queue in which Thomas wore his hair, his facility with languages, the deadly competence in his manner as he contemplated robbing Captain Conroy.

"You're a smuggler."

"Among other things. I came up on my father's ship, but have since retired from sea. Those days did, however, give me experience in discovering where men hide their important possessions or papers."

Jane bit her lip. It was risky. But was it as risky as not knowing which of the people around her were Conroy's spies?

*Would it even do any good?* asked a miserable little voice in the back of Jane's mind. *What would another intrigue, even the beginning of a whole new game, accomplish?*

"You'll see. Men like Conroy are ultimately bloodless. They do not take real risks. He has fastened onto you because he thinks you are powerless. Once you have something of his, he will back down quickly."

They had circled the park again. None of the nurses or children paid them the least attention. Thomas turned her to face him, and took her hand. "Trust me, Jane."

"I want to."

"Then do."

*But I will be putting you in danger, and myself as well. For my salary. For appearances.* She couldn't meet his eyes. It was too much when she couldn't touch him, not properly, not in any of the ways in which her desire drove her. He offered to run a grave risk for her sake. Conroy wouldn't hesitate to have him arrested if he were caught. He might even be hanged for the crime of robbing the Duke of Kent's house.

All for the sake of appearances.

"Jane." His thumb rubbed the back of her hand. The tiniest of gestures, nothing that could be seen. "I swear by all that's holy, whatever else happens, I will not let this man keep power over you. Nor will I let him stand between us anymore. Do you understand that?"

"Thank you," she said. "But, Thomas . . ."

"Hush," he squeezed her hand. "No more. I will see you at the drawing room, and we will put Captain Conroy into his proper place."

He meant to reassure her. Jane closed her eyes and breathed deeply. She caught the faintest scent of sandalwood and spices on the spring breeze. She imagined Thomas in her arms, his hard body pressed against hers, his arms supporting her entirely. He would do as he said. She knew it like she knew the beating of her own heart.

But she also knew what he said wouldn't be enough.

# Sixteen

It had been a long time since Thomas had hated anyone. But watching Jane turn so pale and timid as she related the story of how Conroy and his creature had pilfered Thomas's love token . . . it carried Thomas straight past fiery rage into ice-cold determination without pause for breath. He wanted to destroy this man. He would deliver Conroy to Jane and Conroy would kneel at her feet to await her judgment.

More than even that, though, he wanted to give Conroy cause to pray that Jane's judgment did not leave him in the hands of Thomas Lynne. It had also been a long time since he'd held a knife or cutlass, let alone used them against an enemy. Surely, even in this so very civilized age, there were still places a man could get his good right hand on a cutlass. He'd seen the slender sabers that were currently in favor among the sporting gentlemen of London. They would not answer. To make Conroy understand in detail what a mistake it was to threaten Jane, he required a keen edge.

Thomas found his thoughts of violence served a purpose beyond clarifying his determination. They took at least some of his mind off desire.

Since his last tryst with Jane, he'd lain awake night after night, his cock standing at painful and unstinting attention. His entire body waited for Jane. His skin anticipated her touch, her breath, her heat, and it would not be calmed. He'd considered visiting one of the plentiful whores that haunted the streets, but had tossed that idea aside. Probably he was protected from whatever pox such women carried with them, but Jane was not. And anyway, an East End drab could never take her place, not even for an hour. Not even for a minute. It was Jane he wanted, and Jane he must have.

He thought of attempting to dream with her again. Thanks to their repeated needle-pricking, the wards of Kensington House were just about weak enough to admit his thoughts now. But any such dream would offer only the palest echo of the delights they'd shared skin to skin. Another aimless walk in the public park would provide as much satisfaction.

No. He was a man, not a boy. He could see the thing done properly. Conroy's interference must end. Only then could Jane be truly at ease in his arms, and Thomas would accept nothing less. Then, he'd take all night with her. He'd fuck her for hours, driving her to ecstasy with every toy and tool at his disposal. He'd make her scream his name a hundred times. He'd show her heights that no mortal woman had ever witnessed and he would not let her descend until they were both utterly spent.

And he would not under any circumstances think of how soon he must leave her.

\*   \*   \*

"Ah! Sir Thomas!" The Duchess of Kent clapped her round hands delightedly as he stepped into the white pavilion that had been erected for her "drawing room." Any reception given by a royal duchess was, by definition, a grand affair, which meant it was a large one. Far too large to be held in any one of the actual drawing rooms inside Kensington House. The duchess had declared that it would instead be held in Kensington House's celebrated gardens.

"How kind of you to come!" The duchess held out her hand for him to take. "And does not my English improve?"

Thomas bowed over Her Grace's hand. "Another accomplishment to add to Your Grace's many perfections."

"You flatter!" cried the duchess. But of course she was pleased. Even though he'd only met her once before, Thomas already had her measure as a woman who enjoyed flattery as well as finding it useful.

"I owe all to my excellent tutor." The Duchess of Kent beamed at Jane, who curtsied gravely and did not meet his eyes. She looked tired, and pale. She plainly had not had much rest or exercise since he'd last seen her. Suddenly, Thomas wished them both back in that same park he'd been cursing in the darkness. There, at least, they'd been able to talk, and he could have asked at once how she did.

"Jane," said the duchess. "You will take *Herr* . . . Sir Thomas, and see he is made known to all. Then straight back to me. All this crush and noise." The duchess beamed again as she gestured with her ivory and mother-of-pearl fan at the array of

England's finest that surrounded her. "I cannot stand it without my Jane."

Thomas felt the strong urge to kneel at Her Grace's feet in gratitude. Jane smiled as she stepped up to his side, but that smile did not reach her eyes. She was glad to see him, but she was worried by something as well. *Why wouldn't she be? She'd be a fool not to be worried by an approaching burglary.* Still, seeing Jane so reticent did not sit easily within him.

He reassured himself it was only for a little while. Then he would wipe all the worry away from Jane's mind.

Jane murmured something to acknowledge Her Grace's instructions and led him away from the duchess's chair. Thomas allowed himself the luxury of feasting his gaze on her. Jane wore a fetching moss green tea gown adorned with cream scallops and lace, with a scooped neckline that allowed him a tantalizing view of her lovely breasts. Her chestnut curls were piled high on her head, practically begging to be undone by his hands. His cock twitched resentfully at the distance between them, and only grew more restless as she laid her hand on his sleeve to steer him through the gathering.

Jane lead him slowly around the pavilion, every inch the proper lady as she did as she was told and made him known to the company. The Duke and Duchess of York stood alone and sour in a corner of the pavilion, as forgotten as horses left at the starting gate in the race to produce England's heir. The Duke of Clarence and his wife looked stiff and uneasy amid a crowd of bankers and merchant men, some of whom were openly ogling the lady's belly to see if it showed signs of increase. Of the prince regent there was no trace. His Royal Highness still preferred to pretend it was his direct descendants that would inherit the throne.

At last, Jane was able to extricate herself and Thomas from the thickest crowd and lead him out onto the grounds, murmuring something about his never having seen a particular masterpiece of the gardener's art. This polite nothing was readily accepted by those around them, and no one spared them a second glance as Jane steered him to one of the ruler-straight paths.

By some miracle, the weather had held, and a perfect May afternoon spread all around them. Warm and gentle sunshine fell on their shoulders. The scents of the spring flowers and carefully tended greenery hung in the still air.

According to Jane, about three hundred of the noble and the wealthy filled the grand gardens of Kensington House. They promenaded among the topiary, the statues, the sparkling fountains and formal flower beds. A few strolled the curves of the remaining parterre maze, the others apparently having been plowed under in a fit of modernization ordered by the old king.

It was strange, Thomas mused, seeing the world isolated from all sense of magic. Of course, he'd been as isolated when he'd entered the house before to deliver to Jane Fiora's invitation to supper. But that time, he'd only stayed briefly. Now he was fully immersed in the space sheltered by the Kensington wards. Oddly, instead of muffling physical sensation, it made the physical stand out more sharply. The colors and scents of the garden seemed brighter and more distinct; almost, indeed, as bright as those in fairy. The garden, in fact, seemed like a work of art with each detail clearly labored over and cunningly joined into the whole.

He'd heard that when a man lost his sight, his other senses

became keener. Perhaps that was what was happening to him now. Without access to his sense of magic bestowed by the queen, his more mundane perceptions were becoming more acute. He also found that he did not care to ruminate on the phenomenon. For the first time in far too many weary days, he was with Jane. The sun kissed her skin, adding a pretty pink to her cheeks, and bringing out the red in her hair. Her eyes remained fixed straight ahead, however. He would have much preferred to find her gazing up at him. Her lovely, expressive mouth was also too solemn for his liking. He needed to remedy that before he left for his other work.

Parties in open, formally planned gardens were useful things. It was easy to tell when you were out of earshot of the other guests.

"You look lovely, Jane," Thomas murmured. "I like that dress."

"I was thinking of you when I picked it out," she replied with only the smallest hesitation. "You appear very fond of green."

"I am more fond of what it covers."

"Don't, please," she whispered as they moved into the shadow of Kensington House's eastern wing. A perfectly round pond lay nestled in the green lawn, guarded by a cadre of poplars planted at precise intervals. It was a still day and the pond flawlessly reflected the windows and the house.

"Have I said something wrong?" he asked, as they circled the pond. He could see their images in the water, both of them looking so calm and proper. It was an appearance as deceptive as any glamour he could have conjured for them.

"It's so difficult to be near you, and not to be able to touch you properly," whispered Jane.

She meant it, but that was not all she wanted to say. He could tell by the set of her shoulders and the light touch of her hand. She was holding on tightly to something beyond her desire. Worry touched Thomas.

"It's just for a few more hours." *And then I'll find out what you're not telling me.*

"I wonder." Jane looked up at the red brick walls of Kensington House with their orderly regiments of windows.

"You think I'll fail," he teased. "Can you really believe Conroy's wits are a match for mine?"

"You're worth a thousand of him," she answered at once, but the words fell flat. Her mind was not on him, or what she said. "I'm going to have to make a decision, Thomas, and . . ."

"Wait, Jane." He covered her hand with his briefly. "Before you make any decision, let me do what I came to do. Then we will talk."

She didn't like it, but she nodded. "Conroy's study is the second on the right. There." She nodded toward the windows. "Do you think you can find it from the inside?"

"I'm certain I can. And his apartment?"

"Directly above. Thomas . . ."

"No, Jane," he told her firmly. "We've no time now. Where shall I meet you?"

She thought for a moment. "The kitchen gardens," she pointed. "I'll begin looking for you in an hour."

Thomas risked brushing the corner of her mouth with his thumb, lifting it into a smile. "An hour. Then all will be right, Jane. I promise."

He wanted to kiss her, to hold her against him and assure her with the strength and shelter of his body that he spoke the truth. But the same openness that protected them from eavesdroppers denied him the opportunity to reinforce his promise with any such act.

*Just a little longer. An hour at most, and then she'll know.*

With the gathering being held in the gardens, the interior of Kensington House was all but deserted. The door to Conroy's study was, of course, locked, but the carefully bent wire Thomas had provided himself with before he left Fiora's that morning soon eliminated that obstacle.

Thomas's hand with locks had been something of a party trick for his father. When they paraded chests of Spanish treasure before Queen Bess, he'd popped the fastenings on them to gain the applause of the court and to demonstrate the varied skills of her privateers. He'd once worn a pearl and ruby ring she'd given him off her own hand for that cleverness. What had happened to it?

Thomas shook himself. Why was he thinking of that now? He closed and latched the door behind him.

*To business.*

Thomas turned in a slow circle, surveying the chamber around him, finding it matched his expectations exactly. Other portions of Kensington House might show signs of wear, but not John Conroy's personal study. The room was immaculate, with each thing in its place. The broad desk was entirely empty of papers, and Thomas did not even need to try them to know the drawers were securely locked. Even taking into account the brief duration of the duke's residence, it was clear that hours of work had been put in by the household staff to keep the bookshelves lining the walls immaculately dusted and the great expanses of wood paneling and floor highly polished.

If Thomas had access to his magics, finding Conroy's secret account book would have been a trivial matter. But cut off as he was, he had to fall back on older teachings.

*A man's room tells tales on him, laddy,* said his father's voice from memory. *Room, ship's cabin, any place he's lived. There's no need to be smashing the place to ruin to find what's hidden. Just pay attention to its stories.*

This room said Captain John Conroy was an exact man. He was a careful man who was very sure of his due, and his potential. But more than this, it said he was confident in his own cleverness. Why shouldn't he be? He managed one of the highest ranked men in the kingdom to perfection, and was showing every sign of starting to manage the duke's wife as well. Thomas fingered his lockpick and decided to start with the desk.

The latches on the desk drawers were good, for their kind, but Thomas still had all three sprung within a matter of minutes. He did not expect his prize to be waiting in plain sight in there, but he felt carefully around the sides and bottoms, in case Conroy went in for secret compartments. That search yielded him nothing. The locked map cabinet proved similarly disappointing. The barrister's bookcase held the ordinary ledgers, but no drawers or cleverly constructed and concealed spaces. Nor was there a safe conveniently located behind any of the heavy oil paintings, or under the three Turkish carpets on the gleaming oaken floors. Even the flue, that favorite hiding place of smugglers of all kinds, held nothing but ash and clinker.

*Where then?* Thomas turned again, and fought to keep his temper. He did not have long. Beyond keeping Jane waiting and worrying, this was a drawing room, not a rout. He did not have hours to dismantle Conroy's study at his leisure.

*You're a clever man, Conroy. A clever, clever man. Which is the cleverest place? Where is it that gives you that little thrill of pride each and every time you reach for it?*

Memory rippled through his mind again. He stood with his father in the dim, tiny cabin of the wallowing tub of a Spanish galleon. Smoke and gunpowder from the battle they'd just finished above hung heavy in the air. John Dee had sent them there. The Spanish captain had letters for a traitor in Queen Bess's court. They'd get all the treasure in the hold if they found those letters and burned the ship afterward. He'd been insistent about the burning and the letters. So insistent, that he'd also hinted that without the traitor's letter, their own Letter of Marque and Reprisal might be revoked.

Father had taken the lantern and peered into every corner of the cabin, touching nothing, just looking. Thomas stood impatiently in the center, the excitement of battle still singing through him and urging him to start tearing the boards apart.

"Pay attention, Tommy!" Father snapped. "Use yer damned eyes. There's not enough room to hide a pig's grunt in here, but he's done it. Where?"

They had found them. His father had worked it out. The reliquary in the little drawer where that captain had kept his rosary had a hidden compartment with neatly scrolled strips of paper tucked inside. It was too small for ordinary letters, but plenty big enough for those coded scraps . . .

He had it.

Thomas shook his head. His mistake had been thinking an account book must necessarily be a book.

*Because the most clever place to hide an item is in plain sight.*

He returned to the barrister's bookcase. This was where the ordinary accounts were kept; thick leather-bound ledgers each with the relevant year stamped in gold on the spine. He reached for the volume marked 1839, and flipped it open. The accounts marched down the page in tidy double columns of black and red ink. Much more red than black, of course. They were commendably up to date. The end papers of the ledger were whole and sound. The spine was unbroken. Thomas hefted the volume and ran his fingers around the edge of the front cover.

There. There was a slit at the bottom. Someone had taken their time with it, because it had not disturbed the stitching around the cover's edge. He hadn't even seen it the first time he picked up this book. He could find it only by touch.

Thomas slipped his fingers inside and drew out three sheets of thin, light writing paper, all covered in red and black ink.

John Conroy's secret accounts. In these pages, unlike the duke's, there was far more black ink than red.

*Got you, you bloody bastard.* Just to be sure, Thomas swept his finger into the little pocket again. This time he brought out a length of black ribbon. Jane's keepsake of him, her memory of their passion and their time together.

Thomas tucked the papers and ribbon into his coat's inner pocket. *Thank you, Father,* he thought. No sooner had his mind formed the words, though, than a wave of sadness washed over him. Not for what he remembered, but for what he didn't. He couldn't remember the last time he'd spoken to his father. Really spoken to him, not just relayed shouted orders. A storm had upended the *Free Hand* and Father had gone down with the rest. Thomas had been alone when he'd fetched up on shore. He'd also been half bled-out, half drowned. But Her Glorious Majesty had come to him across the empty sands. Thomas had taken the life she offered, and he hadn't looked back. Why should he look anywhere at all when she gave him all he needed?

But he'd forgotten when he last spoke to his father, and he'd lost the ring given him by Queen Bess, who had once called him the prince of all her privateers. What else had gone missing?

*It's not important,* he told himself. *It's just that you haven't done a bit of thievery in so long that it's got you thinking on the old days.* Which was true, but still unfamiliar emotion stirred in the back of his mind, and it felt disturbingly like a prisoner stirring when the cell door opens.

Thomas returned the ledger to the shelf exactly as he had found it. The perfectly clean bookcase was quite helpful now, because he did not have to worry that the exacting Captain Conroy would notice any dust had been disturbed.

Thomas left the study, closing the door firmly behind him. He did not hurry down the corridor. He moved deliberately and plastered a puzzled frown on his face so that anyone who saw him they would think he had lost his way. He found the grand staircase that lead to the cupola room and started down. Valuables were not the only thing a man could hide in plain sight, and no one would expect a thief to exit by the front door.

As Thomas descended, voices soft and swift, and distinctly

German, reached him from below. Thomas could see nothing from where he was. An instinctive warning rose in him, but he could do nothing about it. There was nowhere to duck, no way to turn without looking suspicious. He'd have to brazen it out.

He did not actually see them until he reached the bottom of the sweeping staircase. They'd picked a good spot for secrets, sheltered from above by the curving stair and from the door by the elaborate clock that graced the center of the room. It was a woman and a man making those earnest, German whispers. The woman was Fraulein Lehzen, Princess Feodora's attendant. Jane had pointed her out to him in the gardens walking with a young girl who wore a froth of white lace. The princess was nowhere in evidence now. There was just a gentleman Thomas didn't recognize. Thomas nodded to the gentleman, as if he thought nothing strange about him lurking in the shadows with the princess's attendant. He passed without breaking stride, heading straight for the door.

"Lynne, isn't it?" said the man from behind him.

Thomas stopped—inches from the door and his escape to the gardens—and turned. The man had moved out from the shadows, and in so doing neatly blocked Thomas's view of Fraulein Lehzen. He was tall, broad-shouldered and black-haired. His plain gray coat and burgundy waistcoat were of excellent quality, but what Thomas noticed most was the physical presence of a man who knew his own power.

"Do I know you?" Thomas asked.

"I'm think not. Corwin Rathe." The man extended his hand. "Lady Jane DeWitte mentioned your name."

"Did she?" *You're lying, Corwin Rathe.* But . . . Rathe. He knew that name. Why did he know that name? "I'm pleased to know any acquaintance of Lady Jane's." Thomas shook the man's hand and cursed the blinding wards of Kensington House. Outside its walls, he would have been able to know everything about this Corwin Rathe from just this brief contact. As it was, he could only hope to lose the fellow as soon as possible. He needed to get to Jane and rid himself of the papers in his pocket. Then he needed to get away from the grounds of Kensington House, back to where he could open his magics again and where he could focus properly without ancient history popping up from the back of his brain to plague him.

"Are you headed back? Tedious business this, but better to be seen, I suppose." Rathe was assuming the airs of a bored aristocrat, and doing it well. It was the set of his shoulders that betrayed him, the way his hands stayed loose and ready at his sides even as he started for the door. It occurred to Thomas he was being discreetly hustled outside.

*I didn't see any Rathe on Conroy's little list. So the question is, is Rathe your real name? If so, and you're not Conroy's, whose creature are you?*

*And why did Lehzen there give you my name?*

# Seventeen

The kitchen gardens of Kensington House were laid out as neatly as any model farm, with each of the identical rectangular plots surrounded by a solid brick wall to deter scavengers. This arrangement created a kind of alley between the last row of beds and the higher wall that enclosed the whole of the grounds. Jane, believing Thomas unfamiliar with the layout of Kensington House, had suggested it for their meeting place. She didn't know how many times she had gone through the tiny back gate in this spot when she hurried through the haze created by glamour and desire to meet him across the lane and beneath the trees outside the wall.

This time, it was she who waited for him. The sun was only grazing the treetops, but shadows already slanted thick across Jane where she stood just beside the outer wall. Uneasiness crept through Thomas, as if Jane in shadow was an ill-luck omen. He told himself not to be daft, but made a circuit around the nearest walled vegetable bed, just to satisfy himself that no one followed him.

Damn the Kensington wards. He felt deaf and blind. Damn this Corwin Rathe for setting him on edge. He didn't want to be lost in his worries when he had a prize to present to Jane.

She didn't smile as he approached her down the lane between the garden walls. But she held out her arms and that was more than enough. Thomas went to her at once and she wrapped her arms around his shoulders and clung there, taut as a fiddle string.

"Now then, now then," he murmured, rocking her back and forth. "I'm here, sweet Jane, and all is right." He gently disengaged himself from her embrace and stepped back, keeping hold of her hands so he could spread their arms wide. "And see? I've taken no hurt from my adventure."

"Thank God for that," she said fervently. "I was afraid, Thomas."

"I know it, Jane." He reached into his pocket and drew out the papers, and the ribbon. "But let these ease that fear now." He laid his acquisitions across her palm.

Jane picked up the ribbon. She laced it in her gloved fingers, clasping it as tightly as if it had been his hand. He could almost feel her holding his fingers, a touch strong and yet vulnerable, and filled with longing. She shook open the papers in her other hand, and as he watched, her eyes traveled down the tidy list of names and amounts. Anger clouded her face.

"So, now I will let Conroy know I have his accounts, and a complete list of those in his employ."

"Yes."

"And he will be very angry, but there will be nothing he can do, especially if I make a copy."

"A good thought," Thomas agreed, but uneasily. She was still too angry. He had expected relief, and thanks, perhaps a showering of kisses that he could fend off. Instead, Jane just clenched his prize in her fist.

"He will look for ways to destroy me for this impertinence. I will still have to be on my guard."

"I'm afraid that is also true."

"So, we've accomplished exactly nothing with this."

Thomas frowned. What was the matter with the woman? He'd run a considerable risk for her. She might show a little gratitude. "Was there a choice? He would have gotten you dismissed."

"Yes, there was a choice, and I'm making it now." Jane slipped paper and ribbon into her reticule. "I am leaving."

"Leaving?" But Jane just held up her hand. Thomas felt himself jerk back, as startled as if she'd slapped him. Leaving? Leaving. She couldn't leave him. Not now.

Jane turned her face away, staring down the lane of sunlight between the looming brick walls. "I've been thinking about it for some time. There are private schools for girls of the *ton*, you know, and for those with wealthy fathers who want to enter into society. They teach etiquette and polish. I've served at court. I'm well-traveled, I can make polite conversation with royalty in three languages . . . I think a school would be glad to have someone of my experience, don't you? There will not be much in the way of a salary, of course, but I've lived on nothing before. Georgie will take me in for a while until I find something, and Her Grace will give me a reference . . ."

With each clipped, bitter word, the sun rose higher in

Thomas's heart, blossoming bright through the whole of his being. The warmth sent a laugh bubbling to the surface.

Jane glowered at him. "What have I said that's so amusing?"

"Oh, no. I'm sorry, Jane. I thought you meant you were leaving me."

She stared at him, like he'd started speaking in tongues. "Leave you? Oh, Thomas. Don't you understand? I'm leaving so I can be with you."

It was dawn in his soul. Not just any dawn, but a full, glorious summer dawn with a fair wind and not a trace of cloud in the sky. Jane wanted to be with him, but it was more than that. She was not just wanting, she was acting. She was walking away from her shelter here behind the walls and wards to be with him.

"If I stay here, I'll have no choices," Jane was saying. "It doesn't matter what I know about Conroy, or anyone else. I'll always be watched, always looking over my shoulder, especially if the babe becomes the heir. Everyone will want to be part of the household, and they'll be tearing at each other to get inside. It's started already." She was thinking about the crowds around the Dukes of Clarence and Kent while their elder brother York watched them all with anger simmering in his protruding blue eyes. "Outside, I'll have to be discreet, but a teacher has no power. No one has anything to gain by trying to make a pawn of her. She may be safely and comfortably ignored. I think it will be most enjoyable to be ignored for a while."

He needed to say something. She was waiting for him to say something. But he could barely think. She wanted to be with him. It was not just the passion. It was more than that. She might truly love him, as he loved her.

He loved her. He loved Jane.

Thomas's mouth went dry. He should tell her. Now. But something held him back, a buzzing in his mind like an angry fly. He was forgetting something vital. He couldn't speak until he remembered.

"What of your family?" he asked instead. "What would they say?"

"My family?" Jane looked at him blankly for a moment. He watched as it occurred to her that they had spoken only briefly of her family. The broken expression that overcame her then slid between his ribs like a knife. "I have none. I have nothing. That's why this has been so difficult, do you see? I'm one of those penniless *ton* women who must make shift for themselves."

"How did this happen? You cannot tell me you are not a gentlewoman born."

"Oh, I was that. The Honorable Miss Jane Markham, if you please. But my father was a gambler. Only instead of faro or piquet, his game was stocks, and he borrowed heavily to play. Sometimes we were rich as pashas. Sometimes . . . well, let us say I've learned to keep up appearances on very little. We were in one of those distressed times when I turned seventeen. Father announced I was going to have a London season regardless, and the wife of his friend Lord Islington had agreed to sponsor me. My mother didn't want it. I should have realized that something was wrong. Mother had always been the one to keep us from foundering, and I knew my father's ways well enough by then. But I was young and I was foolish, and I did so want a season . . ."

She gathered a pinch of muslin skirt in her fingertips and rolled it back and forth. "What I didn't realize then was I was going to London to be inspected like a filly at auction.

"The winning bid was Lord Octavius DeWitte. His sister had kept house for him, but she had died, and he needed someone else for the task. The cheapest option was to find a wife, and I was to be had without much trouble at all. I didn't want to marry a man three times my age, but father . . . he explained his situation to me, and pointed out that my marriage would solve all the family difficulties. I would go with Lord Octavius, and I would sign my jointure over to Father so he could pay his debts. Our debts."

"I resisted. And then . . . we got the news. While we'd been gone, there was a typhus outbreak in the village. My mother, my sister and my brothers . . . they were all sick. We couldn't even go back to them. It wasn't safe. They all died."

"I'm so sorry, Jane."

She didn't look at him. She faced the outer wall. He watched her shoulders stiffen as she tried to hold herself together, to be as strong as the stones in front of her. "Father pointed out he would have to borrow more money to have them decently buried. What was I going to do? Lord Octavius advanced the money for the funerals, and I was married as soon as I was out of mourning.

"Father was in debt again less than a year later."

"God Almighty, Jane . . ." He laid a hand on her shoulder.

"No, please. Just give me a moment." She tried to shake him off, but he stepped closer.

"Look at me, Jane."

She turned, and he saw the tears spilling down her cheeks.

He went to her. Nothing on earth could have held him back. He wrapped his arms around Jane and pulled her against him. She rested her cheek against his chest, and felt the drumming of his heart.

"Someone will see."

"No one will see."

She looked at him, her eyes so frightened, but so filled with the need to be able to trust someone.

He kissed her long and deep. Kissed her as tenderly as passion would allow. Kissed her to the limits of his breath, because he was in the sunlight, the mortal world, without glamour, without any outward deception he had to keep part of his mind focused to maintain. Just this once it was only he and Jane. He could give his whole self over to her. She brought light to him, inside and outside, and he wanted this kiss to penetrate to his bones so that it would never leave him.

She resisted at first, and he feared he would have to find the strength to pull away. He would take nothing from her she did not give. Not here, not now. But then she melted, her magnificent breasts pressing soft and supple against his chest. His cock stood up, hard and ready, at once.

*Never enough*, he thought as he caressed her breast, delighting in the sigh she breathed against his mouth. *Never enough.*

Because he could never have her truly. Never claim her beyond their few stolen moments, because he had nothing to give in return. No share of heart, hand or even possessions. He was a beggar before her, with nothing beyond fleeting pleasure to offer.

This one time would be as honest as it could be. One time for them both to treasure.

He moved his kisses to her face and her throat. She smelled like the springtime around them and tasted of lavender and strawberries. He laved the perfection that was her white throat. She pressed against the brick, writhing her body against his, already seeking the pleasure of his cock. Oh, greedy, demanding minx. She'd never learn. Ever. Not if he had a thousand years to tie her down and discipline her would he teach her to properly submit.

A thousand years with Jane. He was turning them, lowering them, resting Jane astride his lap. He could feel the smoothness and strength of her thighs even through his buckskins.

*Why not a thousand years with Jane?*

He was dizzy, drunk on Jane and passion. He could not think straight while she had wrapped her arms around his neck and rubbed her face against his hair, as if the texture of it fascinated her. Perhaps it did. What concerned him more immediately was her action brought the valley of her breasts to where he had only to bend the smallest amount to reach them. He palmed her breasts, pressing them together to nuzzle and taste the curving tops, reveling in the way that made her arch her back and press her pussy closer to him. Oh yes, such pretty toys this woman had. Pretty, responsive, endlessly delightful toys. A thousand years would be just the beginning.

She was ready for him. Ripe and ready. He could feel her hesitation, still uncertain whether they should give themselves fully to desire. But she wanted him, and more than that, she needed him. He slid his hand under her skirt, and she pressed her mouth to his shoulder, sighing out hot breath against him, as he stroked her folds. She was soft and exquisitely wet now. She moaned as he stroked her, fondling her sensitive folds, finding her clit—her hot, eager clit—and stroking it lazily. She moaned again, and he wrapped his other arm around her, holding her in place against his hand. She let him stroke her and build up her delight, trusting him to take her past her worry and sorrow into the place of pure and perfect pleasure that they shared. He would make her forget she'd ever known loneliness. He would drive it from the earth for her sake.

She was driving him mad with her muffled moans and her rubbing against his thighs and his busy fingers. He withdrew them from her tightening pussy and she hissed in disappointment, but soon realized the rummaging she felt was him undoing his fly to free his cock for her. She looked at him, flushed, a line of perspiration trickling down her temple, begging to be tasted. She tasted like salt and honey. Had he remembered to tell her that? There were so many things he needed to remember to tell her. But not now. Now, she was about to speak. He saw it in her eyes, which were wide and dark. She felt his hard, impatient cock and was torn between her fears and her desires.

This was no time for a discussion of the matter. Thomas kissed her, delving into her mouth with his tongue, silencing her, distracting her while he positioned the tip of his cock against her folds. Then both of them groaned as she rose up on her knees just enough, and he slipped inside.

Relief. Sweet relief. For a handful of heartbeats, there was an end to longing and, in its place, a sense of knowing exactly where he should be. He had no more to fear and nothing to prove while he had Jane's infinitely beautiful body in his arms, and his cock safe inside her.

But that relief lasted only for a moment, because she was already moving. Jane rocked her hips back and forth, looking down at him as surprise brightened the pleasure in her. They hadn't fucked each other in this way yet, and her body was just realizing how very good this position could feel.

Thomas slid his hands around under her skirts to clasp the lush globes of her ass, squeezing, urging her on.

*Yes, Jane. Ride it. Ride it hard.* He lifted her, and brought her down hard, showing her she had no need to be gentle. He could take all she had to give.

She understood him without a word. With only his touch and the arching of his hips to guide her, she began to use her knees, like any good rider. Her hot sheath stroked him, hard and fast, driving him deep, tightening around him. Had anything ever felt so good as Jane fucking him in the sunlight? Already, she was about to come. He felt her clench, felt the slow pulsing begin around his shaft. He pulled her close, driving himself deeper, holding her tighter, so she could press her face against his neck and scream and scream, and yet never be heard. She shuddered and shook and her sheath tightened like a silken fist around him. All thought was gone as he drove into her once more, coming into her, her pussy squeezing him, milking him dry, and all he wanted was more, more and yet more.

But slowly the moment faded. He slipped down from paradise into his own body and found it a slow and heavy place, although remarkably comfortable, especially as his slowly softening cock was still inside Jane. He cradled her against his chest with one leaden arm, and smiled to feel her breath against his neck growing slow, deep and gentle.

So beautiful. To be here in the sunlight, with this woman, content and complete.

Why not a thousand years of this? Why not forever?

"I need to get back," Jane murmured reluctantly, even as she snuggled close against him.

"Jane." He cupped her face in both hands. "I have something I want to ask you, soon. There's one point I must make certain of first, but . . . let me call you tonight. Will you be ready for me?"

She went very still, searching his eyes. She got two dents in her forehead when she frowned. Right on either side of the place where the bridge of her nose met her brow. He wanted to kiss those two little dents, and could think of no reason why not, so he did.

"Thomas, I don't want you to say anything you will regret. I'm not asking for anything more from you."

"I know. But there's so much I want to give you." *Forever, Jane. I want to give you forever somewhere there is no sorrow, and where Conroy and his kind can never reach you.*

He found he liked the sensation of her searching him, wanting to see deeper. She wanted to know him the way he wanted to know her; completely without reservation or barrier. He smoothed her cheeks and she turned her face in his hands, just a little, so that the corner of her mouth touched his thumb.

"All right," she said. "I'll be ready."

He smiled and helped her climb off his lap. She buttoned his breeches up without being told to, the brushes of her competent fingers threatening to wake his flaccid cock again. *She never will submit properly,* he thought again. The only true surrender Lady Jane made was to her own heart.

And that heart was his. Maybe the declaration had not been made yet, but it was in her actions. He could see it even now in the curve of her laughing smile, and he felt it the depth of the tenderness that welled up in him.

He smoothed her skirts, enjoying the shape of her thighs under the cloth. Enjoying it so much, in fact, that she swatted at his hands. He grinned at her, letting her see that he would make her pay for that gesture. Jane just lifted her chin at him and turned away, as if giving him the cut direct. Which only made him smile again. Yes, they would play this game out, but later. When they had nothing more to fear from Conroy, or anyone else in this house.

Thomas followed her along the ivy-covered wall, to the stretch behind the kitchen garden where there waited an old gate of rusted iron. The gate Jane has passed through every night he summoned her, although she would think she'd never seen it before. He lifted the latch and swung it open on silent hinges.

He bowed to her. Jane sniffed, and made her curtsy as proper and correct as if they had been in the prince's ballroom.

"I will hear from you tonight?" asked Jane.

"Trust me."

"I do trust you."

Thomas smiled, and kissed her once. Then he ducked through the low gate, through the line of trees and across the road and into the broad and rolling parkland beyond.

It was as if he walked into a thunderstorm.

The world darkened, and blurred. The ground pitched under him like the deck of a ship. He'd lost his sea legs years ago, so he staggered and almost fell. His head spun and the blood roared in his ears.

Because in walking out of Kensington House, he'd walked back into his own memory.

He'd meant to take Jane to the Fae queen, so she could live beside him forever. Because he loved her. He'd wanted to show her all that was good and glorious in his life among the Fae, and share it all with her.

Except he couldn't love Jane. He couldn't ever love Jane. Jane was a mortal woman. His heart, his loyalty and his life belonged to Her Glorious Majesty, and always would.

But while he was with Jane, it was as if that oath hadn't mattered. How had there been the space of even an hour when it hadn't mattered?

Thomas stared wild-eyed up at the wall and the gate he'd just walked through. The wards. While he'd been inside Kensington House, the wards had severed him from the power of his queen. Not completely, because those wards were weakened now, but enough. Enough to leave a hole in his heart that Jane DeWitte could be poured in to.

The pricking needle weakened the cloth. That was the strategy to weaken the defenses of Kensington House that had turned back on him. The magic surrounding the house had its own sharp point, and he had walked into it without thinking.

It also had a secret ally. Because it wasn't just the magic that had moved him so far. It was Jane herself. Jane's love didn't just weaken his oath-binding, it tore it in two.

*God's teeth. Jane. Jane, what have I done?*

There was a clump of ferns and undergrowth at the foot of an oak just a few dozen yards away. Thomas reeled toward them like a drunken man until the ferns brushed his knees. Then he fell and he crawled around the broad trunk, into a tiny hollow among the spreading roots. With painful effort, he pulled a glamour around him like a blanket, so anyone who looked would see nothing more than earth and stone beside the tree.

Exhausted, Thomas Lynne fell into darkness.

# Eighteen

Jane watched until Thomas disappeared between the trees on the far side of the road. Then she closed and latched the little gate. For all the rust on its crossbars, it moved as silently as any of the well-tended doors inside the house. She suspected more than one servant slipped up to this place in the dark, to exchange love tokens or perhaps to pass some of the duke's leftovers and cast-offs to various scavengers in return for a few extra coppers. That was the way of it in great houses.

Automatically, Jane straightened her posture and smoothed her skirts and hair. She had to get back and could not give away any of what had just happened by her appearance. She took special care to calm her face and hide the way her heart skipped and skittered at the memory of what Thomas had said.

*I have something I want to ask you soon.*

She must not think he meant marriage. There were an infinite number of things that could be covered by such a statement.

She must move forward with her own plans. Whatever Thomas had to ask, she would hear it, and then judge.

*Be ready for me,* he'd also said.

That much, at least, she could do and would do.

With the memory of Thomas's body still tingling through her palms and between her thighs, Jane crossed back into the populated areas of the gardens. All around her, people smiled and nodded. The closer she got to the ducal pavilion, the thicker the crowd got. Men and women stood with glasses and dainties in their hands. They talked closely with each other, rubbing shoulders and elbows. They reminded Jane of nothing so much as a flock of pigeons in the square, waiting for the next scattering of crumbs.

In that moment, it occurred to Jane how truly monumental her plan was. People fought to get into the *ton*. They bribed and flattered and schemed. Once in, they beggared their families to keep their place. And when the family money dried up, they mortgaged land and houses and sold everything of worth, from their jewelry to their daughters, to keep their place.

But she had never once known anyone who left the confines of the *ton*. Not voluntarily. Ladies sometimes fell away for various reasons that could not be spoken of aloud. The occasional gentleman vanished into drink, or "lived abroad," meaning he crossed the channel to escape his creditors. But no one ever simply opened the gate and walked out.

Jane remembered sitting in the darkness of her father's study. She'd had to go back to him when Lord Octavius died, because she'd signed over her jointure to him upon her marriage, and he'd spent that. He had been her last relative except for the cousins who would inherit the estate, and who never wrote her a single word after the lawyers had confirmed the entail. She had been stacking the bills into different piles. The lamp made a circle of pale gold barely large enough to hold the spread of his papers. Fourteen piles altogether, arranged by category. She'd reached for another bundle of correspondence to sort through, and found it to be comprised of letters from friends, each and every one reminding her father how much he had already borrowed from them, and regretting extremely their inability to lend any more.

They had given, and given generously, these letters told her, to allow her father and her family to keep up appearances, because aside from bloodlines, appearances were most important. All those men, from the clubs and the coffee houses and the exchanges, they understood that.

Mother had understood that.

*We must keep up appearances, Jane.* Her mother's voice, flat and dull, came back to her from memory as she signed the note to the banker that would open the vault and release the jewels inside for sale. *All your futures depend on it.*

But Mother was dead, and Francis and Royal, little Charlotte, and infant Arabelle beside her. Father had gone back to his stock tables before the last of the funeral guests had left the house, as if a turn in his fortune could somehow make up for the death of his wife and children. The jewels he had sold, which he had sworn he would buy back, were long gone.

Jane looked at the people around her, and a weight of hatred dropped against her so heavily she almost staggered. How much had her family sacrificed for appearances? It was to keep up appearances that her mother remained tied to her father, who could not be relied on. It was to keep up appearances that she, Jane, married the man her unreliable father picked out, and who had installed her in a house empty of real love. Her entire world, her entire life, had been lived behind a wall of appearances and expectations.

But Thomas had shown her walls had gates, and gates could be breeched. The only real thing she had ever known was this love, her love for Thomas. As he held her as close as man and woman could be, still inside her after their passion had spent itself, she had known it was real. It was flawed and strange and difficult, but it was entirely real.

In that moment, she had felt as if she'd opened her eyes for the first time and seen the sun. Her love was real because it was what she had chosen and given herself to willingly. It was her heart that guided her to him, and nothing else. If she turned her back on Thomas now to don the cloak of the *haut ton* lady, she would be turning her back on what was real. Because it was appearances that kept her locked up in here, not the salary. There were other salaries, there always had been, if she had bothered to look for them. But she'd been made to think the world within the walls of appearance was the only one.

"There is a choice," Jane whispered. "There *is.*"

What came next would not be easy. She would have to be careful how she extricated herself. It would take a certain amount of planning, and a little time. But that was all right. She had time, and she was very good at planning. She had run a baron's house for years. She had been able to marshal a full staff and a thousand details into perfect order before she turned twenty-one.

She needed to begin with ridding herself of the untrustworthy Tilly. And to do that, she would have to confront Captain Conroy.

Just a day ago, she had been afraid of him. Now, however, with the truth held neatly folded in her reticule and all the gates open before her, she found she was rather looking forward to seeing him again.

Jane lifted her chin and sailed into the ducal pavilion.

"Ah, Jane. There you are," said the duchess in cheerful German as Jane made her way to the little dais that held her chair and the frowning Frau Seibold. Contrary to that woman's insistence that she would take cold, Her Grace's hand felt quite warm. She was, if anything, a little flushed. Jane suspected the duchess enjoyed being the center of attention.

"Here are people for you to meet." The duchess switched to English and plowed through the formal phrases with more determination than accuracy. "Mrs. Corwin Rathe, Mr. Darius Marlowe, Lady Jane DeWitte. Lady Jane, Mrs. Rathe and Mr. Marlowe. They say they are friends of Sir Thomas."

"Do they?" Jane fixed on her most polite smile. "I'm very glad to know you."

Mrs. Corwin Rathe was dark-haired, with a well-rounded figure. Her face had moved from a girl's prettiness to a woman's beauty. The bronze dress she wore spoke of taste and restraint.

Restraint also described the gentleman at her side. Mr. Darius Marlowe was a big man, at least a match for Captain Conroy in height, and far surpassing him for the solid breadth of chest and shoulders. Dark gold hair and sideburns lent him a leonine appearance that was reinforced by the fierceness in his steel blue eyes. This man did not want to be here, did not like what he saw, and feared somehow for Mrs. Rathe. He was practically hovering over her, as if he might have to snatch her away from some grasping claws at any moment.

But then again, given the company, he just might.

Mrs. Rathe extended her immaculately gloved hand. "Very nice to meet you at last, Lady Jane."

They touched hands politely. Jane felt something brush against her mind like moth wings; fleeting and delicate, but unmistakable. A ripple of uneasiness ran through her.

"How long have you known Sir Thomas?" inquired Jane, moving a few steps away from the duchess so as not to block Her Grace's view or access to her by her other guests. Circulation was key to a successful gathering.

"Only since he came to town," said Mrs. Rathe. "Has he told you if he intends to stay long this time?"

"I do not believe his plans are yet fixed. He is, as I'm sure you know, a man who travels much for his business."

"I'd been under the impression his business was going to keep him closer to London for a while." Mrs. Rathe turned to her escort. "Wasn't that your understanding, Mr. Marlowe?"

"Indeed. Interesting fellow, Lynne." Mr. Marlowe was trying to sound bored and trivial, but he failed. He was entirely on edge. His gaze roved the gathering, constantly searching for something or someone. "Likes to play the pirate a bit, and keeps his business close to his vest, of course." He shrugged, stiff and one-shouldered, as if he'd been prompted to the gesture. "But that's a traveling man for you."

"A positive mystery," said Mrs. Rathe. "You must come to visit, Lady Jane. We can have a good gossip about Sir Thomas."

"That would of course be delightful. But you understand my obligations keep me close to home these days." Jane cast a discreet glance toward the duchess.

"Oh, how silly of me," Mrs. Rathe touched her fingertips to her mouth to cover her mistake. "But still, if you ever do find you want to talk to someone about Sir Thomas, you can always find me at home in Broadham Street. And promise me you'll look for an invitation from number sixty-eight, won't you?"

"Of course," Jane murmured. The woman smiled merrily, almost vapidly, and Jane felt another ripple of disquiet. She had plenty of experience in reading what lay beneath the surface, and this woman was no more foolish than her companion was bored. Mrs. Rathe wanted to be very sure Jane knew where she could be found.

In the weeks since she had met him, the only other person who had even heard the name Thomas Lynne was Mrs. Beauchamp. Now here were these two, claiming to know him well enough that he had spoken of his acquaintance with Jane. That felt wrong. The one thing she knew for certain about Thomas was that he could keep a secret. And she qualified as a secret, because he knew her reputation depended on his silence. He would not name her in casual conversation with strangers.

So, who were these two? And what did they know about Thomas?

Or what do they want to know?

At last, the drawing room sauntered to a close. Jane looked on with undisguised relief as Simmons closed the door behind the last lingering guest. He turned toward her, saw her expression and risked an eye roll before donning his footman's impassive mask again and pacing away.

Frau Seibold had taken the duchess away a full hour ago. Her Grace had not gone readily, but it was plain that this time her attendant was not taking no for an answer. Jane reported to her rooms at once, of course, but to her relief, Her Grace was sound asleep, leaving Jane at liberty to hunt down Captain Conroy.

It was probably ironic that Captain Conroy was the first person in the household she would inform of her intentions.

When she had last seen the captain, he had been supporting the Duke of Kent to a chair. All three of the royal brothers had managed to cap the festivities by becoming roaring drunk and joining in wobbling harmony with the Duke of Clarence as he bellowed out a sea shanty in a voice that could have been heard all the way to Westminster. The spectacle had done nothing to make Jane regret her choice to leave.

Conroy could be anywhere in the house, but Jane decided to begin with his study. When she reached the door, she heard movement inside. She paused to listen. Inside, papers rustled and drawers scraped open and shut. She thought of the papers she now carried tucked in her sash along with Thomas's ribbon, and wondered if Tilly was making similar noises in her room upstairs.

Jane knocked at the door. The noises paused.

"Who's there?" snapped Conroy from the other side.

"Jane DeWitte," she answered. "I hoped to speak with you, Captain."

Another pause. Then there came a muffled muttering that

might have been a curse, and the sound of footsteps, and the snap of a latch. Jane stepped back before the door flew open. Conroy stood in the threshold, blocking her entrance. Jane could just see past him to the sea of paper covering his broad desk.

"What?" Conroy demanded.

Jane let her brows rise, just a little. "Is something the matter, Captain?"

He glanced behind him, and realized she could see in. He eased the door closed a fraction of an inch. "A misplaced paper. Nothing important."

"I'm sorry. Perhaps I should come back later."

"No, no," he replied quickly, and Jane was treated to the sight of Captain Conroy attempting to pull himself together. "What is it, Lady Jane?"

She glanced up and down the corridor. "It's not something to speak of in the hallway."

He did not want to let her in. He heartily wished her gone and was sorry he'd agreed to continue the conversation. It was strange to be able to read this controlled and controlling man so easily. Jane had not been able to thoroughly look over his lists yet, but she was willing to wager that if she did, there were some very interesting discoveries to be made.

Reluctantly, Conroy stepped back. Jane kept her face carefully composed as she walked into the study. The desk was not the only place disaster had struck. The doors on the barrister's bookcase hung open. The ledgers tilted crazily against each other. Some had fallen onto the floor and their pages rippled in the breeze stirred up by her movement.

Conroy shut the door. He snapped the latch back in place. The sound lifted the hairs on the back of Jane's neck.

"Now, Lady Jane." Conroy folded his arms. "What is it you have to say?"

"I wanted to inform you I mean to give Tilly her notice."

It took Conroy a good long moment before he could manage to reply with sufficient insouciance. "Why would you inform me of this?"

"I was wondering about the economy of it. I would like to hire a new maid, of course, but perhaps I could take up one of the girls on staff. It would be a savings."

"Can I ask what Tilly has done?"

Jane tilted her head toward him. "Do you need to ask, Captain?"

His jaw worked itself back and forth. *There,* thought Jane. *Now we both know.*

"I think there may be some other changes to the staff as well. The footman, Addison, for instance. And the page, Lewis. They are not giving satisfaction. Her Grace is in agreement with me." This last was not true yet, of course, but it didn't need to be. It was enough she'd spoken those names from his missing accounts.

"I see I will have to be sure I am more careful in the future," said Conroy with studied blandness. "Your standards are very high."

"Oh, you do not have much to worry about, Captain. I have no intention of making any great changes. Especially as I plan to leave the duchess's service immediately after the birth."

"You're leaving?" Conroy said the words like he could not

understand them. Well, he might not. Conroy was a man thoroughly of this world within the walls.

"Yes," she said. "I find court life does not agree with me after all."

Jane watched Conroy's brow twitch and smooth as this remarkable statement repeated itself in his mind.

"Public life can be quite fatiguing for those who do not have a robust constitution," he said finally.

"Exactly." Jane bent her lips into a smile, showing how glad she was they were in agreement. "So, you see, not only would I not have time to orchestrate any significant change, I will have no reason to do so. Equally, as I intend to leave quietly and quickly, I don't suppose there would be any reason for any person to interfere with my going, or with anything I might do afterward."

"I could not imagine any such reason," Conroy replied, and they looked each other in the eyes, and that was that. The bargain was made. She would leave, he would not interfere and the papers need never be seen, by anyone who mattered.

"Then I shall bid you good evening, Captain, and let you get back to your business."

"Good evening, Lady Jane." He undid the latch and opened the door again. As she passed, he bowed his head, acknowledging that she had played well, and that he was letting her retire. It was a little like having a wolf watch her remove herself from its den.

As soon as the door shut between them, Jane closed her eyes and breathed out a long sigh in relief. She did not permit herself any other outward show, but moved down the corridor, heading for the stairs and her own room.

It had begun. There was no retreat now. A strange warmth flooded through her. She would be with Thomas tonight. She would be able to tell him that she was—they were—this much closer to freedom.

Her heart soaring, Jane climbed the stairs to wait for her lover's call.

# Nineteen

When Thomas finally woke, his head was splitting and his mouth tasted like he'd been kissing the London cobbles. It was dark, and the moon shone blearily down from behind a high haze. He'd been unconscious for hours. He wanted to spit, but his mouth was dry, so he settled for cursing instead.

*What happened?* He cradled his head in his hands. *How did I come out with a bloody hangover?*

He'd drunk nothing stronger than claret wine, and not much of that. He'd met Jane, and left Jane, and found Conroy's secrets, and met Jane again, and loved Jane . . .

Not fucked Jane, not swived or tumbled Jane, as he was sent to do. Loved Jane. And in so doing lost his love for Her Glorious Majesty.

No. No. It wasn't Jane who did this to him. It couldn't be, because that would put her life and soul in danger from the queen's rage. It was the mortal magic protecting Kensington House. The wards had cut him off from what was true and central of his existence. They made him forget who he had become and think only of who he had been. They had blinded him, and now he was back in the light. No wonder his head hurt.

But it wasn't Jane. His temporary faltering had nothing to do with Jane. He'd just thought it did while he was under the influence of those other magics. Clearly, they were stronger than he had realized.

*I need to be in Faery again. I need to see Her Majesty, if she'll see me after what a bloody mess I've made of this. I need to remember her love and care of me and my honor as her servant.*

*I need to forget Jane.*

Because forgetting Jane was the only way to keep her safe.

Except she wasn't going to be safe if he succeeded in his mission.

*I can't think about that. I have to get back, back home. The other side of the gate is my home. Everything will be clear once I'm there.*

Thomas levered himself to his feet with the help of the tree trunk. He looked across the lane. His sense of magic had fully returned and to Thomas's eyes, the brick wall surrounding Kensington House was coated with an ice-like shimmer that left no crack through which even a mouse might creep.

Jane was on the other side of that carefully guarded wall. He glowered at the brick and its warding spell with something that felt very like hunger prowling inside him.

"I'll end it," Thomas murmured to himself. "It's been enough. Another absence and she'll be desperate enough to seek me out for herself." Desperate, ready, trusting. She'd call to him from inside the walls, invite him back, and that invitation would crack the wards open and let him, and anyone he chose to accompany him, in to her.

But even that thought was a mistake, for a new image seared his brain. But this one was not of Jane bound and naked and begging for him. This was an image infinitely more powerful. He saw Jane sitting in front of him, pouring out her troubles. He remembered Jane taking simple human comfort from his presence.

Simple human comfort. Simple human companionship. The sympathy of a friend. Thomas's heart swelled, painful and uneasy. It kept coming back to that. Friendship. How long had it been since he'd walked with anyone he could call a friend? A wave of loneliness swept over him, and a memory bobbed to the surface, a piece of worn flotsam on the ocean of his disordered mind.

He remembered waking up on a muddy shore, wet and cold to the bone. Mud and sand filled his mouth. He remembered looking down at the flow of blood oozing out of his side. It was a splinter wound, deep and jagged. Pain had been with him so long it failed to surprise him as it snaked up his limbs into his dulled brain. He had come ashore only to die.

The loneliness of that moment had been like this. It was the understanding that there was no further to fall.

Only when he lay dying on that empty beach, the queen had come to him. She had saved him and made him her own. This time, it was Jane who wounded him.

Thomas clenched his jaw. He needed to get out of here, right now. He needed to return to the queen. She would want a report, and he needed to remind himself who his true mistress was.

But then, something stirred at the edge of his inner senses and warning touched Thomas like the odor of hot iron. His head snapped up, his thoughts made completely clear by the sense of approaching danger. Something was coming. Someone was searching, and they were using magic to do it. He needed to hide, quickly, and he couldn't risk a glamour. It would be sensed by whoever or whatever approached. Thomas cursed inwardly. His little patch of fern and bracken wouldn't hide a rat if someone decided to wade through it. All around stretched nothing but yards of open park land.

That left the oak tree. Thomas kicked his boots off and grasped a lower limb of the oak. He found a toehold in the deeply grooved bark and pulled himself up. Skills he'd gained climbing the rigging of his father's ship surged through his bones and sinews, and Thomas swarmed swiftly into the branches. When he could go no higher, he balanced on a limb as thin as his wrist, one hand resting lightly on the trunk, praying darkness and the meager spring foliage were enough to hide him.

An owl soared silently over the peaked rooftop of the palace. Undergrowth rustled below. A stag, his antlers tall and proud despite it still being early in the season, stalked past the grass. Thomas was ready to laugh at himself for panicking at the approach of a couple of animals, until he saw the woman.

She circled the wall of Kensington House, her fingers trailing against the bricks, rippling the icy light of the warding. The stag showed no fear at her approach, but came immediately up to her, touching its muzzle to her brow. The owl glided down to perch on the ground beside them.

Thomas did not dare breathe. He wished in vain he could

stop his beating heart. The very heat of his skin seemed to shine like a beacon in the hazy moonlight.

The woman laid her hand on the deer's flank. Bending her knees, she also touched the owl's head. The distinctive rushing prickle of magic filled the air. It surrounded both beasts, distorting them as a shallow stream distorts sunlight. Then, the animals were gone, and in their place stood two men. Both were tall and muscled. The taller of the pair was black-haired, with a hawk nose and eyes that were nothing more than pools of shadow. Despite his old workman's clothing, Thomas recognized him instantly.

It was Corwin Rathe.

Rathe, who'd been whispering in Kensington House with Fraulein Lehzen, and who lied about how he'd come to know Thomas's name.

The other man was as fair as Rathe was dark. He was also shorter by a bare inch, with chiseled features and pale eyes that were probably blue in daylight. He also dressed in old, loose clothing but carried himself with an air of absolute assurance.

They were Sorcerers. Among mortals, only Sorcerers could change their forms, and among Sorcerers only the most powerful and seasoned could perform the act. As the woman had maintained her shape, probably she was their Catalyst. All Sorcerers required a Catalyst to draw the magic from the natural world and channel it to them for their use.

One more thing was immediately apparent. These three were enemies, servants of the English crown. The queen would have told him if any allies patrolled the boundaries of Kensington House. In these times, there were not as many mortal Sorcerers as there had been once, but still there were enough to be danger-ous. Just two years ago, two of Her Majesty's most powerful and highly placed mortal spies had been destroyed by such as these.

Thomas clenched his jaw. He had to get out of this ridiculous position, huddled high in a tree like a naughty schoolboy. He had to warn the queen.

Below him, however, the Sorcerers and their Catalyst showed no signs of being ready to depart. They stood conferring in low voices. Strain his ears as he might, Thomas could make out no words. He did not dare open his senses to try to eavesdrop. The Catalyst would be able to detect any magic shifting near her. From the gestures, and body language, however, it looked to be a conversation undertaken in frustration. That was some small comfort. Whatever they sought here, they had not found it.

Well, if he was stuck here like a naughty boy, perhaps a boy's tricks would serve. Thomas edged his way along the branch. Two of last year's acorns still clung stubbornly to their twig. Thomas closed his hand gently around them, muffling the slight snap of the stems as he pulled them loose. Slowly, silent as an owl him-self, he stepped downward, into the lower branches, until he was right above their heads.

One of the Sorcerers, the blond man, was making a restless circle, kicking at the ferns.

"They're not hiding in the grass, Darius," said Rathe.

But the answer was a soft thump. "Oh, no?" Darius, stooped, and retrieved one of Thomas's discarded boots, and time was suddenly up.

Thomas tossed both acorns hard toward the wall so they rat-tled off the brick.

"Miranda." Darius and the woman took off at a run, leaving the dark-haired man behind, guarding their backs. But he was more than a match for one.

Thomas leapt.

He landed on Rathe's back, rolling them both down into the grass. Thomas wrapped his hand around the other's mouth, smothering any scream, and slammed his fist down hard at a precise point on his temple. The man went limp and Thomas jumped aside, leaving the unconscious body to sprawl in the ferns. The others would waste time now, making sure their comrade was all right.

Thomas ran into the dark. He felt magic surge behind him. It sought to bind and topple, but Thomas had the queen's blessing on him, and that blessing grew stronger with each running footstep that carried him deeper into the park toward the gate. The pursuing spell fell away like a noose coming up short, and then Thomas was in among the trees.

Ahead, he saw the sylvan light. He lengthened his stride, his bare feet pounding the uneven ground. The light enveloped him, the harsh bonds of mortal earth slid away, and he was gone.

Thomas stumbled and fell to his knees. The light was blindingly bright here. He had fetched up in a garden filled with a riot of flowers from all corners of both the Fae and mortal realms. The scent he breathed was of warmth and impossible loves. This place was garden and palace and ahead of him, beneath a bower of thorn and ivy, stood the queen.

"Sir Thomas," she said, and he thought she sounded a little surprised. "How is it with my knight?"

"Majesty." Thomas drew his legs up under him until he knelt

properly and tried to control his breathing. He was in shocking disarray, and he felt her disapproval seep inside him along with the scent of the blossoms.

Thomas relaxed his internal guards and let his mind open so the queen might see his memory of the Sorcerers and their Catalyst outside the walls of Kensington House. As she absorbed the scene, her eyes slowly darkened to the color of storm clouds. The air all around him chilled to the killing depths of winter. Her anger swept out hard, like a blow to his mind. Thomas bowed his head and grit his teeth to hold unmoving against the storm.

"Oh, they think themselves so very clever, these dogs of the crown." He felt her smile in his heart, diamond-edged and killing-sharp. "They will hunt high and low for the magic that chips away at their precious warding, but they will never think to look at their own bitch in the manger."

Thomas kept his head bowed, hoping his consternation did not show. To hear Jane spoken of in that way, even by his queen, stirred anger deep in his bowels. But that was wrong. He could not be angry at the queen. It was as impossible as if he should flap his arms and fly to the moon.

"And how does our lusty Lady Jane?" she asked him. "If the dogs are on the trail already, we do not have not much more time. Does she itch, Thomas, and beg for you to scratch?"

"She . . . she is very willing." He needed to lift his eyes so he could look on the queen's face and feel her regard. Her gaze would clear his mind and drive out the confusion that racked him. But he kept his eyes lowered.

"Look at me, my Thomas."

He could not refuse. Thomas lifted his eyes to her face. She was so beautiful, so filled with light and power. When the queen looked at him, all other things seemed distant, mean and tattered. She had granted him so much; his life, his rank and power in her unchanging realm. Anything she demanded, he owed to her. He was her captain, her lover, her confidante, anything she wanted him to be. His body and heart and soul all were hers to command. He would live or die at her word, and looking into her eyes, that was all he desired. His heart swelled with love, as it had from the moment he first saw her.

And yet, and yet . . . As she held him with her gaze and let him delight in her presence, Thomas remembered Jane, and the trust in Jane's dark eyes.

"You are troubled," she said. "You have never before been troubled in my service, Thomas. What is it?"

Perhaps there was a way out yet. A way that would save him from his own weakness. "If these Sorcerers work for the mortal crown, they will now search Kensington House. They will question the occupants. If they apply their magics, Lady Jane will not be able to conceal that she has been with me. It is my advice as your captain, Majesty, that I . . . that we try no more with Jane. The house has other weaknesses we can make use of. There is a greedy man, Captain Conroy, very close to the duke and duchess both. He can be had for nothing more than gold and the promise of power."

The queen cocked her head at him. Color swirled in her eyes, as uncertain as night and moonbeams. His throat constricted. A fog of doubt seemed to have descended over him, and it felt more terrible than certain knowledge of her anger could be.

But then she smiled, and the fog broke apart before the sun of her regard. "It is well thought, Sir Thomas. But there are rea- sons to pursue this opening. Therefore, it is my wish you should continue."

"Then let me go no more to her. She is . . . ready. She will call out to me. Her desire will break open the wards from within." *Forgive me, Jane. Forgive me, but if I come to you again, I will not be able to leave.*

"We must be certain, Thomas," said the queen firmly. "We have no room for error here. Not with the babe so close to being born. No. You will go to her once more, and make utterly certain of her."

"But . . ."

"I have spoken, Sir Thomas."

"Majesty."

She smiled, and she was so beautiful it sent a stab of pain to his heart. "Come now," she raised him up. "Kiss me, Sir Thomas. Show me I have not lost your affection because I dared to command."

She lifted her mouth to him. She was lush and perfect, the dream of what woman should be. Their lips met, and the kiss was soft and unendingly sweet. Her power flowed around him and through him, and within the space of a heartbeat his cock hardened to the point of pain.

"There!" But Queen Tatiana broke the kiss, laughing. "Take that to your Lady Jane and put it to good use!" She gave his cock a swift pat, and then walked into her bower, and vanished to his sight.

In the heart of that fantastic garden that was itself the heart of the Fae realms, Thomas Lynne's knees buckled and he fell slowly to the ground

The queen had laughed, and because she did, he laughed. But along with the unanswered lust that raged in him, he was aware this was the first time he'd had to force such laughter. Before, her mood would have wrapped around him and taken him in like a lover. That intimacy was denied him now. Lady Jane stood between him and his queen, and he could no longer deny it.

Worse, the queen knew he had weakened. That was the reason she wanted him to go back to Jane. It was not the defense of Kensington House she was testing, it was him.

Never before had Thomas doubted his own strength. He had been a commander of men since he had come of age. He had faced threats both mortal and magical. He knew his own skill and his worth. But the idea of facing Jane again, of seeing the trust and love in her eyes before he took her soft and willing body into his arms . . . it was enough to bring him to his knees. When he was with her, he didn't want to be the Fae queen's captain anymore. He wanted to be the mortal man who could save Jane from the loneliness that plagued her.

The danger in these thoughts was beyond anything he had ever approached before.

He could not get close to her again. He must go, but he must keep his distance. He must find a way to remember the true glamour here was love. Jane's love was a spell that would steal him away from his oath. He had all the love that man could ask for in his service to the queen. He needed no other. Yes. That was it. He must find a way to drive Jane from her senses tonight, but still preserve his detachment. Then, he must ready himself to leave the field, keeping the door between them open just enough for her to try to follow after.

If his heart broke in the leaving, the presence of his queen would muffle the pain and this unreasoning affection. Eventually, he would barely be able to recall Jane DeWitte's face.

He had, quite literally, all the time in the world to forget her.

# Twenty

Thomas's call did not reach Jane until the small hours of the morning.

*Jane. I'm waiting for you, Jane.*

Jane threw back the covers and scrambled from her bed. She didn't bother with the lamp this time. She didn't stop to think what she would do if someone saw. She didn't think at all. She needed to see Thomas. She needed to look up into his eyes as she told him what she'd done. She needed to hear what he wanted to ask her.

Jane reached the short, shadowed corridor, and darted swiftly through the rose door. In the fire-lit chamber, she drew herself up, heart pounding, only to find she was quite alone.

For a moment, Jane couldn't understand. She wondered if she might have only imagined the summons, but she dismissed that notion. She could not be mistaken about the resonance of Thomas's call in her mind. Her next thought was he might be hiding somewhere. His mischievous nature made it possible, but as she circled the room, she had no sense of him. There was no sound of breathing or movement in the luxurious chamber, save what she herself created.

Jane frowned. Perhaps he was called away by some emergency? Disappointment sank in, although Jane tried to resign herself to it. They lived in the real world, and delays did occur.

A new, cold thought struck her then. What if he had been caught?

No, impossible. How could he be caught? What could catch a magician? But he had said there were other magic workers, Sorcerers and wizards, and she understood so little of this part of him. In truth, she had avoided probing too deeply. She had feared that dwelling too much on magic would make her change her mind and run away from Thomas.

Now, though, her willful ignorance bred worry and that worry pressed beneath her heart like a stone. Jane clasped and unclasped her hands, glancing repeatedly toward the door.

*This is useless.* She drew in a deep breath and forced herself back into a semblance of calm. She would compose herself to wait for a reasonable time, and if Thomas did not appear, she would leave. She was going to visit at Mrs. Beauchamp's tomorrow afternoon. If Thomas was not there, she could easily find some excuse to ask after him.

But probably nothing was wrong. Probably he was merely making her wait to increase her desire for him. Probably this was another game.

Keeping this thought firmly in place, Jane tried to decide which sofa would be the best to be found on. She would sit there cool and composed, her skirts arranged just so. She also found herself wishing Thomas had thought to provide this otherwise very usefully furnished apartment with some reading material.

It was on her second circuit of the room that she noticed a pillow had been placed on one of the low, round tables, and on this waited a white . . . object.

Jane moved forward to inspect the object, and found it to be a penis. It was life-sized and carved of what was probably ivory.

A blush burned in her cheeks and she looked around, to see if Thomas had appeared, and was appreciating his joke. But she was still alone, with the object on its green velvet pillow. It must have come from the cabinet where he kept the ropes and oils and so many other . . . articles. She could not imagine what had possessed Thomas to leave such a thing lying about, even here. At the same time, she found herself wondering what those intricate carvings would feel like against her hand. Would they compare at all to the real thing?

*Oh, surely this is nonsense.* Jane looked around again, told herself she was being decidedly ridiculous and picked up the object.

It was heavy for its size, and most realistically carved, with ridges, a blunt head and even rough testicles. It was not, she judged, as thick as Thomas's cock, but it seemed to be fully as long. The ivory warmed quickly against her skin. To her shock, the first, familiar stirrings of desire also warmed within her.

She put the false cock down at once and stared at it, as if it might turn into a snake and bite her.

How could this be? It was a carving, a toy. A very strange toy. Becoming aroused by it was as ludicrous as being stirred to desire by a Greek statue. It was not the object itself, she reasoned, it was the reminder of what it represented. Holding it reminded her of the delight of holding Thomas's erect cock, and of stroking him while she felt his hands fondling her breasts and spoke in his seductive voice.

*Are you wet, Jane? Are you ready for me? Suck me, Jane. Suck me now.*

Warmth spread through her, and Jane felt her pussy soften. Desire blunted self-criticism and strengthened curiosity. She settled herself on the backless sofa and picked the ivory cock up again. It still held the warmth of her hand. She ran her fingertips over it, feeling the long ridge on the underside, the slight indentation at the tip, the roughness of the carved balls. She imagined touching Thomas so, first with one hand and then with two. He'd groan and command her to go slowly, to let him savor her touch. She'd obey, which would be both difficult and enjoyable. She might even rub her cheek against his velvet hardness. She stroked the ivory cock against her cheek to test the sensation, and her breasts swelled with longing. Oh, yes, that would feel good.

Jane's breath caught in her throat and her nipples began to tighten. They ached to be touched. Where was Thomas? She needed his hands on her. She needed his cock, not some ivory toy.

And yet, and yet, if just fondling this toy brought on her desire, what would happen if she . . . touched herself with it.

*I cannot be thinking this.*

But she was, and the wickedness of it sent a bolt of warmth through her. Why not? Why shouldn't she? No one was here to see, not even Thomas, and she was so hot now. She rubbed her thighs together, but that only increased her agitation, and made her clutch the shaft of the decadent toy more tightly.

Slowly, she brought the hard ivory cock to her mouth and touched it to her lips. It was warm as skin now, and the shape of it against her sensitive lips was so evocative she let out a sigh. She circled her mouth with the tip and a shiver of pleasure ran down her spine. It did feel good. Not as good as Thomas's living cock, but good just the same. She opened her mouth a little ways and slowly ran the tip of her tongue up the longest of the carved ridges. Her nipples peaked, pressing against her chemise, begging to be touched. She licked the cock again, thinking of Thomas, of how he urged her on and praised her responsiveness. She thought how his control left him when she sucked on him and how he ordered her to take him deeper and harder.

She plunged the ivory cock into her mouth, images of Thomas filling her mind. *That's it, Jane, that's it!* cried his hoarse voice from memory. *Suck me hard! Show me how you love my hard cock in your pretty mouth!*

Almost without her realizing it, Jane's free hand crept to her breast and squeezed. *Touch me there, Thomas. You know how I like it.*

Oh, this was torture, licking and sucking on this false cock while touching herself. Hot desire filled her. Her pussy was drenched with her need. She wanted to come, here and now.

She'd put the toy in her mouth and it had felt good. How good would it feel inside her pussy?

Torn between desire and laughter, Jane fell back onto the longue's curving arm. She tried not to think. She just lifted the skirts of her nightdress and chemise, baring her thighs to the fire-warmed air. Her nipples were deliciously hard under the layers of cambric and muslin, aching to be touched and toyed with. Jane pressed the tip of the ivory cock against her clit and gasped. She melted back against the velvet sofa and the puddle of her skirts. After her disappointing experiments with touching herself while she was apart from Thomas, she had not expected this game to feel so good, so like the real thing. The desire was certainly real, and the burning need. She sprawled across the sofa, legs open wide, holding the false cock between her legs.

More, her body urged her. More. She ran the cock up and down her slit, slowly at first, but slow would not answer. She needed it fast. She needed power and fire.

*I want you inside me, Thomas. Fuck me. Fuck me hard.*

She pressed the ivory cock against her weeping entrance and groaned. It slipped easily inside, fitting delectably. She arched her hips and pressed deeper. Oh, yes, that would feel so good. He'd fuck fast and hard, urging her to scream in her pleasure. *Let me hear you, Jane. I want to hear you!*

"Oh yes," she gasped. "Yes, Thomas, I want it. I want it deep."

"So I see."

Jane's eyes flew open. Thomas, clad in shirt and buckskins stood over her, his eyes alight with mischief and desire.

"Oh G—" She was on her back, *en dishabille,* with this wicked toy in her pussy, and Thomas had seen it all.

"Oh, no, Jane, don't stop on my account." Thomas knelt beside the couch, his hands pushing under the disarray of her skirts to caress her thighs, then to cover her hand where it still clutched the ivory cock. "Don't stop at all."

He moved her hand, moved the ivory cock inside her in long, slow thrusts.

"Ahhh . . . what are you doing?" she sighed, half appalled, half sinking back into desire.

"Giving you what you asked for," he murmured. "You want it deep. You want it hard." He increased the tempo, setting a glorious, wicked friction against the silken walls of her sheath. "Take it, Jane. Take it hard."

"Yes." Her head fell back and her hands rose to her own breasts, plucking and toying with her nipples. It felt so good to have him minister to her with this cunning toy. To have his eyes on her as she arched her hips, seeking a deeper stroke. "Yes."

"Lovely, greedy, impatient Jane." The fingers of his other hand probed the very top of her slit until he found her clit. Jane gasped and her hips bucked. "Ah, now, that's even better, isn't it?"

"Yes!" she cried as he rubbed her and thrust the ivory cock inside. "Oh, yes!"

"You know what I want, Jane. I want you to beg me to make you come like this."

"Please, please, please!" she cried the word in time to the thrusts, the rolling of her clit, the trembling caress of her own hands against her breasts. "Oh, Thomas, I want to come!"

"Yes!" He thrust and pressed down and Jane cried out as her pleasure burst from her, rocking her hips hard against his hand, wringing wordless cries from her. Slowly, slowly the waves subsided and she fell back against the sofa, gloriously spent.

Thomas smiled down at her, and eased the ivory cock from her sheath. Pulsing as she was with the echoes of her orgasm, Jane felt strangely empty. Thomas grinned as if he guessed her thought and leaned over. He kissed her softly, yet openly, his tongue stroking and tangling hers. Jane groaned again as fresh desire rose with a swiftness that was almost frightening, and she reached for him.

"Oh, no, Jane." Thomas caught both of her wrists in one strong hand as he pulled away. "You have been very naughty. You know that, don't you?"

"What . . ." Desire robbed her of her wits. "What have I done?"

He held up the ivory cock. "You should have waited for your master to instruct you, Jane. You took this to pleasure yourself without my orders." Wicked light shimmered in his green eyes, and Jane could not help but glance down at his cock. Oh, he was hard. Very hard.

"Please," she whispered. "Master Thomas, I will be good. Don't punish me."

"Now, now, Jane, what kind of master would I be if I did not show you discipline? You would grow careless of your glorious body and all your sweet pleasures."

He stood and with a strong tug brought her to her feet. She stood before him, her nightdress and robe horribly rumpled, her hair falling about her shoulders and her breasts straining beneath his heated gaze.

"Bend over the couch arm," he ordered. "Put your hands on the cushion, and leave them there."

Jane's mouth had gone dry, and her heart pounded hard in the base of her throat. The familiar nervous anticipation fluttered in her wrists, but it was almost lost in the wicked eagerness to see where this new game would lead.

She did as she was instructed, bending across the sofa arm,

and planting her hands on the plush seat. Her breasts rubbed against the fabric of her nightclothes, and the curve of the sofa arm pressed right against her swollen pussy. Her ass lifted high in the air.

She felt Thomas move behind her and heard his harsh breathing. His arms reached around her and his fingers fumbled with the hooks and ribbons of her nightclothes, loosening them just enough so he could shove the garments down hard, so the fabric fell into a heap around her ankles. Cool air washed across the heated skin of her body and she hissed, shifting her weight. As she did, her pussy rubbed against the sofa arm, and it was all she could do not to gasp.

"Now, Jane," said Thomas in a warning growl. "Do not make this worse than it must be. Keep still until I give you permission to move."

His hand was on her ass, caressing, up and down, exploring the rounded flesh with a connoisseur's appreciation. Her nipples tightened again with painful abruptness and she groaned.

"Please," she arched her back.

"Oh, no, Jane. Not yet."

She felt a blunt point press against the right half of her ass. At first she thought it was Thomas's cock. Then she realized it was only the toy, still slick with her juices, rubbing and prodding her flesh.

"Ahhh . . ." she sighed.

Thomas said nothing, but caressed the curve of her ass with his free hand. Her pussy dampened and strained to open. This was good, but she wanted more. She wanted his body over hers, his cock, his real cock inside her . . .

The tip of the ivory cock pressed against her anus and Jane's eyes flew open.

"You're not . . ."

"Open for me, Jane. You wanted this pretty toy inside you. You couldn't wait for it. Take it now."

She'd had his finger in her that way before, and it had felt good, but this . . . it was so much bigger . . . it couldn't possibly fit.

Thomas pressed the ivory cock closer, stretching her open. It felt strange. It felt good. It felt wrong. It felt right. He was so close behind her, leaning over her, his thighs against the backs of her legs, his arm alongside her to brace them both.

"Take it, sweet Jane. Be good. Show me how very good you can be."

Desire and curiosity both rose. She pushed out as Thomas pressed the ivory cock inward. It stretched and it burned, and she cried out, and it was inside and he was moving it, fucking her with it, pressing her against the sofa arm so that her pussy rubbed against the velvet with each thrust.

She sighed and her arms trembled. "Please, Master Thomas, let me move."

"Oh, not yet, Jane. Not quite yet my sweet, sweet Jane." He rubbed his chest against her back. He was so close and yet infinitely distant. Her breasts swung, grazing against each other, and she moaned. She was full of the ivory cock, but it wasn't enough. Her muscles clenched around it and her empty sheath, and it only made desire burn brighter. She wanted more. She needed more. "I want you. Please, Master!"

She heard the unmistakable sound of buttons being torn open and she groaned with relief. He would remove this decadent instrument of sexual torture. He would bury himself in her sheath. She wanted that so badly she ached and trembled. She would weep if she had to wait any longer.

Thomas took firm hold of her hips to adjust the angle of her. His cock pressed against her thighs, and she parted for him. Shifting her position caused the ivory cock to move inside her, almost as if it were a living thing. Thomas moved closer, running the tip of his cock around her drenched folds, and settling it against her entrance.

It occurred to her fevered brain that he was not going to remove the ivory toy. He was going to fuck her while it remained inside her. Jane didn't know whether to be elated or terrified, and then Thomas was inside her.

The first sensation was relief. Her sheath and pussy had been begging for this for what felt like ages. Now that she had what she needed she could do nothing but revel in it. She was twice stretched, twice full, and the double sensation fed all the greedy flames of desire burning in her.

"So hot, Jane," Thomas moaned. "So ready for me."

"Always ready," she panted in answer. "Always ready for you."

"Yes." He gripped her hips and ass, holding her ruthlessly where he wanted her and began to thrust. Each powerful movement ground her pulsing clit against the sofa arm. His merciless hands squeezed and kneaded her ass, and that stirred and shifted the ivory cock so that it too fucked her. Harder and faster, Thomas slammed into her, as lost to the wicked glory of their fucking as she was.

She wanted it to stop at once, lest she burn alive in the fire. She wanted it to never end.

"I can't . . . I can't . . ." Jane's fingers dug into the velvet cushions.

In answer he thrust deep so that her sheath clenched around him and her ass squeezed the ivory cock tight.

Jane screamed as the orgasm took her. She flew free, her body beyond control, lost entirely to the tumult of pleasure. Thomas roared like a lion and she felt the second storm of his climax as he drove madly into her, clamping her tight against the sofa, refusing to release her until at last he was spent.

Panting, trembling, moaning. Jane couldn't move. It was entirely beyond her. Gently, Thomas slid both his cocks from her. He gathered her into his arms and carried her across the room to the bed. He lay down with her, and draped her across his partially clothed body.

"Beautiful, beautiful Jane," he whispered as he cradled her close to his chest. Languor took her. She was exactly where she longed to be. All questions could wait. Right now, all was perfection. He was saying something else, but sleep had already moved her beyond understanding. She could ask about it later. For this moment, she had all that she needed.

## Twenty-one

The woman currently called Fiora Beauchamp dozed fitfully in her bed. She'd had many names in her long life; Fiora mac Sulen, Red Fiora, the Nightingale of Drury Lane, but none of them mattered, because none of them were spoken by her queen anymore.

Fiora twisted restlessly beneath the weight of the quilts her maids had heaped upon her to try to keep out the endless cold. In response, the ache that permeated all her joints dug in deeper. She was not truly asleep. Real sleep had not come to her in a long time. She chased darkness and light through her mind, but never did she dip far enough below the surface of thought to lose awareness of the heaviness following close behind. It was patient, inexorable and final. It would settle onto her heart and lungs when it caught up with her. She was so slow, and she couldn't catch her breath. It would have her, it would smother her and she could not even scream . . .

*Fiora.*

Light like a benediction fell all around her. The cold was gone, the pain was gone, washed away by a sylvan flood. Even the final dark could not stand before this bright glory, and it slunk away. Fiora knew this light instantly, though she had not seen it in many long years. It was the light of the Fae realms. The light of her true home, and her true queen.

"Majesty." Fiora struggled from beneath the heap of blankets. She fell to her knees and clasped her hands together. "Majesty!"

The queen stood at the foot of the bed, and she was beautiful and terrible beyond words. Midnight black draped her perfect form, and she held a silver sword in her hand. Black wings drooped from her shoulders. She was war, she was vengeance, and she fixed Fiora with eyes the color of thunderstorms.

"You betrayed me, Fiora. You let your heart stray from your loyalty to me."

Memory flashed through Fiora, clear and violent as lightning. She saw herself and Cullen locked in a torrid embrace. She saw his ungainly, lumpish, mortal form, felt the slop of his mouth on her face, the clumsy fumbling of his hands across her body. The terrible weakness of his lust found answer in her foolish spirit. Weak as she was, she mistook this greedy pawing, this stinking, graceless coupling for something approaching the unending love that was due Her Glorious Majesty.

In the depths of Fiora's heart, a faint voice wailed that there had been more. They had only fallen in love as human men and women did. Such affection did not lessen the love or loyalty due to others. But the visions the queen poured into Fiora's open mind quickly smothered such weak protests.

"I'm sorry!" Fiora threw herself down prostrate at the queen's feet. "I was weak and selfish. I took your blessing for granted. Forgive me! Please, Majesty, forgive me!"

Silence. It was as if she'd been deserted in some arctic place with only darkness on all sides. And yet, and yet . . . she could feel her queen. She was distant, she remained present.

"Forgiveness must be earned." The queen's words fell soft as snow onto Fiora's franticly beating heart.

"I would do anything!"

"I am becoming concerned about Sir Thomas. I fear his mission may be proving too much for him."

"Sir Thomas?" Fiora struggled to set aside her torrential emotions and think clearly. What did the queen want to hear? What would please her most? Fiora's mind scrabbled frantically for the proper answer. "I have seen no sign of his faltering, Majesty."

"I am glad to hear it. But I require you to watch him closely, Fiora. And should he begin to falter, you are to warn me at once."

It was the chance she had longed for down the endless years. It had filled her voice with sorrow as she sang sentimental ballads in the cramped and stinking theaters. It had tinted her very soul, allowing her to become one of the most celebrated tragediennes of the age. All that feigned sorrow, all that counterfeit longing rooted only in this single wish; give me another chance. Please. Just one more chance.

"I live only to serve Your Majesty," whispered Fiora.

"And should you serve me well in this, you will be rewarded."

The light poured down, and Fiora felt it filling her. It straightened her back and limbs and banished the pain. She looked down and saw her hands were young, strong and capable as they should be. She touched her face, and her cheeks were full and flush. The strength of her body was dizzying. She could dance again. She could sing like a bird. She leapt up and spun on her toes, made speechless in her delight. The queen lifted her chin and smiled. Fiora's heart swelled to the point of breaking. How many times had she tried to remember that smile with its infinite warmth and the way all that was goodness flowed her queen's regard?

Fiora dropped to her knees again, light and easy in her youthful frame. The queen held out her hand, and Fiora kissed it.

"See you keep your vows this time, Fiora." Queen Tatiana laid her finger on Fiora's brow. "The daemon realms will accept your soul in payment of our bargain as readily as they did Cullen's."

Then she was gone.

Fiora woke, on her back, in her bed, beneath the heap of quilts. Age clamped down on her once more, robbing her of breath and life. The dream of youth and strength made the sensation of her wizened body that much more horrible.

"I will not fail," Fiora whispered to the night, certain her queen would hear. "I swear it."

# Twenty-two

*I love you, Jane.*

Thomas cradled Jane close against his chest and felt her drift away into sleep. He should rouse her, clothe her once more in her rumpled nightdress and send her back to her room. But he could not separate his flesh from hers. It was as far beyond him as swimming the broad ocean.

*What am I doing?* He closed his eyes. *What is happening to me?*

He had been sent to seduce this woman, to fuck her until she was ready to run any hazard to have his cock in her again, and through her repeated invitation to him, he would be able to widen the crack in the defenses of Kensington House to allow Her Majesty's other servants entrance. They would determine whether the child the duchess carried was the one foretold in the prophecy of the daemon realms. After that . . . well, it was none of his business what happened after that. He was the loyal knight to his queen. He must not question her will or her actions.

Jane would question them though. His arm tightened around her of its own accord. For all their games of obedience and mastery, Jane would question what happened, and want to know his part in it.

Not that she would get a chance to ask him anything. He would be gone back to the Fae realms and the queen's court where he belonged before she even understood the nature of the questions she should put to him. That was good. That was what he should be longing for now. Because there he'd be able to lose himself among the glamours that were of a more familiar kind, and infinitely safer.

God's legs, he'd thought he'd spill himself like a raw youth as he watched Jane playing with the ivory toy he'd left out to tempt her. When she'd taken it into her sweet, pink mouth, he hadn't been able to keep from touching himself, and when she'd slipped it into her pussy and called his name . . . he'd been undone. Utterly on fire.

He'd see far more erotic acts in the Seelie court. The queen enjoyed sexual sport, and her courtiers regularly vied to entice and entertain her. He himself had serviced three women at once so she could take her pleasure in watching and then fucked her in full view of her cavorting servants. Nothing could match the queen's beauty, her inventiveness or appetite.

Despite all his experience, the pleasures of this one human woman were driving him to madness, for it was madness for him to think of love. Queen Tatiana permitted her knights to seduce mortal women. She might even encourage it for sport or spite, or if she had a use for the woman as she did now. But if the queen became convinced his heart was no longer wholly hers . . . Fiora's lover would have company in the fires to which he had been sent. Which would leave Jane alone, and defenseless before the wrath of Her Glorious Majesty. She already suspected him. She was granting him mercy, but her mercy was always short-lived.

Terror rushed through Thomas, filling every crevasse of his being, followed fast by an anger that seared his soul. God's teeth, he was a thousand kinds of fool!

"Thomas?" Jane shifted in his arms, her hands moving instinctively to caress him, to soothe and comfort him.

Thomas squeezed his eyes closed. *No, no. This cannot be.* He would protect her with all his strength, all his soul. But against the queen, the strength and soul of one mortal man could never be enough. He had to get away from Jane. Now. While there was still a chance the queen might be willing to overlook his flirtation with treason.

Jane shifted again. "Thomas. What is it?"

He steeled himself. "Nothing, sweetheart," he said lightly. "It is only that it is time to get you back where you belong."

It felt like he was stabbing his own arm, but Thomas made himself sit up and settle Jane onto the pillows. She shivered and wrapped her arms around her breasts. He almost ordered her not to. He wanted to feast his gaze upon her. But she really was cold. He lifted a broad fold of the silken coverlet and drew it around her shoulders.

"Thank you," she whispered.

He said nothing. He didn't trust his voice. She looked so lost, so young, bundled up like that. He thought of chaffing her arms to warm her, which would, of course, lead him to pull her close to cradle and kiss. Then he would reach beneath that coverlet to fondle her breasts. She'd sigh against his mouth and then . . .

Thomas's groin tightened, and he turned away with a muffled curse to pick up her nightdress. It was all but ruined. He'd been careless of the hooks and seams when he'd shoved it down across her hips to get to her. He wished he could repair it somehow, but the queen had not thought to grant him such powers. He smoothed out the fabric as best he could, but there was nothing he could do about the torn lace, or the rent he now saw in the shoulder. Suddenly, Thomas hated himself, as fully and viciously as he had ever hated an enemy. He hands itched to hold a cutlass and to swing it hard against some target, any target that would splinter beneath his blow.

All he could do was hold out the ruined nightclothes for Jane.

"Thank you," she said flatly, and his heart shattered.

Awkwardly, and by degrees, she shed the silk coverlet and set about dressing herself. Thomas struggled against the unaccountable urge to turn away and give her a moment's privacy. Instead, he began righting his own clothing in awkward silence. This was ridiculous. Why was it like this? He should be fastening her gown tenderly, laughing with her, kissing and touching in merry lover's parting as he always had before.

He stomped his foot into his hessian boot, cursing the tight footwear roundly. What was the matter with the men of this age that they insisted on wearing clothing it was impossible to move freely in?

"Thomas?"

His head snapped around. Jane was back in her robe. A bit of lace dangled from the neckline as sadly as her disarranged curls dangled about her shoulders. All at once, he could not see her as a woman who had been well and passionately loved. She looked like she'd been brutalized. Like he had brutalized her.

"Have I done something wrong?"

"What? No!" He straightened at once, and folded her into his embrace. The way she wrapped her arms tight around him made him curse himself in every tongue he knew, mortal and Fae alike. Here he was wondering what to do about the fact that the sight of her filled not just his cock but his heart to overflowing, and she was wondering if he was angry with her.

"You've done nothing," He cupped her head with one hand to cradle her closer to him. The gentle weight of her cheek against his shoulder seared him. He would bear the sensation like a brand the rest of his life, however long that might be. "I am only sorry that I must leave you now." This was true, as far as it went. But it did not go nearly far enough.

Jane seemed to accept it though. She tilted her head back to look at him. "Will I see you today?"

His throat tightened painfully. "You are coming to visit F . . . my godmother, are you not? She said she was expecting you for an early supper."

"Yes. But will you be there?"

He opened his mouth to say no, to tell her he had an errand that was more important. But he could not do it. The words simply would not come while he looked into Jane's dark eyes and understood that this afternoon, during a polite, private supper, might be the last time he would ever see her.

*This one last time. One last moment with Jane in the sunlight.* "I'll be there."

"Then kiss me, Thomas, and let me go."

Thomas obeyed, as swiftly and as readily as she had ever obeyed him. Then, she walked away and left him standing there. As the door closed, it made a hollow sound, as hollow as the space inside where his heart had once been.

# Twenty-three

The morning was horrendous.

Previously, the trysts Jane had kept with Thomas had felt as restorative as sleep. But this time, she climbed laboriously out of her bed and slumped stupid and thick-headed down to breakfast. No amount of coffee could make any difference. Certainly, as far as the duchess was concerned, Jane could get nothing right—not the placement of pillows, not the translations for the letters and invitations that needed to be answered, not even the temperature of the cloth she ordered for her forehead.

"Enough!" Her Grace cried, flinging the towel away. "Oh, get along, Jane. Today you visit Mrs. Beauchamp, so? You go and come back when you discover where you have left your wits."

"Yes, ma'am." Jane all but slunk from the room to change into her walking costume.

Now she rode in the landau with Tilly, who was sneaking glances in between stitches. Jane hadn't had a chance to make the dismissal yet. But this felt like a minor irritation. How was she supposed to endure this call? Mrs. Beauchamp was a fine woman, but she was prone to prattling, and would be relying on Jane for a heaping spoon of gossip to go with their supper. What on earth was she going to say? She could barely remember what had passed at the drawing room yesterday. In fact, she could barely remember anything she'd done since she returned to England, unless it involved Thomas.

Of Thomas, she could remember every detail. Her skin held tight to every word and every touch, but most clearly she remembered the way he'd looked at her the night before, the moment he'd bent down to kiss her before she'd hurried away.

For she could not shake the feeling that in her mind she'd heard Thomas speak a single word with that kiss. *Farewell.*

*Perhaps it's for the best,* Jane tried to tell herself as she watched the traffic jostling slowly alongside their carriage. The rain that had so obligingly held off yesterday now poured down steadily, turning the day as gray and miserable as her thoughts. *I must have frightened him with all this talk of leaving my position to be with him. Surely, it's better to know I've had all he can give sooner rather than later. Isn't that the way of* affaires du coeur?

She'd have to ask Georgie. Georgie would know. But Georgie would want to know what prompted such a question. What would she say then? She would never be able to speak the entire truth of her affair with Thomas to a single soul.

In a lifetime heavily marked by funerals, Jane didn't think she'd ever felt so wretched. She didn't even care if Tilly saw how she struggled to hold herself together. After this, she would be alone again. Until this point, she'd borne that loneliness because she'd never known there was another life for her to live. But her fleeting moments with Thomas had shown her what it was to have companionship as well as passion. There was no undoing the splendor of that revelation, or the pain of knowing those fleeting moments were all she would ever have. For how could another man take Thomas's place? It was he who freed her heart as well as her desires. Jane closed her eyes. Freed her and bound her. Forever.

Mrs. Beauchamp possessed a large house in Mayfair. To be sure, the dwelling and the neighborhood were no longer on the cutting edge of fashion, but both remained fine enough to show that the widow had efficiently managed the fortune her doting husband had left her. There were rumors of a pension from at least one doting lover as well, but as Mrs. Beauchamp was mostly retired to her own parlor and had not generated any new scandal in Jane's entire lifetime; those whispers were not much remembered.

"My dear Jane!" Mrs. Beauchamp stretched out her hands wrapped in fingerless gloves as soon as Jane entered her pretty green parlor. Jane bent to receive a kiss from her hostess. Mrs. Beauchamp looked thoroughly respectable in crepe and lace with her widow's cap starched and spotless. Table and chairs had been set near the sofa, but that table had been laid for only two.

Thomas was not there, and he was not expected.

*It's better,* she told herself. *Much better. It would be too hard to keep my countenance if he was here.* Fortunately, her hostess motioned her to a chair just then, so she did not have to find the strength to remain standing.

"Will you have some tea? Or sherry? It's so dreadfully cold out, you'd never know it was May, would you? The supper is almost ready. You must be fairly exhausted after the time you've been having. I'm sure you're not eating properly."

"Oh no, I assure you," replied Jane reflexively. "The food at Kensington House is always excellent."

"Well then, indulge an old woman. I simply cannot manage until eight without something. Shall we sit?" She reached for the bell pull.

"Of course."

They settled themselves and Mrs. Beauchamp's servants came in bearing an array of covered dishes. Jane struggled to stay attentive to the oyster soup, cold lobster salad and boiled potatoes. She was certain she had done more difficult things in her life than smile and dredge up some innocuous details of the drawing room and what she had been learning of the duchess's tastes and habits. But at that moment, she could not remember what they had been.

"Why, Jane, you've hardly touched anything." Mrs. Beauchamp peered up at her anxiously. "Shall I ring for something else?"

"No, no. It's all delicious." Jane looked down at her plate. She was certain she'd been eating steadily during the conversation. She certainly wasn't at all hungry. But the pink-edged china seemed as piled with food as it had when she'd been served. The thought of having to take more for politeness' sake left her feeling ill.

"I'm sorry," Jane said, striving for brightness in her voice. "It's been such a whirlwind since we came back, I find my appetite is entirely gone."

"Oh, dear. But you'll take a little tea?" Jane nodded her assent. "Excellent. Robbins, we'll take tea on the sofa."

*One cup, and I can leave,* Jane thought guiltily. Mrs. Beauchamp did not get much company, and here she was thinking only how soon she could get away.

The door opened again. Jane, certain it was only another of the servants, did not permit herself to turn around.

"There you are, Thomas! I was beginning to wonder."

"I am sorry, Godmother," he said, bending down to kiss Mrs. Beauchamp. "Your commission took a little longer than I had foreseen. Good afternoon, Lady Jane."

Jane's body stood without any command from her mind. Her mind was wholly occupied in seeing that Thomas—looking perfectly ordinary and everyday in blue coat and tidy cravat—had come into the room.

"Good afternoon, Sir Thomas." Jane curtsied. Thomas bowed, but as she tried to catch his gaze, it slipped away. A splinter fell from Jane's heart.

"Sit down, sit down." Mrs. Beauchamp fluttered her hands at him. "We've had supper, but were just about to take some tea. You'll join us, of course."

"Thank you," Thomas said gravely. "I will." He settled himself into one of the deep wing-backed chairs and stretched his long legs out. But there was nothing relaxed in his manner. Jane could feel the tension vibrating from his frame. He kept his eyes on the table, on Mrs. Beauchamp, on the broad bay window at her back. Anywhere but at her.

*Look at me. Please look at me.*

And he did, but his eyes were flat and shuttered. No mischief, light or longing showed through. Jane might have been looking at a stranger for all the self she could discern in Thomas's gaze. Again, she sensed the tension in him, as if it were a current of air against her skin. Thomas was holding himself under absolute and rigid control. He was so closed not because of lack of feeling, but from the need to not to betray any of that feeling.

"And what do you think, Jane?" inquired Mrs. Beauchamp.

Jane started, her cup rattling in its saucer. God have mercy, she hadn't even realized she held a full tea cup. "I'm so sorry. I have been most shamefully woolgathering. What was the question?"

Mrs. Beauchamp began to answer, but the door opened and her man Robbins entered with a letter on a silver tray. He hesitated, but Mrs. Beauchamp beckoned him over.

"Excuse me just a moment, won't you?" she said, picking up the letter and breaking the seal. As she read the contents, her brow furrowed and she muttered something through her teeth.

"I'm so sorry, Jane, I must go deal with this at once." She creased the letter firmly closed and climbed to her feet. "Thomas, you'll keep Jane company, won't you?"

Thomas rose as his godmother hobbled out and closed the door.

Silence enveloped them. Thomas sank back into his seat. Jane set her cup down. She picked it up. She looked at the tea and her stomach turned over. She put it down again.

"Jane."

Thomas spoke her name softly, yet not so softly that she could fail to hear the tender echoes in it. At the same time he did not move an inch toward her.

Jane could bear it no longer. "Something has changed, hasn't it? What has happened?"

He ran his hand through his hair. A lock fell out of the queue to brush against his shoulder. "Jane, we cannot speak of it here."

"No." Jane glanced toward the door. Her fingers knotted tight together. She almost picked up her cup again, just to have something to hold. "I suppose not."

"I'm sorry."

She shook her head. She must lift herself above this. She could not falter now, or ever again. "You owe me nothing."

"That's not true. But . . . I am not entirely a free man, Jane."

The remains of Jane's heart crumbled. All this magic, all this mystery, and now this revelation. "You're married."

"No, oh, no, Jane." Thomas hand moved toward her, but he stopped himself short, curling his fingers tightly inward. "But I am an ass. I spoke badly. Forgive me."

A wisp of a smile formed on her lips. "I should have known such an ordinary problem would be too much to ask for."

"Yes, you should have."

"If not marriage, what is it?"

"I want to tell you, but I gave my word to hold what I know in confidence."

"I see." He was lying. Did he think after all they had shown each other that she would not be able to recognize a lie? Anger spiked through the pain, but she didn't know what to do with it. She had no training in how to be angry. She'd only been taught resignation.

Sitting still was impossible. Jane stood and crossed to the arched window that overlooked the back garden. The rain had beaten down burgeoning blossoms and the cold wind blew their sorrowful heads low over the silvered grass.

"Jane . . ."

"No. No." She waved him away without turning to look. He was on his feet too. He might even be coming toward her. "I'm just tired. The duchess has not been well, and she has been sending for me constantly and I could do nothing right today." She tried to muster a smile. "I think she does not dare berate Frau Seibold, so I am the whipping boy. It is so near her time, her attendants are concerned, and we must keep close watch. So you see . . ." At last she showed him a smile as false and meaningless as any she ever mustered for a tedious dinner guest. "I am not entirely free either."

They were silent for another long moment. Jane had never dreamt being so close to a man would also mean being so close to tears.

"I wish I could hold you," Thomas whispered. "I wish I could wrap my arms around you now and bring you close to my heart."

"I thought we could not speak of such things here."

"Of course. I said as much, didn't I?"

"You did. Your memory is most shockingly bad, Sir Thomas."

"Perhaps I grow old."

That small remark turned her around. Jane studied the lines and planes of Thomas's face; the shape of his cheek and jaw, the small space of his neck visible above his simple cravat and collar. All glimpses of the body she had kissed and caressed and loved. That was all she had now of his body, and of his self.

"What is it?" Thomas asked.

"You have never told me how old you are."

He tried to smile. "My grandmother would say I'm as old as my tongue and a little older than my teeth."

"I see a sense of humor runs in your family."

"Is it important?"

"No, at least . . . no, of course not." It was, in fact, nothing short of trivial, but it was nagging at her, like an itch between her shoulder blades. Part of her was certain it meant nothing, but another part was sure it was important somehow. It felt as if this single triviality could lead to the heart of the mystery that was Thomas. "It's just that . . . sometimes you seem very old. It reminds me of the men I've met who survived the wars. Some of them were even younger than I, but all of them seemed far, far older. Did you fight?"

"I served," he said simply. "And I still do."

"I see." But she saw nothing, because she could no longer bear to look. She could demand answers. Her anger pounded at her heart, insisting that she give way, that she cry and make a scene. Maybe then he would notice her pain. Maybe then he would finally tell her what was really happening.

But Mrs. Beauchamp might return at any moment, or one of the servants might walk in. She was still on display, and no matter what her anger urged, she could not forget that.

"Forgive me, Thomas," Jane murmured. "It's only that I . . . I'm afraid of you leaving me."

"There is nothing to forgive. I understand." He was making his voice light, but that lightness was brittle, like ice on a winter brook. The least pressure would break it and reveal the swirling waters below. "Pleasure is hard to forsake."

He did not say he was staying. He did not declare he would

never leave her. Was there anything left inside of her that had not turned to ash? "It's not the pleasure. Maybe it was at first, but it has gone far beyond that. It's you." She lifted her eyes. This might be the last time she stood with him, and the last true words she spoke to him. She would look him in the eyes.

Those eyes were bright with an unfamiliar sheen. Could he possibly be close to tears? "Jane . . ."

"I know it's foolish. We've known each other such a short time, but it is true. And you know what I mean to do about it. I've already told Conroy I'm leaving. There's no going back for me." Her heart beat frantically. Her head felt light. There was no going back from what she said next either. "I wanted you to know that so you could decide what you wanted to do."

Thomas's jaw tightened and his posture stiffened as anger pulled hard at him. "You mean so I could decide to slink away from your declaration of feeling?" he whispered harshly. "Have I given you reason to think me a coward?"

"No. But neither do I think you can pay me attentions in the usual way of a gentleman."

"Is that what you want?"

"I have no right to expect so much."

"I did not ask what you expect," he snapped. "I asked what you wanted."

Jane bit her lip. She could lie. She should lie. But this might be the end. If she had to walk away from him now, or if she had to watch him walk away from her, it would not be because of a lie. That was one burden she refused to carry.

"I love you, and I want to be free to love you," Jane whispered. "And I want you to be free to love me, if you believe you could."

Jane had never seen a man go so utterly still. Only his chest moved. It rose and fell with his rapid, shallow breath.

"Jane," Thomas croaked. "You don't know what you're asking."

"No. Clearly. Forgive me. I can't seem to stop saying that, can I?" She was babbling. Her head spun. This was hysteria, part of her mind told her calmly. But that calm was far away from the rest of her. "It's only that I'm so tired. Shall we forget this? We'll smile and shake hands and say no more about it," she added brightly, as if she were covering up a misstep on the dance floor. Jane turned swiftly to the window. She clamped her mouth shut. Tears stung her eyes and threatened to spill over. She could not let him see her face until she had herself under control again.

Jane only heard the faintest whisper of cloth as he moved closer to her. She could breathe in his scent as he laid one hand on her shoulder. Jane closed her eyes, focusing solely on that place where his palm rested. Warmth trickled slowly through the cloth that separated them and spread down her skin, raising an ache in her breasts that was equal mixture need and sorrow.

*I do love you, Jane. No matter what happens, I will always love you.*

She did not turn around. She did not permit herself to stir. She did not know if she had truly heard those words in her mind, or if she had only imagined them. She did not want to know. The pain was bad enough as it was.

Neither of them turned to see Mrs. Beauchamp's watery blue eyes gleam as she peered through the parlor door at their backs.

## Twenty-four

As soon as Jane left the house, Thomas collected his hat and cane and hurried into the cold and rain-drenched street. He could not give Fiora the opportunity to question him. She had watched them both from narrowed eyes during the remainder of Jane's strained, awkward visit. Jane herself had pleaded fatigue and left as soon as politeness allowed. But Fiora would have to be blind not to see the unshed tears glistening in her eyes, and Fiora was anything but blind.

She suspected him. He was certain of it. She suspected he had committed her treason. That he, Sir Thomas, Captain of the Seelie Court, had fallen in love.

He could no longer deny the truth. He loved Jane DeWitte. It reverberated through his heart and soul. Jane certainly knew the truth now, for she had felt it through the bond of desire he himself had forged between them as a tool of seduction. He loved her with all the strengths and weaknesses of a mortal man, and she loved him in return.

In that moment, when they stood together, the current of emotion running so high between them, Thomas had felt something snap within him, as sharp as the breakup of the ice in spring. The Fae knight shattered and the man—weak and shaken—emerged. Oh, he still had the gifts of glamour and perception the queen had bestowed on him, but the loyalty, that was gone. Because he could not love Jane and maintain that loyalty. His heart had made the choice as he stood with her. If he was honest, that choosing had begun soon after he'd met her; he had simply struggled against it. But when Jane turned away from him with tears brimming in her eyes at the thought of his leaving, all struggle had ceased.

Sir Thomas was forever gone. He was only Thomas Lynne, because it was only Thomas Lynne who could fight for Jane. But Thomas Lynne was also ten times a cursed, careless fool. He should have warned Jane from the house as soon as he suspected his heart. Failing that, he should have never permitted himself to be in the same room with her. All he'd needed to do was stay away from her for a few hours this evening. But he'd been too weak. He'd given in to his desire to see her, and to assure himself that she was all right. And she hadn't been all right. Her heart was breaking, and he had reached out in a way no one, not even the disgraced and exiled Fiora, could miss.

Fiora said she was nothing but an old woman, but old women had eyes, and Thomas had known the single wish of Fiora's existence was to restore herself to the queen's favor. He thought back to something Jane had said while they walked together in Kensington House gardens. She said the only kind of persons in a court were those who were trapped or those who wanted something.

But she'd missed one kind. Those who were useful. Once you knew the way to Faery, you never forgot it. Fiora would be able to make her way back to those guarded gates, and the queen might very well let her back in because Fiora had suddenly become useful.

Thomas shoved his cursing aside. The damage was already done. If he was not the queen's enemy now, he would be soon, and he needed a battle plan. He had to find a way to save Jane. He could no longer trust Kensington House to hold her.

When Thomas had sailed with his father, he'd met the dark and fierce men of the Barbary coast. These men laughed at any danger, and were true as steel once they'd given their word, especially in battle. They had a saying, those Barbary pirates; the enemy of my enemy is my friend. Thomas had never thought to test that saying, but now he prayed they'd been right.

He lifted his head and surveyed the streets about him. The rain had halted, but the lowering wind sent the heavy clouds scudding hard against the sky. The first thing he had to do was get down to the riverbank. The proximity of flowing water was detrimental to magic. It would be safer to think and to plan there. Maybe he could still make use of the queen's gifts before they were snatched from him. Whatever he did, he had to be cautious. This new, sprawling, bustling London was still a foreign land, and Fiora might already be having him watched. All the more reason to get down to the docks. There, the crowds surely still jostled shoulder-to-shoulder among the cargoes and casks. His fine clothing might show him up among the sailors, but there would be plenty of places to hide from any man of Fiora's.

As long as they were still ordinary men. As long as she hadn't been granted magical servants yet. Thomas lengthened his stride.

Thomas spotted his first shadow just as he reached the carriage house. A skinny, roughly dressed youth peered at him from under a shovel hat. A stable boy perhaps, or a bootblack. He ducked quickly behind a stack of barrels, denying Thomas a good look, but that quick motion gave him away.

Thomas stepped into the house and found the proprietor. A few words and a few coins later, and he had hired a spotted gelding of low parentage and suspicious temperament. While he waited for the man to saddle the ungainly animal, Thomas quietly helped himself to some horseshoe nails from the open barrel in the corner. Cold iron was the first and last enemy of magic. These little nails would do nothing if he came before the queen, and in the Fae realms they'd be a minor annoyance, but here in the mortal world, they could weaken or even break any lesser spells he might encounter. He slipped some into his pockets, and after a heartbeat's thought, tucked one in his cheek like a bit of tobacco.

The spotted gelding was a wary creature, as streetwise as any pickpocket in the London stews. It took the horse a few blocks to realize Thomas wasn't going to fall for his well-honed tricks, like suddenly changing gait, or deliberately stumbling over the slippery cats-head cobbles, or tossing his head to slip the bit. After several blocks of this, the horse grudgingly agreed to be ridden into the traffic. They dodged between the vans and drays, rocking cabs and pleasure carriages. This, the horse decided, was a grand game and he stretched his neck forward, eager as a blooded animal for a race. Thomas took a risk and gave the creature his head. The horse snorted, as if to warn him to hold on tight, and surged forward.

The horse broke into a canter, sliding like an eel through the jostling traffic, recklessly threading the thinnest gaps. All around him men cursed and women gasped, but Thomas just bent low over his horse's neck and bared his teeth in a fierce grin. He kept a slack rein and hung on tight with his knees, letting the animal take them where it would. The streets narrowed, the buildings changed from grand stone edifices and tidy parks to slouching houses of timber and brick, some of which he swore he recognized from when he was a boy. The horse's ribs began to heave and Thomas could hear him blowing even over the street noises echoing off the close houses. He sat back and the horse slowed to an easy trot, tired and satisfied enough to follow the direction of the reins. Thomas's sense of direction remained good and he followed the winding passages east, down into the oldest, darkest parts of the city. Warehouses loomed between the taverns and grimy shops. He felt his shoulders relax. Finally, here was a place he recognized the feel of.

He spied a group of barefoot boys gathered to taking turns pitching stones at a battered box. But their game didn't stop them from eyeing the swell on the hired horse who drew rein beside them.

"Who wants to earn a half-crown?" Thomas asked as he swung himself from the saddle.

Instantly, he was the center of a surging crowd of urchins.

"Me!"

"I do!"

"Right 'ere, y'r lordship!"

Thomas picked the biggest lad, who also had the most intelligent face, and gave him the address of the carriage house. He scribbled a note on a leaf from the book in his pocket and handed it to the boy. "Give this to the proprietor when you get there and you'll get another shilling." Then, he laid his hand on the horse's neck and spoke softly in his ear. "I swear, should I live and ever become a free man, I'll find you again. We're well suited you and I." The horse whickered and rolled one keen eye toward him. Thomas patted the gelding's neck and let him go.

Of course now he had a flock of street sparrows swarming around him, all offering to be guides or errand runners, or anything else he needed. Thomas cleared them away by the time-honored method of tossing a handful of coppers into the dirt, and took himself around the first corner, and another. Then he ducked down a flight of dirty, treacherous stairs under a dark stone arch and came out at the riverside.

Thomas stopped and stared.

God's teeth it had been a long time. The Thames was thick with tall ships: schooners, clippers, brigs and sloops. The air filled with the smells of tar and mud, water and fish. Rough shouts tumbled over each other from every direction. He could have traveled back in time on those voices, all the way to when he was running on these banks on bare feet, ready to swing aboard the *Free Hand* and make his salute to his father, who'd clout him on the shoulder and order him into the rigging. His ears filled with the sound of cannon and the fear and rush of battle as a pig of a Spanish galleon tried its best to waddle away from their sleek greyhound ship. He remembered the wicked mischief of rowing to shore with a dark lantern and a laden boat, to pass off some of the richest plunder to trusted friends all muffled in black, before taking the rest back for good Queen Bess's coffers.

Had his brothers thought him drowned when he didn't come back? Had his mother taken some of that money she saved and put up a headstone for him in the churchyard? God's teeth! Thomas clenched his jaw. He'd had over two hundred years of life granted him, and he'd never once wondered about those he'd left behind. Two hundred years, and he hadn't thought where his parents, his brothers and his sisters might lie now.

He'd had family once. He'd had place and purpose. And in one instant of fear and love, he'd thrown it to the winds.

He felt the last of that glamour slide away, shedding off his body and mind like water from a drowning man who had finally broken the surface. His heart swelled and constricted beneath the tide of the emotions that filled him. Love and sorrow, anger and regret; his heart gulped them all down, dizzy with the awareness that he was truly alive again, and that whatever happened next, for this one moment he was free.

*I'm free, Jane.* Thomas turned to the sinking red sun and threw his arms wide. *Free! Do you hear? And I love you! I love you and I don't care who knows!*

"You might want to keep it down, regardless."

Thomas heard the words a moment before he felt the prickle of magic against the back of his neck. He spun around, dropping reflexively into a low crouch, fists ready. The dark-haired man he'd knocked down outside Kensington House emerged from the mouth of a filthy alley beside the warehouse.

Corwin Rathe approached slowly, giving Thomas plenty of time to get the man's measure. He had maybe six inches and two stone on Thomas, and his cold and wary face said he remembered each blow they'd exchanged. He still wore his workman's corduroys and shirt, which gave him freedom of movement as well as a passable disguise.

Thomas faced the enemy of the Fae queen with empty hands and only the wisdom of men long dead to give him any hope. Slowly, allowing Rathe to see each move, he straightened up. He opened his hands to show them empty and spread them out from his sides.

"I ask parley," he said.

The corner of Rathe's mouth twitched into a humorless smile. "Since when does Her Glorious Majesty parley with mortal Sorcerers?"

"I don't ask for the queen, I ask for myself."

This gave Rathe pause, but nothing about his alert stance lessened at all. "I'm expected to believe so much from the captain of her knights?"

"You're well informed."

"It's my business." *My business, not our.* He was giving nothing away, but Thomas was sure Rathe's partner was here somewhere. Maybe the Catalyst too. It was risky bringing a woman down here, but these three were not fools, and they would be ready with magic as well as force.

*I don't have time for this.* Thomas clamped down on his temper and spoke as evenly as he was able. "Listen to me, Sorcerer.

Your country is in danger. An assault is coming. If you'll listen, I will tell all I know."

"And in return?"

"I ask safe passage for a woman out of Kensington House." Jane had friends. Georgie. Surely Georgie could get her away from England if need be.

"That would be Jane DeWitte," said Rathe, and Thomas's guts twisted. Of course they already knew. He might have realized as much before, if he'd been less preoccupied with his useless struggle against his own heart.

"And what would you want for yourself?" Rathe was asking.

"I want safe passage for the woman. Beyond that . . . I don't care." That wasn't true. He cared passionately, for he wanted to be with Jane. He wanted it more than he wanted his next breath. But if his life was the price this man wanted for her freedom and safety, Thomas would strike the bargain and thank him for it.

"I've no authority to promise anything of the kind."

"You'll find you do have it, if you want the information I can give you," Thomas told him. Rathe was playing for time. He might have already summoned his allies and maybe even his superiors. If he was half as smart as he seemed, he'd be trying to hem Thomas in, and Thomas could not let himself be trapped before he had guarantee of Jane's safety.

Rathe tilted his head. Thomas felt the hairs on the back of his neck rise. Rathe was hearing some inner voice, some sympathetic communication. If Thomas opened his perceptions, he might be able to overhear, but Rathe would be able to sense him listening, so he held himself closed.

Rathe straightened. "Very well. No one will pursue Lady

Jane DeWitte, and she will face no punishment for her part in your plan, if in return, you will give to us all you know of the Fae queen and her plans. This I swear by my breath and blood."

"And I agree."

Rathe moved forward, wary as a panther. Thomas let him approach without flinching, keeping his hands spread out and open. Rathe did not stop until he was almost within Thomas's reach; almost but not quite.

"Then prove your agreement. Tell me your name."

Thomas had been ready for this. It was no simple request coming from a Sorcerer. Names gave those who knew them power. A name could be used to summon the owner, and to bind them.

"My name is Thomas Lynne. My father was Mathias Lynne, captain of Her Majesty's privateer *Free Hand*. His father was Reynold Lynne, a common sailor aboard old King Henry's vessel *Dover's Pride*." *There, Rathe. You could call me from the grave with that.*

"Thomas."

For a moment, he thought it was the Sorcerer who spoke, but Rathe whirled around. Hooves and hobnailed boots thudded on the dirt, and a mob poured from the alley.

First, Thomas saw Fiora, looking straighter and stronger than he had seen her since he came to London. She rode sidesaddle on the spotted gelding, its head low and its eyes glazed from the force of the spell that bound it. Around her clustered a gang of squat men with bowed arms and crooked legs. They could pass as any crowd of dockworkers, until you looked in their eyes and saw how they were round and black as crows' eyes.

Goblins.

Rathe shouted and threw up his hands. Magic crackled and rushed into the air, but the goblins charged forward in a body. Around them, men shouted and whistled. The goblins knocked Rathe to the ground and charged past and over him without hesitating. Thomas backpedaled, shoving his hand into his pocket, scrabbling for his pilfered nails, but the goblins barreled straight into him. Thomas fell sprawling on the dirt. The nails flew from his hands, and the monsters piled laughing on top of him. He kicked out with all his strength. He punched and flailed, but they were creatures of wood and stone, and his blows fell like leaves on them. They lifted him onto their crooked shoulders, holding him tight and grinning in triumph. Thomas saw Rathe struggle to his feet. One of his captors lashed out carelessly and knocked him flat again. He thought he felt another wash of magic, thought he saw Rathe's compatriots running up the bank, but then a blow fell against temple and he saw nothing but a painful blaze of stars.

*Come along now, Thomas Lynne,* said Fiora's voice inside his mind as consciousness spiraled away. *Our queen is asking for you.*

# Twenty-five

*J*ane.

    Jane lifted her head from her pillow. She was certain that it was the early hours of the morning. Far past Thomas's usual time for calling to her. Or, at least it had been until the night before.

*Come to me, Jane. Now.*

Jane squeezed her eyes shut, torn by indecision. Since she'd returned from the interminable supper at Mrs. Beauchamp's, she had longed for nothing more than a moment to compose herself. The moment had not come. The duchess wanted to be up and walking, and Frau Seibold was determined she should be perfectly at rest. Jane found herself caught in the middle of the tussle between the two, being ordered to fetch and carry pillows and blankets, bring them here, take them there, fetch the maid for tea, take all this horrid food away, to read this book, no, the letters . . .

When at last the duchess was in her bed, Jane had to sit by

her side reading her German Bible for well over an hour until she at last fell asleep.

"The baby is very close now," said Frau Seibold. "We must be ready at any moment. You will be required to help when the time comes. You are prepared for this?"

"Yes, yes, of course." What other answer was she going to make? She'd crept to her bed, just to try to get a little rest, and had surprised herself by falling deeply asleep.

*Jane.*

And now Thomas called. Their stilted empty conversation in Mrs. Beauchamp's parlor pressed against her, robbing her of breath. She was certain he was about to leave her, and equally certain he had said he loved her. If she went to him now, she might be granted a final chance to make peace with all she had done, as well as with the man who had captured her heart and yet some how set her free doing it.

But if she should be absent when the birth began . . .

*Now, Jane. There is no more time.*

Urgency surged through her. Jane bit her lip and made her decision. She would have to risk it.

She struggled out from under her blankets to claim her robe and slippers. The hallway was empty, dark and ice-cold. Jane made her way down the back stairs and through the maze of the ground floor rooms. As she reached the cupola room, the clock chimed the hour. Four in the morning. This was not right in so many ways. She felt it to her bones. Dawn was too close. The servants would be up and about in less than an hour. She was putting herself in worse danger than ever before. But she had to see Thomas. She had to speak with him. She would have no peace in her mind or heart if she did not. Even if he told her that he was leaving, that whatever he felt for her was not enough to cause him to travel past a brief affair . . . she could accept anything as long as she *knew*. As long as she could see him just once more.

Jane hurried on. Drafts curled around her ankles and shoulders and Jane clutched her robe tightly about her. The lantern guttered and threatened to go out with every hurried step.

There it was, at last, the familiar corridor with its four doors. But something was wrong. She felt it in the way her skin crawled on the back of her neck and the way her hand holding the lamp trembled. It too was drafty, and Jane swore she smelled the rain. There was something else though. It took her a handful of heartbeats, but then Jane realized the welcome was missing. Welcome. Thomas's welcome and the happy anticipation, which she had felt each and every time she had made this journey were entirely absent now.

Jane backed away from the corridor's mouth. She turned to run.

A wind blew hard around her ears, and the walls of Kensington House melted away like a dream.

Jane pressed her fist against her mouth to stifle a scream. Trees loomed high against the sky heavy with clouds. She spun around, searching desperately for some landmark, and behind her saw a straight road and high brick wall topped with iron. It was the outer wall of the Kensington grounds, and it was yards away. Her hems and slippers were sopping wet and stained with grass. Rain tapped on her cap and hissed on the sides of the lantern's glass chimney.

She barely had time to wonder how she had gotten out here or to comprehend that this was some new magic when she was aware of silhouettes shifting under the trees that lined the road in both directions, and the glint of eyes.

"So, this is Jane."

"Sweet Jane."

One by one the owners of the voices emerged from the shadows. They came out from under the trees, and dropped from the branches. They rose straight up from the ground. They wore human shapes, but each one of them moved with the fierce and feral grace of hunting animals. Their hair tumbled free about their shoulders, and their clothing was nothing more than thin tunics and kilts hanging loose about their bodies.

"Pretty Jane."

"Pretty pigeon, Jane."

The words were smooth and cutting as flint. The voices that uttered them had a strange musical sound that Jane couldn't identify as male or female.

"Come here, pretty pigeon."

"Come here now, Jane. Your lover needs you."

The words surrounded her like the creatures did, and seemed to come from every direction at once, as if they were not many, but a single being with a single voice between them.

"Pretty, pretty Lady Jane."

"Pretty pigeon."

"Such a pretty peach. No wonder he sought to nibble your ripe flesh."

Jane turned again, seeking escape, but their ring drew tighter as they stalked forward and left her no place to run. She could see their eyes now, and the slim semblance of humanity about the creatures vanished. They looked at her from beasts' eyes and birds' eyes; from the eyes of cats, the eyes of wolves, and tiny glittering eyes that could have belonged to snakes.

"Who are you?" Jane demanded.

"What?" cried the voice, although no mouth moved. "Didn't he tell you?"

"So careless of him."

Him. There was only one person they could be speaking of. "Where is Thomas?"

"Yes, where is he?"

"Where is Sir Thomas?"

"Where?"

"Where is the pretty Thomas? Pretty Jane wants to know."

"How thoughtless not to keep his tryst."

"Fickle Thomas, cannot choose who he loves the best."

A cold laugh rippled round the ring. Then in front of her the bodies parted, and a woman stepped into their circle.

She was a tiny woman. Her head barely came up to Jane's chin, but in the strange silver light, Jane could see she was beautiful. A wealth of red hair spilled down her shoulders, blowing freely in the night wind. Strong, round limbs and ample curves showed beneath her light tunic. She looked up at Jane and smiled, and Jane saw that her eyes appeared human, but they were far too old and watery for the impish maiden's face that held them.

She knew those eyes.

"God in Heaven," she whispered. "Mrs. Beauchamp."

"Oh, very good, Jane!" cried the little redhead. "But then you always were such a clever girl. And so kind to old ladies." Her smile sharpened, becoming bright and cruel. "Or perhaps it's just their handsome godsons you're kind to."

"What's happening here?" Jane cried. "What do you want?" The world had already turned over, it had already shaken her to the core. But the other creatures had been strange beyond the realm of comprehension. This incredible transformation of someone she had known her entire life pierced her straight through. Jane thought she might be sick, or faint.

"I should have thought it was obvious, Jane." Mrs. Beauchamp cocked her head at Jane in the dreadful parody of the old, friendly woman she had once been. "We want you."

Fear bit down hard. Jane swung the lamp out. Mrs. Beauchamp skipped back, and Jane ran. In her panicked mind, Jane hoped to startle the other . . . creatures with her sudden charge, but they just closed ranks. She hurled the lamp at them, but it was dodged easily, and she ran straight into their arms. They wrapped cold hands around her shoulders, waist and ankles. Jane had never been weak, and she kicked and struggled now, but it was as if she was clasped in iron bands. They bore her to her knees, cruel fingertips digging hard into her flesh, and Jane cried out as she fell to the rain-soaked grass.

"Now, Jane," said Mrs. Beauchamp, or whoever this diminutive redheaded girl in front of her truly was. "Don't make this any worse than it has to be."

She caught Jane's wrist and held it with the same unnatural strength as the others. Someone grabbed her hair at the roots and forced her head up so Jane looked into the other woman's ancient blue eyes.

"Lady Jane Markham DeWitte," intoned the creature who held her wrist. "You will give over to me."

It was as if a vein in her soul had been opened. Strength, breath, vitality all fell away. Jane felt somehow she was fading, becoming a thing of mist and dreams. At the same time, the woman who had been Mrs. Beauchamp changed. She grew taller. Her fiery red hair darkened, her face softened.

And Jane was looking at herself. Only the penetrating, cruel blue eyes remained unchanged. Otherwise, it was as if she looked in a dark mirror to see her own face and figure, and neat night attire.

Jane screamed, weak and hoarse. She couldn't help it. The other Jane, the one with Mrs. Beauchamp's eyes smiled sweetly and reached down to pat her cheek.

"Thank you so much, Jane. Don't worry. I'll not need your visage long, but I promise to take good care of it." She straightened and smoothed the night-robe down.

"Take her to our queen," ordered the Other Jane to the inhuman creatures who held her. "Let her find out what happens to those who try to take what does not belong to them."

Then Other Jane walked through the rusted garden gate Jane had left open in the walls around Kensington House and disappeared in the darkness.

"No!" cried Jane. "No!"

But a cold hand passed in front of her eyes bringing with it a wave of absolute darkness. Jane felt herself sag in her captors' grip and then there was nothing at all.

## Twenty-six

"Jane."

Someone was calling her name. Jane struggled to form an answer, but it was as if a blanket of cobwebs smothered her thoughts.

"Jane."

She was freezing cold and her body ached. For some reason she'd lain down on a sheet of ice. She'd been having a nightmare. Fiora Beauchamp had stolen her face and thrown her to a pack of shadows. She'd screamed and screamed but she couldn't make any sound . . .

"Jane. You must wake up.

It was a man calling her. A man she knew. She wanted to remember who. She needed to remember. Slowly, the cobwebs that enveloped her mind parted, and Jane felt her thoughts flow together and become whole.

"Thomas!" Jane's eyes snapped open.

She lay huddled in one corner of a room made entirely of

white marble. The floor, walls, even the door were smooth and seamless white stone streaked with black. Even the bars covering the slit of a window high above her were polished marble.

The window let in a weak silver light that was just enough to show her Thomas as he edged out of the corner. His clothes were torn, rumpled and mud-spattered, and his golden hair hung loose about his shoulders. A bruise like a smear of ash spread across his temple.

"My God, Thomas!" She lunged for him, but something jerked her arms and ankles back. She cried out and fell to the marble floor. She stared down. She was also chained. Silver manacles held her wrists and ankles. A solid bar ran between the wrist cuffs, keeping them a precise distance apart. A similar bar ran between the cuffs holding her ankles, and from one of those ran a length of chain to a silver bolt in the ice-cold floor.

"Easy, Jane. Easy." Thomas's breath puffed out in silver clouds as he spoke. He lifted his hands, reaching for her, but now she could see he was chained as he was. "Have they hurt you?"

Jane made herself breathe evenly. None of this was possible, but then, neither was anything else she'd seen since she left her room. It would do her no good to protest it. She must understand it.

Jane took an inventory of her body. Her head ached, and her wrists and ankles were sore where she had just strained them against her bonds, but otherwise her limbs seemed sound.

"I think I'm all right," she told him. "I'm weak but . . . Thomas, what are they? What's happening?"

"Oh, Jane." Thomas reached out as far as the chain permitted. Jane inched herself forward, stretching her arms to their limit, and found she could just graze his fingertips. His hands were cold, but they were steady.

"I'm sorry," Thomas whispered. "I'm so sorry. This is my fault." His head lolled forward and she saw the bruise again.

"Thomas!" she cried. He'd taken a heavy blow. Her heart twisted as she imagined the pain, and twisted again because she could do nothing to help him. She also knew if he fell asleep now, it might be hours before he woke. "Tell me what's happening!"

Thomas shook himself and his face creased with pain. Jane pressed her fingers against his. She stretched until her joints creaked and pain lanced up her shoulders, but she could get no closer.

"We've been taken by soldiers of the Fae court," Thomas said slowly. Bitter recrimination filled his voice. He bowed his head so she could not see his eyes. "We are being held to await the judgment of Queen Tatiana."

"You can't mean this." She saw the impossible marble room around them. The air smelled of frost and winter. She felt the cold of it, saw the fog of her breath as she panted against the bite of the silver chains around her wrists so she could remain even this close to him. All these things were real. But what Thomas was saying . . . her mind shied away from hearing it. "You're telling me we've been kidnapped by the fairies!"

"The Fae, Jane. I came to you as a servant for the Queen of the Fae." He spoke the words in deadly earnest. Now he lifted his head so she could see his eyes. The desperate doubt that had sheltered her melted away under the pain and earnestness of his gaze. "They are as real as the old stories, and as powerful and as terrible. I served their queen for two centuries. It was she who granted me the magic to reach into your dreams and seduce you."

"But why?"

"The baby, Jane," Thomas said softly. "The duke's child. It has been prophesied that a great queen of England will defeat the Fae and drive them from the island for all time. But if she can be kept from the throne, the Fae Queen will be able to return to the rule she enjoyed in ancient days. So one of us had to get past the magics and iron guarding Kensington House."

It was too much. Even after all Jane had seen and all she already knew, this was too much. She tried in her mind to turn and flee, but there was nowhere left to go. The truth was all around her, ice-cold and stone solid. It was in the chains that held her, in Thomas's anguished eyes and the flat finality of his voice.

She jerked her hand away from his so fast he flinched. "You were *helping* these . . . the Fae?"

"Yes."

"You used me?"

"Yes. At first."

"My God." Jane scrambled backward until her back pressed against the flat stone wall. "My God. What a fool I've been!"

"No, Jane, no!" Thomas cried. "Please, listen to me." Heartbreak cracked his voice and glittered in the tears that hung suspended in his beautiful eyes. This man was still the Thomas she loved, and she loved a monster.

"It was only at first." She could feel him desperately willing her to hear his words. "I was sent as Her Glorious Majesty's trusted captain. I'd never once failed her, not in the two hundred years I'd been at her court." Jane huddled in her corner. She wanted to crawl inside the marble walls and clap her hands over her ears. Maybe then she wouldn't have to hear him. "But once I met you, once we spoke and walked and loved . . . Jane, you touched me like no other. You reminded me that I was a mortal man, with all the passion of a mortal heart. I fell in love with you, Jane."

No. No. It could not be true he loved her. He was a monster, a creature out of legend and nightmare.

"Because of you, I wanted to come back to the sunlit world," said Thomas. "I wanted to live and grow old and die, as weak and changeable as only man can be, as long as I could live and die beside you. I tried to turn away from the queen, but I was too slow, and they captured me. And now they've captured you."

"I will not listen to you." She couldn't even cover her ears. The bar between her manacles prevented her from moving them closer together. Jane squeezed her eyes tight, as if she were a child and believed that what she couldn't see must somehow vanish.

"You must listen, Jane. Hate me if you will." Thomas's voice faltered. "I deserve your hatred. But you must listen. We have to get you away from here. You must find the Sorcerer Corwin Rathe."

"Rathe?" Jane opened her eyes. Memory stirred, as if woken from years in the past instead of a single day. A dark-haired woman with a false, vapid smile stood in front of her. "I met a Mrs. Rathe at the drawing room."

Thomas let his head fall back and winced as it thudded

against the stone. "I should have realized. They knew your name. I don't suppose they did anything so convenient as give you an address."

"How did you know?"

To Jane's surprise, Thomas began to laugh. The pained noise bounced off the marble walls, and the harsh echoes rang through Jane's aching head.

"Oh, they are admirably direct, these servants of the mortal crown. They knew you were tied to me, and so they made sure to put themselves in your way." He shook his head. "Then, either you would come to them for help, or I would to spy, and either way they'd stand a good chance of unearthing the whole of the plan. Listen, Jane, I've held parley with Rathe. They have promised to protect you. You must get to them and tell them what's happened."

Jane stared at her manacled hands lying limp in the lap of her filthy night-robe and clenched her jaw. She must not give way to her riot of feeling. She must be as cold and hard as the stone around her. "How can I believe you?"

"Because you know me, Jane. No other has known me as you do. Look at me now. Please."

Jane lifted her head, and she looked directly into Thomas's wide, green eyes. She remembered how she had looked into the counterfeit of her own face and had seen Mrs. Beauchamp's ancient eyes there. She remembered the beast's eyes in the faces of the creatures . . .the Fae who surrounded her outside Kensington House. Whatever magics these beings possessed, they could not disguise their eyes. Whatever else might be illusion, Thomas's eyes were real. His eyes pleaded with her, holding all the strength and desperation that came from a final hope, the hope that she who had trusted him with her body and her heart would now trust him with her life. But beyond that, Jane saw the same joy and pain she felt in her own heart as she looked at him now.

"Thomas." Fear and anger dissolved into a terrible ache, for she knew that this was love, and it came in the midst of a horror beyond description.

"My sweet Jane," he whispered. He felt it. He knew she loved him, and she felt the pain and the wonder in him. "I promise, it will fade," he spoke the words as if they would choke him. "Very soon, in fact, and you will be able to feel what you should for me."

"I do feel what I should." Was it possible to experience elation, here and now, when all the world had overturned and magic and fairies were real. Yes. Yes it was. Because her heart remained free, and it was not broken after all. "I love you, Thomas."

"No," his voice cracked on the single word. "What you feel now is the sympathetic bond between us. It's a spell, a form of glamour. It will break when . . ." He stopped. "It doesn't matter, Jane. We must get you out of here."

"I won't leave you." It was a moot point anyway. She was as tightly chained as he was.

"You have to, Jane. Once we're taken before the queen, there will be no chance of escape. Now, stretch out your hand, as far as you can."

"Thomas . . ."

But his face was hard, and she saw again the dangerous man she had glimpsed so briefly in the park. "Jane, the queen means to conquer and to rule. If you do not get a warning to the ones who can defend England, she will take the whole of this island."

Jane had a million questions, but she clamped her mind shut against them. She stretched out her hand to the limit of the shining chain. Thomas's chains clanked as he shuffled closer, cursing in a thick, strange voice she barely understood. He stretched out his neck to her palm, and he spat. Something wet, hard and warm dropped into her palm.

It was a nail.

"Touch it to the bonds."

Jane flipped the nail around, grasping it in her two fingers. She bent over, bringing up her ankles until she touched the nail's tip to the bar between her ankles. With a jolt, the bar vanished.

"Iron. Salt. Moving water," Thomas said as she moved to touch the nail to the cuffs around her ankles. Both fell open and clanked against the stone. "These are their weaknesses. You can use them all."

Jane listened and tried to accept without thinking. If she thought about what she was doing, she would curl into a ball and be unable to move. She had to free her hands now. That would be trickier, but Jane risked dropping the nail into her skirt where she could lay the bar between her wrist manacles against it. As soon as the bar vanished, she was able to deal with the cuffs easily.

"Now you." Jane climbed painfully to her feet, but Thomas jerked back.

"No, Jane. I have to stay here."

"What? Why?"

"Jane, what you are doing now is breaking the spells that bind us, and what I am doing is hiding your actions." She knelt again beside him. Now, she could see the sweat on his brow gleaming in the weak silver light. The strain in his voice came not just fear, but from some unseen effort.

"There are guards outside," Thomas nodded toward the marble door. "I'm using a glamour against them, but it will only fool them for so long, and the second I leave this room, it will be gone and they will be after us both."

"How can I leave you here?" she whispered. She touched his brow. His skin was so cold and the sweat made it clammy. He was beginning to shiver. With a blow to his head, it could be a fever coming on. He could die here in the midst of all this magic from a cracked skull and chilled body.

He didn't bother to answer her. "Touch the nail on the window bars, Jane," he said firmly. "It'll work as well as it did on the chains. Once you're outside, you must go straight to Rathe and his friends."

Jane stared at the pathetic little nail in her hand, and then up at the marble bars that covered the slit of a window. "I don't even know where we are."

Thomas chuckled hollowly. "We're in Fiora Beauchamp's cellar. You'll see when you get out."

"What? How . . ."

"The Fae have folded their magics about it, as I folded a piece of glamour around the grove outside the walls of Kensington House to make the chamber for our tryst." His voice faltered. "Hurry, Jane," he croaked. "They'll be coming soon."

"Thomas . . ." A hundred mad plans ran through her head.

She could scream, make a scene, bring the guards in, find a way to incapacitate them. That was what a heroine in a novel would have done. But she had nothing but bare hands and one pathetic horseshoe nail. She didn't know how many were out there, or what powers they had.

"Don't say anything, Jane," whispered Thomas. "Just let me see you get away. I can do anything if I know you are safe."

Jane bent swiftly and put her mouth to his, pouring the flood of feeling that filled her heart into the kiss. His mouth was so cold. She pressed hard against him, willing her warmth into him. She felt him yield to it, drinking in the love and desperation, returning it tenfold.

*I will come back*, she swore in that kiss. Could he hear her? She didn't know, but she made the promise anyway. *I will bring help.*

*I love you, Jane.*

When they separated, she did not look at him. If she did, her nerve would fail.

The tiny window was high up in the wall, almost right against the ceiling. Jane stretched onto her toes, with the nail pinched between her fingers. The tip of her fingers touched the marble bars.

But they were not stone. They were not even bars. Nor was the window as high as she'd thought it was. Jane saw an ordinary cellar window set incongruously in the solid marble wall. Its catch had been broken at some point and mended with a bit of knotted wire.

"Hurry, Jane," breathed Thomas.

It was no easy feat undoing the wire with her numb fingers.

The grimy window let in a bare trickle of uncertain gray light. It must be near dawn. Or perhaps it was dusk. Her sense of time had vanished. The rusty wire cut her fingers and she clamped her teeth shut around a hiss of pain. But, at last, the final twist came loose and she was able to push the window open. She braced her hands against the frame and heaved and struggled, kicked and pushed and, finally, she was outside.

Jane stood in a mews. A quite ordinary lane behind a quite ordinary house with dawn's ordinary chill soaking into her frozen, sweating body.

Dawn. That was dawn that showed between the sleeping Mayfair houses. The world would soon be awake, and she had no way to explain her appearance, or her presence here. She had no money, nothing. Just herself and her knowledge of an impossible invasion that threatened England.

And Thomas was counting on her.

Jane gathered up the hems of her night-robe and began to run.

## Twenty-seven

Red Fiora tripped lightly through the servant's entrance to Kensington House. What a pleasant frame Lady Jane had. It was a treat to wear, like a well-made dress.

It was early. Servants with sleepy eyes moved about their morning chores. Before she crossed the tattered remains of the Kensington wards, she'd thought to clothe her borrowed form in the seeming of one of Jane's modest morning dresses, so not one of them looked twice at her as she entered the kitchens. The cooks nodded their good mornings and made room for her as she helped herself to a cup from the cabinet and hot water from the kettle on the stove. None of them questioned her. None of them cared. They had their own work to do, getting the breakfast ready, and they kept their eyes on their chopping, mixing and frying.

Not one of them saw her take the little golden vial from her pocket. The sharp, mineral scent was lost under the smells of frying meats and baking bread. Fiora tipped a good amount of liquid from the vial into the cup. The water turned a pale, shimmering green. She picked up the cup and carried it away, and no one looked at her. No one at all.

Fiora headed for the servant's stairs. How easy it had been to plunder the map of the place from Jane's pathetically open mind. She'd thought Jane stronger than that, but she'd put up no fight at all.

"So, now Lady Jane."

On the landing above her stood a man. Tall and dark, dressed only in his shirt, breeches and boots, a candle held high. Ah. This was the famed Captain Conroy. He was a figure of contempt in Jane's mind, and, Fiora had to admit, there were good reasons for her feelings. This man was a greedy fool, but as Her Glorious Majesty had said, he might yet prove a useful fool as well.

"And what are you doing abroad at this hour?" She could feel the plans swirling inside him. Conroy looked at Jane and thought he might be able to use what he saw. No, more. He thought he could hurt her, make her pay for her theft of his private papers.

Fiora smiled Jane's warm and open smile. "And wouldn't you like to know, Captain Conroy."

"I would," Conroy replied blandly. "That's why I asked." His mind buzzed and spun like a top, propelled by all his shifting plans.

Fiora slipped up the stairs, until she stood right below him, and composed her face to Jane's more serious expression.

"I am sorry, Captain." She laced Jane's fingers around the warm china cup. "I've had some thinking to do. I believe I have something of yours. You'll have it back before the day is done."

That stilled his racing mind. Fiora had to admire his control. She might have made a remark about the weather for all the surprise that showed on his face.

"And may I ask what brought on this sudden change of heart?" Conroy inquired.

"Sober reflection. I was wrong to make an enemy of you. I'd like to make it up, if I could." She climbed one more step. Now she stood beside him on the landing. She straightened her back and sucked in her stomach so that Jane's ample bosom strained against her dress, even while she dropped her dark eyes in a show of modesty. "I would be most grateful, Captain."

She felt his gaze lingering on Jane's breasts, so she held her breath, which swelled them further yet, and ensured her cheeks were nicely rosy by the time Conroy's slow gaze reached them again.

"Well." He didn't trust her, but he trusted his own intelligence more. He thought this woman, the poor daughter of a foolish man, could be no real danger to him. She was plainly weak and changeable as all women were. "You should be in bed, Madame. But be sure we will be continuing this conversation later today."

"Of course, Captain." Fiora let her breath out in a long sigh she made certain he could hear. "Whenever you decide."

Conroy stood aside and let her slide past. She felt his eyes on Jane's round ass until she closed the door.

*Stupid, greedy man. You will do admirably as a bridge for our queen's conquest.*

The corridor to the duchess's room stretched out before her, broad and empty. Fiora moved more carefully now, more like

Jane would. She had seen her enough over the years, she could match her ladylike carriage easily. Even as she assumed Jane's proper manner, Fiora felt deeply humbled at her new understanding of her queen's wisdom. She had not ever truly been exiled. She had been most carefully placed, so she would be ready against this moment when she could again serve.

*I will never doubt Her Glorious Majesty again. Never.*

A door opened, and for a moment, Fiora froze. Then she remembered she was snug within Lady Jane's visage. Lady Jane had every right to be here, and Jane knew Fraulein Lehzen, this stern woman in her neat gray dress who stepped into the corridor.

"Lady Jane," said the woman, her voice tickling all Jane's memories. Lady Jane did not like her much, and trusted her less. "You are abroad early."

"Good morning, Fraulein Lehzen," Fiora smiled and nodded once. "The duchess woke and she was thirsty. Frau Seibold asked me to fetch her a tisane." She held up the steaming cup she carried.

"So? Well, you had best take it to her then." As Fiora moved forward, Lehzen moved aside, but her elbow joggled the cup, and the liquid inside splashed across the carpet and their skirts.

"You clumsy cow!" cried Fiora.

"Oh, I am so sorry!" Lehzen clapped a hand to her cheek. "I will go fetch another. You will tell Frau Seibold it is entirely my fault and I will be there in but a moment." Rage rendered Fiora speechless. She would blast this foolish woman to cinders! But before Fiora could find her voice again, Lehzen had already disappeared down the stairs.

Fiora groped in her pocket for the vial and shook it. There were still a few drops. Would it be enough? It would have to be. She could not fail. She must not fail. She hurried down the corridor. If that idiotic creature hadn't woken the whole palace with her shouting . . .

Fiora slipped into Jane's chamber, and pressed her ear to the door connecting it with the duchess's room. She heard nothing but breathing, and some very rude snoring. Fiora backed away. She must be very careful now.

Slowly, she breathed out, and summoned her magics.

She was nothing. A shadow, a breath of wind. Nothing to touch the mind of the lightest sleeper. It was difficult. This was more than a simple glamour; this was transformation. It was always easier to be something than nothing, and her heart hammered with the effort of becoming as close to nothing as she could without wholly dissolving herself.

When she was little more than a wisp of being, Fiora opened the door and slowly drifted into the room. Frau Seibold snorted and turned on her couch. The duchess lay beneath her pile of coverlets, her breeding stomach a great sloping hill in a quilted landscape. A glass and some drops of what Jane knew to be one of Frau Seibold's strengthening tonics waited at the bedside table. Fiora directed herself that way. The vial in her pocket weighed her down like lead. She focused her will and lifted it out. Her faded fingertips could not grasp the stopper on the tonic bottle, and she nearly panicked then. The duchess stirred and murmured in German. Hearing her charge, Frau Seibold rolled over again. Fiora froze.

Gradually, the duchess settled back, and Frau Seibold murmured something that ended in another prodigious snore. Fiora summoned all her force of will and gently, gently, lifted the stopper on the tonic bottle. Slowly, drop by drop, she poured in the contents of the vial in her pocket.

The duchess turned again and sighed, and laid her hand on her belly. Frau Seibold snorted and coughed.

Fiora smiled, and faded away into Jane DeWitte's room.

# Twenty-eight

Voices cut through the darkness that enveloped Lady Jane.

"Who on earth . . . ?"

"I don't know, Madame. That's why I thought it best to wake you."

"Good Heavens! Bring her inside, Jacobs. Carefully now. Into the red room."

She was being lifted and turned. She was a mass of pain. Her feet, her throat, her fists, they all hurt. Memory came back in lightning flashes that hurt almost as much as the physical pain. She'd almost been run down by a coal wagon as she dodged across the street. The horse's hooves had brushed her hair back from her forehead as it reared.

"Miranda . . . what . . . ?"

"It's Jane DeWitte."

A pair of bravos had tried to pull her into an alleyway, and would have managed it if she hadn't gotten hold of a building timber and brained the pair of them.

"Look at her feet. My God."

She'd lost her slippers somewhere and the cobbles cut and tripped her. She should tell them that. It might be important. But things seemed to be happening in discreet packets with long stretches of dark in-between.

"We must get word to Smith. Someone needs to get out to Kensington House at once."

Still she should make an effort. She had the feeling it was important. She should open her eyes.

"Help," said someone thickly.

Her. That muffled, sloppy voice was hers like the pain was hers, and the nightmare dash through the early morning streets had been hers. The dash to warn, to save . . .

Memory dropped down like a stone and Jane gasped in shock. She struggled to sit, but a woman's arms wrapped around her shoulders.

"Gently, gently, Lady Jane," the woman said. "Where's that brandy? Here, drink this. Slowly now." A glass was put to her lips. She smelled the brandy fumes and sipped. The heat was a shock to her sore throat, but a welcome one. It jolted her eyesight back into focus and gave her the strength to sit up.

She was on her back in a bed hung with red draperies. Red silk covered the walls and upholstered much of the carved furniture. The window drapes were closed so she couldn't tell what time of day it was. Mrs. Corwin Rathe stood beside the bed wearing an autumn brown night-robe.

"Corwin Rathe!" Jane clutched the woman's hand. "I must speak to your husband at once!"

"At your service, madame." A black-haired man stepped into

her field of vision. He'd dressed hastily, with only a rumpled blue coat over his shirt and breeches.

"What is it you want with us, Lady Jane?" growled another voice. A second man came into view and Jane recognized Darius Marlowe. His gold hair was tousled and, like Rathe, he'd clearly thrown on his shirt and maroon jacket after being hastily summoned from sleep.

"I have to tell you, they've broken in. . . ."

"Who has?" barked Marlowe.

"Them. The f-f . . . the fair . . ."

"The Fae?" said Mrs. Rathe in a low voice.

Jane nodded. The three of them exchanged a long look, all their faces going taut with a mix of anger and pure fear.

"What are they after?" Mr. Rathe asked Jane. "Do you know?"

She nodded, but had to take another swallow of brandy before she could speak. "The baby."

Mrs. Rathe clapped her hand over her mouth.

"I'll alert Smith." Marlowe strode out of the room.

As soon as the door swung shut behind him, Rathe turned back to Jane. "How do you know about the Fae?" he demanded.

"Corwin, let her rest." Mrs. Rathe laid her hand on Jane's forehead. The light touch seemed very soothing, and Jane longed to slump back against her pillows. But she could not. There was no time.

"I'm all right. Please." She shook off the other woman's hand. "I know because Thomas told me. Sir Thomas Lynne."

She spoke his name and her vision blurred. It was as if she could see him in front of her, slumped in the corner, his knees drawn up and his chained hands resting limp on them. Resignation settled deep into him. It was the end, the end, but Jane was safe, and that was what mattered . . .

"What have you to do with Thomas Lynne?" Rathe's voice snapped her out of her strange reverie. Jane shook her head and tried to focus on what had been said. Mr. Rathe's tone said he already knew Thomas was her paramour. He just wanted to see if she'd admit it.

But she couldn't. Not yet. "They've taken him," she told them instead. "They took me too. There's a . . . a . . . woman who looks like me in the house now."

"A double?" asked Mrs. Rathe. "A doppelganger?"

Jane had heard that word while in Saxe-Coburg and nodded.

"When?" demanded Rathe. "How? How long have they . . . ?"

The woman shot Rathe a quelling glance. "Corwin, have Jacobs wake Cook. Lady Jane needs food. And send in Martha. Tell her what's happened. We need to get Lady Jane's feet cleaned before they start to fester."

Rathe bridled for a moment, but then nodded and left the room.

"Now, Lady Jane. . . ."

"Jane." She slumped back onto the pillows. Her head ached horribly, but not as badly as her feet. Her feet burned. "Just Jane."

"And I'm Miranda, Jane. I think you'd better tell me what's happened, from the beginning." Jane heard the mix of sympathy and practicality in her calm words. This was not a woman who would judge, or disbelieve.

If anything less than Thomas's life had been at stake, Jane

never would have been able to make herself speak. As it was, she stumbled over her words and had to take several more sips of the brandy to gather enough strength and nerve to keep going. When the maid arrived with a tray containing plain toast, a soft boiled egg and hot milk posset, Jane could have kissed the girl. Miranda insisted she eat, and waited calmly while she did, although Jane could see the tension in her shoulders.

At last, Jane finished the tale. "Please," she whispered. "You must help him. They're going to kill him. Or worse. I don't even know what they're capable of . . ."

"None of us knows all they're capable of," said Miranda grimly. "But it will not be good."

The door opened again to admit Rathe, Marlowe and another maid carrying another tray. This one held a steaming basin, bandages and scissors and a series of bottles.

"Smith's on his way to Kensington House," reported the blond man. "Apparently we've had word from our people there. The duchess is in labor."

Jane's throat constricted. The baby was on the way. Frau Seibold would be issuing orders, the doctors would be called. And there would be Mrs. Beauchamp, all eagerness to help. Ready to harm the innocent child, the duchess . . .

"You must do something."

"Everything's being done that can be." Miranda dismissed the maid and set the tray on a table and began opening bottles. Jane smelled herbs and strong alcohol. "What we need to do now is get these feet seen to."

Miranda moved around the foot of the bed, laying out towels. She began bathing Jane's feet in the hot water. It stung like fire, but Miranda held Jane firmly as she washed away the blood and dirt. The men watched her and moved not a muscle. Something crackled in the air, something familiar yet terribly strange.

It came to Jane in a flash. *They're in each other's minds, the way Thomas was in mine.*

"I know you're talking to each other," she said out loud. "Can you find Thomas? Can you free him?"

All three of them turned to stare at her. A ripple of shock ran between them.

"Stop," Jane snapped. "I am not entirely ignorant, and you know that by now."

"No, you are not entirely ignorant," drawled Marlowe. "What we do not know is whether you are entirely innocent."

His words hit Jane hard, pushing her back onto the pillows. She had been so intent on giving them her message and on saving Thomas that she had not stopped to consider how the story of her actions would appear to others.

"You have helped breach the defenses of a royal residence," Marlowe paced the room slowly, one fist knotted behind his back. "Perhaps it is as you say, and you played your part unwittingly. But we need to be sure before we go any further, especially when you're begging us to rescue the captain of the Fae queen's knights."

"He sent me to warn you," Jane fought to keep her voice level. Her feet throbbed under Miranda's ministrations, and found an answering pain in her head. "He risked everything to do that much."

"Perhaps, perhaps not," said Rathe. "The Fae are masters of

manipulating appearances, something I'm sure you have real-ized by now."

"All right, all right," cut in Miranda. "We can sort all this out later. But right now, since she knows so much of magic, there's no reason to leave her feet in this condition, is there?" She glowered at both men. "Come here, Corwin. Help me. Hold still, Jane."

Miranda laid her hand on Corwin Rathe's shoulder and the prickling Jane had felt before filled the air. The Sorcerer reached out and wrapped his broad hand around Jane's ankle. Before she could protest the familiarity, a harsh itching dug deep into skin and bone and Jane hissed.

The world around her blurred again, and Jane thought she might be fainting. She couldn't see the red room or the Sorcerers anymore.

She saw Thomas. No. She saw Thomas's hands, with the sil-ver bar between them, she saw his legs and battered boots.

She saw not Thomas, but what Thomas saw. She felt the cold air scrape against his lungs and the throbbing pain in every joint.

*What's happening?*

*I don't know. Darius, here. Do you see . . .*

*Jane?* Thomas lifted his head.

*Yes!* She cried. *It's me, Thomas. I'm here!*

But darkness fell like a hand had been clapped over her eyes. Jane cried out, but she was back in the red room, with the Sor-cerers clustered at the foot of her bed, all of them staring at her. It was almost as an afterthought she noticed the pain in her feet had vanished entirely.

"What have you done!" she shouted at the pale trio.

"More to the point," said Rathe slowly. "What have you done, Lady Jane, to permit yourself to become so bonded to the captain of the Fae Queen's mortal knights?"

Jane pressed her lips tightly together and turned her face away. These people had been supposed to help her, but they acted as if she was some kind of criminal.

"If you saw what was in my mind, you see that Sir Thomas is a prisoner. He has risked everything to get word to you. There must be something you can do for him."

"The question is not what can be done, but what should be done," said Marlowe. "You forget, madame, we have no reason to trust you or this story you tell."

"But you saw . . ." she began, but Marlowe cut her off with an impatient wave of his hand.

"It could be an illusion. Even here, even now, you could be but a cat's-paw for Their Glorious Majesties."

Which was true, however little she wanted to admit it. Jane swallowed her panic. In order to get help for Thomas, she needed these people. Unlike her, they had power. She must be calm, no matter how strong the fear that circled the back of her mind. She must think clearly. "What must I do to convince you? Please. A good man is going to die at the hands of these . . . creatures."

The three looked at each other. It was Rathe who answered.

"There is nothing to be done until we have word from Kensington House. Until then, I advise you to rest and get your strength back. One way or another you will need it. Miranda, you stay with her."

With that, the men left the room. Miranda made sure the

door shut securely and then seated herself by the window, as if doing nothing more than visiting the invalid.

"Am I a prisoner?" asked Jane.

"Yes." Which was at least a commendably direct answer.

"On whose authority am I held?"

"That's a more complex question, but ultimately, our authority comes from the Crown."

Jane knotted her fists in the down coverlet, trying to set aside the anger and fear and think. It was impossible. All she could see was Thomas chained in the marble cell that was also the cellar of Fiora Beauchamp's house.

*I will not cry,* Jane insisted to herself, even as one hot tear trickled down her cheek. She batted at it furiously. *I will not cry in front of this woman.*

"I know this is difficult, Jane," said Miranda quietly. "But please believe, we are not your enemies."

"Then why won't you help him?"

Miranda looked at her hands folded in her lap for a long time, considering carefully before she spoke. "Because we have been deceived before," she said. "And the consequences were terrible." Her face was taut, and Jane sensed a formidable control being exercised to keep her emotions from showing through. "In a way the queen has done us a great favor. By giving so much attention to the duchess and the duchess's child, we know she did not accomplish her ultimate end with the death of Princess Charlotte." The woman spoke the words calmly, but a lifetime of watching people's faces showed Jane what that calm cost her.

"God in Heaven . . . they killed the princess?"

"They did. And they used a ruse much like this situation you present us to do it." For the first time, Miranda's voice faltered. "There was a defector, a trusted attendant, and three magic workers who thought they were being very clever . . . So you see, we have reason to be cautious."

Did Thomas know about this? Why hadn't he told her? He had set out to use her, what if he was using her now? That creature, that thing she had thought of as Mrs. Beauchamp, she could be doing anything at all in Kensington House while Jane was safely out of the way.

*What if that was all part of the plan?* Jane closed her eyes.

"I'm sorry," said Miranda, and Jane was sure she meant it. "But we are fighting a war for survival in which we are outnumbered and badly outgunned. We cannot take any chances that you may have been deceived."

"Why do they bother?" she asked miserably. "If they're so strong, what do they need with someone like me?" Or like Thomas?

Miranda smiled grimly. "As powerful as they may be, this world is not theirs. There are limits to what they can do here."

"Cold iron, salt, running water," said Jane softly.

"Among other things. But that is why they have always needed the help of human beings to conquer. That's why they have recruited a cadre of human soldiers and need the help of human Sorcerers." She paused. "And why they have always sought to sway human hearts."

There was no answer Jane could make. She could not explain the love in her. None of these people would believe what she saw in Thomas's eyes. They had a single answer for all she had seen and all she had felt. It was all illusion. She had no proof to offer them, for the only proof was held tightly within her heart.

Miranda sighed. "I am going to say this, although I know you do not want to listen. The Fae queen's glamour is the strongest there is. To look at her is to fall in love, and there are very few that are strong enough to break that spell once it has taken root. They will serve her until death, and beyond if she calls them. And all who serve the queen seek to subvert the prophecy. Whatever else they may do, or even feel, that will be their goal."

Still Jane said nothing. She would not beg or plead or fumble for proofs that did not exist. She'd only talk herself into knots.

"Very well." Miranda shook her head. Then, she seemed to reach a decision. "There is one other thing you should know, Lady Jane."

"What is that?" Jane asked.

"You are with child."

Jane's frayed temper snapped in two. "You are impertinent and disgusting!"

"I am also a Catalyst," replied Miranda coolly. "As such, I am connected to the currents of life and magic in the world, and in the people around me. You are with child. It has not been long, but it has happened."

It could not be true. This woman could not know any such thing about her. She was trying to frighten her, about Thomas, about what she had done with him.

And yet, and yet, she spoke so plainly, and her gaze was so steady.

"I cannot be pregnant," Jane said quietly. "I am barren. I was married for five years and did not once conceive."

"I cannot answer as to that. Whatever did or did not happen with your husband, you have conceived now. In a month or two you will have your own proof. Whatever you choose next, you also have a child to consider."

A child. Thomas's child. Thomas was in danger of his life, a prisoner of the Fae, condemned as traitor by them and these Sorcerers, and she carried his child. The world turned over once more, and Jane could not see how it would ever be righted.

"Can you leave me alone for a little?" she whispered. "I need . . . I need a moment."

A flicker of sympathy passed over the woman's face. "I'll be right outside," she said by way of reassurance and warning. "Call if you should need anything."

Miranda left, and Jane heard the unmistakable sound of a key turning in a lock. She swallowed hard and despite the protest from her aching, exhausted body, she climbed out of the bed. She'd been given a clean nightdress at some point. The garment was a bit tight across the bosom and the hem a couple of inches too short. Her feet were healed, but remained stiff as she staggered to the window to push back the drapes.

She looked out from a third story of whatever house this was. A city garden stretched out long and narrow below her. A high brick wall topped with iron spikes hemmed in beds of daffodils and neatly trimmed lilacs, as well as the burgeoning green of the tidy kitchen garden. Jane rattled the window sash and worked the black iron latch, to no effect. She suspected that if she hammered on the glass she would find it did not break.

Not that she was sure what she would do if she could open the window. She was not even sure where she would go. When she had woken, she only wanted to fly back to Thomas, to break his chains and set him free. Now, sickening doubt filled her heart. She felt all the old loneliness wrapping around her, smothering her, but it was worse now, because it could never be lifted again. Because if Thomas had deceived her, she would for the rest of her life know herself for a fool, and a helpless, ridiculous woman with judgment that was not merely faulty but dangerously reckless.

And a child? She laid her hand on her belly. Was it really possible she was carrying Thomas's child? Tears and laughter both threatened and she was not sure which hurt worse. All these years she believed that children were denied to her. Now . . . now she had one, but the father might be at best a soldier lost in a war, at worst an agent of a cunning and murderous enemy. And she had not even stopped to think of the possibility of a baby when she lay down with him.

*My father's daughter after all.* She rested her forehead against the cool windowpane. *Only I gambled with passion's stakes, and may have lost the whole world. Oh, well done, Jane. Was there ever such a gamester?*

Behind her, the door opened. Jane lifted her head and made herself turn slowly. She composed her features. She would not show her jailers her confusion.

They all entered the room, Miranda and her two men.

"Good news, Jane," said Miranda. "We were in time. The duchess is delivered of a healthy baby girl."

Jane staggered and pressed her hand against her stomach. "Thank Heavens," she murmured. "And Her Grace is well?"

"Very, I am pleased to report."

"What of Mrs. Beauchamp . . . my doppelganger?"

"There we were less successful." Marlowe growled and folded

his arms. "Your absence was much remarked on, and angrily. I'm afraid you've lost your position."

She looked from one of them to the other. "Then I have lost my only chance of proving what I say is true."

"Not quite," said Rathe. They were casting sideways glances at each other. Clearly another mysterious, silent conversation was being held. "We must admit that your arriving in time to save the heir to the throne speaks well in your favor."

"And, if what you say is true, if Thomas Lynne has turned against the queen, a Fae knight would have a great deal of useful information for us. Because even if their plans to interfere with the birth have failed, their Glorious Majesties will not stop here."

Painful hope swelled Jane's heart. "What must I do?"

Rathe's dark eyes bored into hers. "You must consent to a truth seeing."

"What is that?"

It was Miranda who answered. "The truth seeing will allow the three of us to share this bond that seems to lie between you and Thomas Lynne. We can use that to determine whether his actions were sincere when he sent you to us."

The idea of these three parading through her emotions did not appeal. What if they saw what she had done with Thomas, the way they had loved each other? They'd condemn her as a wanton, as indecent. Jane shook her head. Surely with Thomas's life at stake, that was the smallest triviality.

She drew her shoulders back. "And if you see that what I have said is true?"

"Then," said Corwin Rathe, "we will do our best to rescue Thomas Lynne."

# Twenty-nine

They came for him at twilight.

A slow scraping filled the cell. Thomas lifted his aching head to see the door push open. What Jane had seen as solid marble, he saw as icy white light lying over the wooden door of the butler's pantry. His silver chains were real enough, but they too were frosted with the spell light to sap his will and energy. The nail he had given Jane had been his only protection, and that was gone now. If he was left here, the chains would simply drain his life away. It would be a slow, despairing death, but not the worst that could be imagined.

Therefore, of course, it would not be granted him.

*Jane's away,* Thomas told himself yet again. *That's all that matters. Jane is free.*

Three soldiers dressed in leather kilts and molded breast-plates like ancient Roman soldiers entered the cell. The queen did not send any of the mortal soldiers he had once lead. Perhaps she did not trust them to drag their captain before her in his chains. These three were elven knights, each a mirror image of the other with pale gold hair, pure white skin and eyes like carrion crows. They were also strangers to him, at least in their current form.

The first of them gestured toward Thomas. The light coating the chains turned to crackling fire, and an unseen force hauled him to his feet. That same Fae, clearly this little detail's captain, stepped close. Thomas knew what was coming and tried to steel himself for the blow. Pain exploded in the side of his head and he fell sideways into the arms of his captors. His feet scrabbled at the floor but could find no purchase. The world swayed and spun as they dragged him from the cellar and out into the waiting carriage. Somewhere beyond the pain that blurred his eyesight, Thomas was aware his captors had shifted form, becoming three immaculately attired gentlemen. If he squinted, he could see the elven knight beneath the facade, as he could see the chariot beneath the closed barouche, and the silver ring bolt to which his magical chains had been fastened. He let his head loll sideways, feigning a greater weakness than he felt. Although he was not sure why he bothered. There was no escape, and he knew it. But his mind could not convince his body of that. Body and heart still wanted to live. The two-thirds of his being that had withstood battle, storm and starvation, that had dared the wrath of Queen Bess for the sake of a few Spanish trinkets, believed there would be a chance. It whispered that if he kept his wits about him, he still might find a way to escape these three—who probably didn't have an independent thought in their immortal heads—and to make his way through London and back to Jane.

*Jane wouldn't give up,* murmured his heart to his mind. *Jane would not let you give up.*

Thomas felt a smile curl on his lips. Even now that he'd put her irretrievably beyond him, she still shaped him. Or perhaps it was just the freedom that came with a death sentence. Having nothing left to lose did convey a remarkable sense of liberty. He would not be able to hurt Jane anymore. As for the damage he had done to her heart . . . well, anger was a fine balm for such hurts. She would be angry, and she would outlive the pain. For she was strong, his Jane, a fighter and a survivor. She would find her way.

That thought should have comforted him, but it was harder than any blow to bear his captors could have dealt. Thomas turned his face to the carriage wall.

"He's still awake."

"You didn't hit him hard enough."

"I'll fix that."

The next blow brought only darkness.

*T*homas.

Thomas lay in Jane's arms. She was so warm and sweet. She rocked him, but too roughly. Why was she rocking him so roughly? He wanted her to stop. It made his head hurt.

*Jane . . .* Thomas tired to say.

*A gate in Hyde Park?* muttered a strange man. *How did we miss . . . ?*

*Thomas.* Jane again. Her voice filled with love and fear. For him. All he had done and all he had been, and Jane still loved him. *Can you hear me? Answer me, please.*

Slowly, memory filtered into the blackness of his mind, along with the pain and a good dose of nausea. He was captured. He was being taken to judgment. He was weak as a kitten from his magical bonds and two blows to his head. About all he was good for was being sick over the boots of his captors, which would be satisfying but not very useful.

And he could hear Jane.

*They say you have to open your eyes, Thomas. So we can see where you are.*

*They?* "They" needed him to open his eyes to see? Slowly, he realized Jane was with the Sorcerers. Jane was speaking to him through the bond he had forged for them.

Jane was going to get herself killed.

The thought focused his mind instantly.

*Jane, stop this. They'll hear you. She'll find you.*

*We're coming, Thomas.*

*No, Jane!*

But it was no use. While she could touch him through their bond, she would come to him. The sympathetic magic held sway in her heart and he himself had done this to her. Thomas shut his eyes, and did what he should have done when she had escaped from their basement cell.

*Good-bye, Jane.* He moved will and heart, twisting hard.

But nothing happened. The bond did not break. He tried again, straining every sinew of his inner self. But it was no good. He could not break the bond alone, not anymore. Jane had claimed it for hers, and Jane was holding on tight.

*Jane, you must let me go.*

*No.* She answered calmly. *Not like this.*

*Jane, whatever you think you feel for me, it's not genuine. It's only glamour.*

*We will decide that when you are free.*

*Jane, you must withdraw. They're searching.*

She ignored this as well. *We'll be there soon, Thomas.*

The guards around him were stirring. He saw their heads lifting one by one, like hounds catching a strange scent.

*Quiet,* said the man's voice sharply. Silence descended in Thomas's heart and mind. His guards shifted uneasily. He made himself lie limp and still, and they quieted. But Thomas's thoughts did not. For Jane had said, "We'll be there soon." Not "they'll be." We. She was coming to him, straight into danger.

That, he could not permit. No matter what the price, he could not be the cause of bringing any more danger to Jane. He wasted precious seconds cursing himself for sending her to the Sorcerers. He had thought they would shelter her. How could he have failed to realize they would use her to get to him? He was a rich prize for the crown's magical agents. Of course they would risk her to get to him.

Thomas felt the moment the wheels left the cobbles and turned onto the gravel lane of Hyde Park. He had but a handful of moments to make his decision. He knew the ground here. The last of the daylight outside had faded, but that wouldn't slow the Fae down at all. But if he could run . . . there was the Serpentine not too far from here. There was the iron gate to Kensington House. The wards might not stop him now that the queen had withdrawn her favor, and as a mortal, iron made no difference to him than any other metal.

A handful of moments to decide whether he would try to live or accept his death.

Except it wouldn't be his death. He knew that. He would not be handed over to anything so merciful as death. And if he escaped into Kensington House, he'd only bring the danger following him onto the residents there. The queen might be desperate enough for a siege, and his actions had left the house defenseless.

Whatever he did, he must do it now. Before Jane could reach him and put herself in his captor's power.

Iron calm descended. The river then. His chains would sink him in the current, and there would be precious little these Fae men could do about it. They could not enter the running water without great hazard to themselves. He had to die before they brought him before the queen. She could flay his mind bare, take up the end of his bond with Jane and follow it back to her. She would wrap it tight around Jane and throttle her with it.

Jane would be safe only when he was dead.

A plan began to take shape in Thomas's mind, and none too soon. The carriage stopped. Gravel crunched beneath the horse's hooves as they tramped and snorted.

One of his captors undid his chain from the bolt. They'd left his hands in front of him. The length of silver bar between them was a nuisance, but they hadn't chained his ankles. Another mistake, as was the length of chain fastened to the manacle bar.

His own men never would have made such mistakes. But the Fae knights were secure in the powers of their magic. He was a mere human being, and a traitor at that. To them, he was less than nothing, and they were treating him as such.

Thomas made himself stir and groan. The Fae behind him shoved him out of the disguised chariot and he staggered a few steps across the gravel. The guard that climbed down from the box chuckled and aimed a kick at Thomas's shin. Thomas flinched and sagged a little further. They grinned and their crows' eyes glittered. Their senses were alert for any stirring of magic in the darkness, but not for the tensing of his muscles.

Thomas stumbled again, and as he did, grabbed at the chain with his right hand.

He yanked, hard.

The Fae cursed, but his grip was slack. Thomas yanked again and the end of the chain flew free. He snapped it like a whip, sending the Fae reeling back. Thomas wheeled and planted his boot in the stomach of the second Fae. The kick sent that guard crashing into his fellow so they both went down. Thomas pivoted and he swung the chain again, this time snapping the end hard against the flank of the nearest horse.

The near horse screamed its outrage and reared. The off horse echoed its fury, and both took off running. Thomas bolted after them, grinning like a madman. He leapt for the luggage rack at the back of the carriage, and caught hold with one hand. The momentum dragged him off his feet and he jounced and cursed and somehow swung himself onto the narrow wooden shelf.

It was a move that bought him only seconds and he knew it. The Fae were already on their feet and running after him. Mortal men would not have stood a chance of catching the rattling carriage, but the Fae ran like deer, and they were gaining. They became blurs in his sight, inching close and picking up speed.

He gripped the carriage ladder with one hand and despite the pain and the danger, he laughed out loud. The sense of defying such power was dizzying. It was like being aloft in a raging gale. For this one moment, he was a man and alive as he had never been before.

No, that wasn't true. For he had been a man alive in Jane's arms and that moment was greater than any that could come now, because in that moment he'd had the dream of a future with her.

The lane turned away from the river at the next bend. The horses would follow the easiest path. He had to jump again. With his manacled hands, he wouldn't be able to tuck properly. He'd be lucky if he only broke his arm. But he had no choice. He had to keep what little lead he had on his pursuers. Perhaps if he was very lucky, he could smash his weakened skull, and put an end to matters right here.

*Wish me luck, Jane.*

Thomas jumped. He hit the ground in a blaze of pain that nearly burned the consciousness out of his brain. Instinct took over and he rolled, and was on his feet and running. The chain threatened to tangle his feet with every step and send him toppling forward. He had to stay on his feet and run, run hard, run for his life, for Jane's life. He just had to make it to the river. Nothing else mattered but that.

*Thomas!* Jane's voice filled his mind. *Thomas! This way!*

A woman's silhouette topped one of the many little rolling hills on the park green. She held a lantern light high. It was Jane. Jane ignoring her safety. Jane coming, as she promised. Jane whom nothing and no one could ever keep from him.

*This way!* cried Jane's voice in his mind again.

"Oh, no, Sir Thomas. This way."

Sylvan light blinded him. The strength of his body vanished and Thomas fell to the ground like a dead man. Absolutely limp and numb, he rolled across the damp grass, and came to rest at the feet of Her Glorious Majesty.

# Thirty

Jane watched Thomas fall.

She screamed and she lunged forward. Corwin and Miranda tried to hold her back, but she tore herself out of their reaching hands. She ran. She ran as if her life depended on it. It did. For Thomas, bathed in a sickly ghost light, lay in the grass as if he'd been struck dead.

"Jane, stop!" cried Miranda behind her. "Come back!"

No force in any world could have stopped Jane. She raced down the hill and across the greensward. She stumbled and slipped and fell and leapt up again. Three crows flew high overhead, calling harshly to their fellows. Behind her she heard a crackling like fire. She didn't look back. She kept her eyes on Thomas where he lay.

*Move, move, Thomas.* She cried inside her mind. *Show me you're alive. Please, Thomas.*

And she heard an answer, but it wasn't Thomas's voice. It was a woman's, and it was as sweet and as deadly as poison.

*Oh, welcome, Lady Jane.*

Shock broke Jane's stride, but too late. Her own momentum carried her into the circle of silver light, and into another world.

In the blink of an eye, she was surrounded by winter's cold. She sank up to her ankles in snow. More snow fell on her arms, left bare by the summer gown she had borrowed from Miranda. Cold crawled across her skin, making her shiver.

But as she lifted her eyes, Jane saw a woman standing before her. She was tall and slender, wrapped in a dress of white furs. Her skin was pale, and seemed to shine with a pure light. Even her eyes gleamed, white as frost on a window when the sun hit it.

Jane had never seen anything so beautiful. Awe blossomed inside her. Surely this was the queen of the angels come to earth. She should kneel. It was not right that she remain standing in the presence of such glory.

But as her knees began to buckle, movement caught her dazzled eyes. Behind the woman, Thomas lay sprawled in the snow. His skin had gone paper white from the cold and a blue pallor tinged his lips. But he'd turned his head, and she saw his eyes, his brilliant green eyes, and they were wide and fearful with warning.

Awe fell away, cold fell away as the fire of anger rushed into Jane's blood. She looked again at the pale woman, and this time she knew who it was.

"You're the Fae queen," Jane said. "You're Tatiana."

Tatiana laughed and the sound crawled like ants up Jane's arms. "Do you think I fear my own name in the mouth of a mortal drab? Did your pathetic Sorcerers tell you it would help you? They cannot even help themselves."

The queen pointed one long white finger. Jane could not help but look. At first she saw nothing but darkness, and that darkness was filled with the hunting call of a hundred crows. Somehow her eyes adjusted and she saw Corwin, Darius and Miranda on the hill. A ring of clear fire shone around them, and an entire murder of crows dove down from the sky. The birds hit the fiery wall, and bounced off, only to rally and dive again. With each blow, the wall shook. The crows laughed and screamed, and dove again.

Fear threatened to crush Jane's heart. But she shoved it aside. She must trust the Sorcerer's strength. She must not give way before this terrible and beautiful creature.

*As powerful as they may be, this world is not theirs. There are limits to what they can do here.*

Jane moved carefully around the circle. On numbed feet, she plowed a path through the snow until she stood beside Thomas. Tatiana turned to follow her, watching every move. Every clumsy, useless move. Jane knew herself to be ugly, ungainly and useless. She had failed her family, failed her husband, failed her charge to the duchess even. What made her think she could do anything now?

Nothing. Nothing at all, except the man lying so still in the snow.

Again, the queen laughed. The sound cut so deeply Jane was sure she felt blood welling up along her arms and falling like tears down her cheeks. Her knees trembled. Pins and needles swarmed up her ankles. The queen, Jane realized, did not have to do anything. She just had to keep Thomas here, because Jane would not leave Thomas, and Jane could not live in this cold.

*Thomas,* she thought toward him. *You must try to stand. I cannot lift you alone.* But she felt her thoughts press hard against some unyielding surface, like glass, like ice. Whatever it was, Thomas was on the far side of it and she could not reach him.

"Oh, yes, Sir Thomas," drawled the queen. "What are you thinking, lounging there? What sort of gentleman fails to stand when a lady enters the room?"

Thomas's legs twitched. His head jerked up, and he stood, slowly and mechanically. Jane could practically see the chains around his wrist and throat pulling him to stand upright.

"Bow to the lady," ordered the queen.

Thomas bowed and straightened, as powerless as a toy soldier. But as he did, Jane saw his eyes again, and saw the pain and defiance that glittered within. Hope surged into her faltering heart. Because in that defiance she saw Thomas. He was still there. Whatever magics Tatiana possessed, she had not yet claimed his soul.

"Pretty thing, isn't he?" The queen reached out and brushed some snow from Thomas's shoulder. "And such a fine lover. Did you enjoy him very much, Jane?"

Jane stiffened her spine. "Let him go."

"Now why would I do that?"

"He's nothing to you anymore. He no longer loves you."

The queen smiled. Jane thought her heart would stop for love and fear.

"And you think he loves you? That you are special to him? Foolish child!" Her laugh fell like blows against Jane's body. She swayed, then staggered. The sound of triumphant crows sounded close overhead.

*I can't fall. I can't let Thomas see me fall.* Somehow she managed to keep her feet, and the corners of the queen's perfect mouth turned up scornfully.

"He's a man too long away from his own shore and homesick. You could have been any woman who spoke English and had the enticing taint of mortality about you."

"That might be true," said Jane through clenched teeth. She was shivering uncontrollably now. "But it makes our love no less real."

"Your love! You think he feels anything I do not allow? He is mine, mortal child, and he has nothing I do not give, not even a will or form of his own. Sir Thomas!" she spat his name. "Come here!"

Slowly, stiffly, Thomas marched to the Fae Queen's side. Jane felt her heart tremble with fear and sorrow at the sight of his still, pale face. It was as if his soul had fled him. Until she looked into his eyes, his beautiful green eyes that had captivated her from the start. In his eyes she saw his anguish, and knew that no matter what commands he might now obey, Thomas still lived within himself, and in that truth lay all their hope.

"Your lady love is here," said Queen Tatiana acidly. "Take her in your arms."

Thomas wheeled around. He marched toward Jane, his face absolutely blank. For a moment Jane's nerve faltered and her body screamed for her to run. But where to? The queen would only order him to chase her down, and that might break them both.

Crows called again. Fire blazed on the hills. The Sorcerers were still fighting. She could not let go now.

Thomas moved closer and Jane held herself still. She was very conscious of the breadth of his shoulders and of his strength as his arms enfolded her, without tenderness, without love.

*Thomas!* She flung his name against the wall between them. *Thomas!*

*Jane.* She heard him answer, but his voice in her mind was faint, blurred, as if he spoke from a great distance or in a high wind.

*Fight her, Thomas!* she cried inwardly *You must fight!*

"Kiss her, Sir Thomas," sneered the Fae queen. "I want to see this grand passion she claims."

Thomas's mouth was on hers, hard and devouring, without mercy but equally without passion. Jane stiffened against his stabbing tongue. She could not help it. And in the distance, as if from farther away than the sounds of battle on the hill, she felt his heart break.

*I cannot fight. I am sworn. I cannot break that oath.*

"What do you think of your lover now, Lady Jane?" inquired the queen. Her tone cut at Jane, a knife across her flesh. "How shall it be when I command him to do far more than steal one kiss?"

*You are still a man, Thomas. You have your own will, your own heart. If she owned those, could you love me now?*

"Enough," snapped the queen impatiently, and Thomas stepped back, his face still a mask, his eyes still fixed and distant, but there was something, some thaw in his despair. Jane felt it.

"Thomas has never hurt me," Jane did not bother to look at Tatiana. She spoke directly to Thomas. All their games, all the times he had held her helpless in his arms and in his bed, he had not once used his strength against her. Not once, even when he had brought himself into her thoughts and dreams, had he misused her. "He will not hurt me now."

Thomas could not move, but Jane could, and she moved forward. She put her arms around Thomas, enclosing him in her embrace.

"Stupid woman! He is mine! Even to his flesh and form, he is mine!"

Jane felt the sting of magic, and impossibly, Thomas began to swell in her arms. The shape of his limbs and torso shifted beneath her hands. He threw back his head and cried out, but that human cry stretched and deepened, becoming an animal roar.

It was not Thomas she held any longer. It was a lion. Huge, heavy-maned, utterly inhuman, its fangs snapped inches from her face and its paws crushed down her shoulders. Her fingers knotted in its living pelt. Too stunned to scream, every instinct Jane possessed cried at her to run. But she did not run.

Because the lion looked at her with Thomas's green eyes.

*I trust you, Thomas. I trust you.*

The lion roared out in animal despair. The sound cut through her and Jane shuddered. But that roar stretched again, taught and high, turning from roar to screech and as the sound changed, so did Thomas's bestial form.

*I* . . . She heard Thomas's voice in her mind, faint, but real.

Thomas shrank and withered. His arms, which had been paws broadened and flattened. Fur became feathers. The snout tightened and curved to become a cruel beak. Wicked talons shot out of his drastically shortened legs. The lion was gone, replaced by a golden eagle that flapped its great wings and shrieked a hunting cry like torn metal, and still Jane held on.

And then something new happened. The eagle that had been Thomas Lynne ceased its maddened flapping. Jane could feel its frantic heartbeat as she clasped its feathered breast, aware that despite its predatory strength of beak and talon she might break any of its bones with a careless touch.

*I will not . . .*

The air crackled with anger and menace, and the sting of magic once more. The eagle shrank again, stretched again, becoming long and lithe and smooth, a living rope of brown and white in her hand. Its hood spread out like the eagle's wings had and its fangs glistened more cruel than beak or claw. Jane had seen illustrations of the king cobra of India and knew what she held now. But even the serpent had Thomas's green eyes and it was those eyes she looked into now.

*I trust you, Thomas.*

The serpent's hood closed. It curled its body around her wrist.

*I. Will. Not. Hurt. You. Jane.*

*I know it, Thomas. I have always known.*

*My Jane.*

*Always.*

Tatiana's scream of pure rage split the air around them. Hatred blurred the very air around her. Her face no longer seemed young or fair, but instead was brown and withered as if she wore a mask of tree bark. Something else was missing. It took Jane a moment to realize.

The cold was gone. The snow was gone. Whatever magic that

was had vanished, and Jane stood on the grass of Hyde Park again. But Thomas was still a serpent coiled around her arm, hissing at his former queen.

Tatiana raised her hand once more. Her ever-changing eyes glowed the purple-black of storm clouds, and Jane felt the magic stab deep through her, and again Thomas's form twisted in her hands, shrinking down, smaller and smaller until she cried out for fear he was being stolen from her altogether.

The light and heat hit her together. This was no wild creature now. It was fire. Jane cupped a live coal in her palms. The heat assailed her face, she smelled the burning and her mind cried out at the danger, reflex urged her to drop it. There were no eyes now, no way to see Thomas, and yet, and yet, she felt him, and the heat did not sear her. It hurt, it hurt, but she could bear the pain and she did not let go.

"Hold on, Jane!" called a voice, a human voice, a woman's voice. "We're coming!"

Tatiana screamed and wheeled around. In a flash, Jane saw a stag charging down the hill, its antlers lowered. A white owl the size of an eagle flew overhead. The queen held a spear in her hand and the words she cursed seemed to split the night with their power.

Jane did not wait to see what would happen. She turned on her heel and fled. Pain filled her palms. She could smell the stench of burning flesh, and she knew it was hers. Thomas was losing control, giving in to the form forced upon him.

*The river, Jane*, she heard him whisper in her heart. *The water.*

Yes. Yes. The Serpentine. It glimmered silver in the light of the spring moon. Another few yards, another few feet. A dreadful scream tumbled over her, pushing on her back, tripping her feet.

With all the strength she possessed, Jane hurled herself headfirst into the slowly moving water.

It was a plunge into icy blackness. Jane's skirts billowed and tangled around her legs. They caught her like water weeds and dragged her down. Her lungs strained and her hands flailed as she twisted. Thomas was gone. She was alone and the current tugged and tumbled her. She didn't know which way was up any longer, and she'd lost Thomas. She fought to swim but she could not get her legs free.

Strong arms encircled her waist. Jane felt herself lifted up, and she burst thought the surface of the water. Air rushed into her lungs as she gasped and coughed and gasped again. She twisted in her rescuer's arms, but she already knew who she would see.

Thomas. Whole and well, entirely naked, and fully himself, Thomas held her in his arms.

"Thomas!" She fought to turn in his grip so she could throw hers about him.

"Hush, love, hush. I have not the strength if you struggle."

Her heart swelled with love and fear, Jane held still. Thomas shifted so his arm slanted across her breasts. With a strong but awkward one-armed stroke, he pulled them both to shore.

Slowly, both shaking for the effort, they clambered to shore and fell face first upon the grass.

"Jane," he breathed. "My Jane . . ."

"Now you hush," Jane rolled toward him, twining her weak

fingers into his. He was too pale, his breath coming short and his skin was cold as ice. At once, she threw her cloak over him, sodden as it was.

"My God, Jane, she's gone."

"What?"

"The queen. She's no more in my heart. You've banished her."

"None banish me."

She stood before them, power crackling in a dreadful aureole about her. She was pale as death and moonlight and her eyes were storm and lightning. Trembling, Jane got to her feet, a gesture as absurd as the cloak had been. She had no strength left. Her hands were empty. She could not have fended off a kitten.

But the queen did not even see her. She looked straight past Jane to Thomas on his knees. "I trusted you, Thomas Lynne. I gave you my heart and my charge. I should have instead plucked out your eyes and heart and given you wooden ones in their place." Only then did she turn to Jane. "You've won your knight, Lady Jane. Very well. I relinquish my hold hereby and wish you joy of him."

She vanished and thunder clapped in the place where she stood. Jane reeled backward. Slowly, it sank into her that the queen was gone. Gone. They'd won. She spun around to shout their victory to Thomas.

But Thomas still lay on the grass. Her sodden cloak had fallen open to show the awful rush of blood pouring from his side.

"No!" Jane dropped to the ground. Blood, there was blood everywhere. Thomas's life poured out onto the trampled grass.

He laid his hand into its warmth and gazed numbly at his darkened fingers. "I feared this would happen," he whispered.

"No! It cannot! Not now!" Jane bunched up her cloak, trying to staunch the blood, but it poured out over her hands.

"They cannot truly heal," Thomas was saying with a dreadful calm. "They can only suspend hurt, and grant illusion. Without her magics . . ."

"Lady Jane!" cried Darius's voice from somewhere behind. "Thomas Lynne!"

"Here!" shouted Jane. "We are here! We need help! They will help you." She bunched the cloak more tightly against his wound and pressed harder. Thomas coughed, and a trickle of blood ran across his lips. "You will not leave me!"

"Hold me, Jane," he whispered. "This last time."

"No!" she screamed. "I will not! Not if you are going to give up!"

The three magic wielders topped the bank and galloped toward them.

"Gods all," whispered Corwin as they came up beside her and Thomas.

"Help him," begged Jane. "Please, you must help him!"

Corwin knelt at once beside Thomas and pushed Jane's hands gently away so he could lift up the cloak. He laid his hand on the other man's wounded side and went very still. He looked at his fellows and Jane was sure a moment of anxious and silent communication passed between them.

"Quickly, Miranda," said Darius.

Miranda at once stepped between the two men and took a hand of each. Her face went taut with concentration as she closed her eyes. Jane could see nothing, but she felt something stirring, some deep and restless force drawing itself up from the earth. The Sorcerers held out their hands, palms down flat over Thomas. Thomas writhed and cried out.

"You're hurting him!" shouted Jane.

They did not seem to hear. The men began to tremble, and the color fled Miranda's cheeks

"Too much, too far," Corwin gasped.

"We're losing him," said Darius.

"No!" Jane threw her arms around Thomas's shoulders. He felt as light as reeds and papers to her touch. He felt like he was dying.

*Thomas!* She reached out with heart and mind. *Thomas, you must hold on!*

He did answer, but it was so slow, as if from the depths of great pain. Farther even than he had gone when still in the Fae queen's grasp.

*It was worth it.* The faint words reached her. *To love you, even for a moment. It was worth it.*

*You will not leave me! I forbid it!*

*You forbid?* She heard the spark of his familiar mischief and she did not know if hope or fear would break her heart first.

*Yes!* She returned the thought, struggling to concentrate, to press closer. *I forbid! You have mastered me long enough. Now I have a thing or two to teach you, sir!*

In her mind's eye she searched for him, but it seemed she traveled through darkness. So lonely; this place inside was as lonely and bitter as a winter field.

*I have brought you only danger and darkness, Jane.* The words came soft and cold as falling snow.

*You have brought me love, Thomas. You have brought me*

*yourself. Please, please, if any of it was real, if you loved me even once beneath the glamour, stay with me now.*

*Even once?* Oh, Jane, I always loved you.

*Then stay with me now! I'm carrying your child, Thomas! You will not leave me alone with your child!*

*A child?* Wonder colored his fading voice. *How . . . ?*

But they both knew. She felt the memory of his hand in hers, strong and warm, of sunlight on skin and the smell of the spring breeze as they held each other in the garden. She seized on that memory with her whole heart, willing him to feel her hand, her fingers twined in his, to feel her pulling him close into her embrace so she could wrap her arms around him, press herself close to him so that he could feel her heart beat and she could feel his. She remembered him strong, she remembered the heat of his skin against her, the love and enticement in all his tender kisses.

She remembered Thomas with her and beside her, closer than anyone had ever been. She remembered love, and she held on.

"By all that's holy, he's coming round," breathed Darius.

"Hold on, Miranda!" said Corwin through clenched teeth.

"Hold on, Jane!" Miranda retorted.

But she was melting away and she knew it. The darkness and the cold and the sheltering love, her sense and dream of self were all falling away into the darkness. Down to where Thomas was. Her Thomas.

*Too far!* Someone was saying. *She's gone too far!*

# Thirty-one

"Open your eyes, Jane."

Jane stirred. She liked this place of peace, warmth and darkness. If she opened her eyes she might have to leave it.

"Remember obedience, Jane." Thomas's voice rumbled. "Open your eyes."

Slowly, Jane's eyes opened.

She lay on a huge four-poster bed under a mound of white coverlets with pillows tucked under her head. She was vaguely aware of a voluminous silken nightdress clothing her. But what she was most aware of was Thomas. Thomas, strong and whole and well, with his green eyes shining. The only change in him was his golden hair was now streaked with silver.

"What . . . happened?" Her throat was terribly dry. Cloth rustled as someone moved beyond her field of vision, and Thomas slipped his arm around her shoulders, gently helping her to sit. He held a glass to her lips.

"It's barley water," he told her. "Abominable stuff, but it will do you good. Drink slowly."

She did as he said, and he was right. It was abominable. But she was so thirsty she could have gulped down the whole glass if he'd let her.

Thomas set the glass aside and laid his broad hand on her brow. "You gave me a scare, my love."

"He would scarcely let anyone else near you." Miranda walked into Jane's line of sight and laid a cool hand on Jane's brow. "Thank goodness you are doing better. Corwin and Darius were ready to tie him to a chair to get him to stop his pacing."

Jane stirred and winced at the pain. Gently but firmly, Thomas pushed her back into the pile of pillows "How long have I been unconscious?"

"Two days," Thomas said. "Two very long days."

"I will tell the others you are on the mend," said Miranda briskly. "We will send for the doctor, just to be certain, I think we can safely say you've passed the greatest crisis."

With that, Miranda sailed out of the room, leaving Jane and Thomas alone.

At once Jane seized Thomas's hand as tightly as she was able. "Tell me everything. Are you . . . ?"

"I'm fine," he said at once, squeezing her fingers gently. "Our hosts were able to fully heal my body, although I seem to have gained a few years somewhere along the way." He brushed ruefully at the gray streaks at his temples. "And you, my dearest one, held my spirit long enough for them to do so. I owe you my life, Jane, not once but twice over." His voice grew soft and his face absolutely serious. "I thought I lost you, Jane."

She lifted her hand to his face, and laid her palm against his cheek. "And I you."

They stayed like that for a long moment. Jane gazed deep into Thomas's eyes. The green had dimmed a trifle now that he was no longer a Fae knight, but all that was important remained—all that was brave, mischievous, strong and true. No words came to Jane's mind, only warmth, and a sensation of sympathy and empathy that was worth more than any words.

"What of the Sorcerers?" Jane made herself ask, remembering the men's harsh doubts about Thomas's trustworthiness, even while they raced to his rescue.

"All is right there too. I am seen as a valuable source of information about Their Glorious Maj . . . the Fae court, and you may believe me, Jane, when I say I have been more than ready to tell their commander all I know. He's offered me a house and pension if I continue to work with his people. I told him I would and gladly. Jane . . ." He took a deep shuddering breath. "Jane, I've nothing. I am a man out of his time. I barely understand the place I am in, let alone how I shall make a living in it. I . . ."

"Hush," Jane clasped his hand again. "We will work out what is to be done. All of us together." She laid his hand against her belly.

"All of us together," he said, wonder filling his eyes as he gently caressed her. "My love."

He kissed her then, deeply and tenderly. His hand slid up from her belly to just underneath her breast.

"And when you are better," he whispered in her ear. "When we once again have a private place, we will discuss in detail what a minx you have been. I do not mean to resume mortal life with an unruly and disobedient bride."

She shimmied happily underneath his hand. "I am certain I do not know what you mean, sir. Perhaps I will need further instruction."

"And you shall have it, my love. As much as you desire."

He kissed her again, and Jane opened herself to him, to his touch and to his love. Jane knew that they all at last were safely home.

Keep reading for a preview of
the next novel by Marissa Day,

*The Fascination of Lord Carstairs*

Coming soon from Heat Books.

"Augusta, you *cannot* sneak away from your own engage-ment party."

Augusta Hartwell looked closely at her cousin. Valeria's brow was wrinkled and she held her mouth in a decided frown, with-out the crinkling around her eyes that indicated she was holding in a laugh. Her disappointment was genuine, then.

"I'm not sneaking away," Augusta replied levelly. "I need to go to the retiring room. Look." She displayed the gold ribbon dangling from the end of her bronze satin sleeve.

"You've been tugging on the thread for at least an hour to get that to come off. I *saw* you." Valeria spoke conversationally with a wave of her fan and a slow glance around the ballroom. Au-gusta frowned again, running through the possibilities of what the difference between tone and gesture meant. Probably Vale-ria did not want to draw attention to them, which was difficult, as she was talking with one of the grand celebration's two cen-ters of attention.

The other, Lord Edward Carstairs, Marquis of Warringsdale, was currently deep in conversation with Mr. Corwin Rathe, a man said to be very high up in government circles. Her fiancé's preoccupation was why Augusta had chosen now to make her escape. Judging by the intensity of the discussion, it would be a while before Lord Carstairs noticed her absence.

"Valeria, please." Augusta's fingers strayed to the cinnabar brooch she wore on the silver chain at her throat. It was a nervous gesture she'd never been able to break herself of. "I just need a breath of air. I'm exhausted from everyone staring."

The bright ballroom overflowed with a glittering crowd that included most of fashionable London. It seemed that every one of them was constantly glancing Augusta's way, gauging, judging, measuring. Worst of all was her family; her aunts, uncles and the entire flotilla of Hartwell nieces, nephews and cousins, not to mention her older sisters and brothers. All of them were on alert tonight, ready to pounce in with a covering remark or action in case Augusta did something embarrassing, said something untoward or did not remember to smile at reasonable intervals.

"They'll think you're going to meet someone," Valeria remarked.

"Is that what you think?"

"No, of course not." Valeria's face crinkled. In fact, they both knew Augusta having any sort of lover—secret or otherwise—was as far out of the realm of possibility as her drinking the Thames dry. "But you know how people are . . ." Valeria let her words trail off, and fanned herself furiously. Few members of Augusta's family had ever taken action to try to make things easier for her. Part of that was a consequence of being just one among a huge cohort. Part of it came because no one quite knew what to do with a girl who was utterly devoid of comprehension for the feelings of others. Only Valeria had ever tried to understand her.

"Don't be too long," said Valeria at last. "If we have to invent a sick headache for you, the aunts will never let either of us hear the end of it."

"Thank you." Augusta started toward the retiring room again at what she hoped was a casual pace.

Had she been any other woman, tonight would have been Augusta's moment of triumph. Uncle Gavin and Uncle Morris—her guardians since she was a child—had spared no expense. Her cadre of aunts had exercised every fiber of their well-developed tastes to make sure each detail of the celebration was perfect. The ballroom was a wonderland of light and color. Pink and gold silks hung on the walls, creating a shimmering backdrop for the profusion of scarlet roses and white orchids that filled every porcelain vase. Augusta herself had been dressed to coordinate with the decorations. Her gown of bronze, figured satin and gold ribbons had a train appliqued with white orchids. Her chestnut hair was piled high and dressed with creamy roses among the pearls and citrines. Girls who had tittered at Augusta behind their fans at their coming-out balls and had swept past her on the arms of new husbands now watched her with faces made white and pinched by jealousy.

And they whispered. Even as Augusta walked right past them, their cold words brushed her.

". . . look surprisingly well together, I thought, but *still* . . ."

". . . when he could have any woman in London . . ."

". . . imagine such a man with Augusta Heartless!"

Augusta kept her eyes straight ahead, as if she did not hear a thing. She had planned her retreat with great care during dinner, while she worried at the loose thread on her ribbon. Fortunately, the retiring room was empty of all except the ladies' maids, allowing her to walk right through into the dim, quiet house without having to stop and make conversation. Once in the main body of the house, she kept to the side corridors and, where possible, moved between adjoining rooms to lessen the possibility of being seen by such guests as inevitably wandered away from any society rout.

At last, Augusta reached the conservatory that was Uncle Gavin's pride and joy. She slid the pocket doors shut behind her and moved farther into the darkness, inhaling the scent of greenery and citrus. As warm as the conservatory was, it was cooler than the crowded ballroom by several degrees, and blessedly quiet. Alone among the moonlight and carefully tended orange trees, she could breathe, and she could think without anyone watching to make sure her expression was suitable to the occasion. When Augusta was not concentrating, her face had a tendency to go blank. A blank face was most emphatically not appropriate for a young woman at her engagement party, or so she had been informed by every single aunt, all four of her sisters and more than one niece.

She had tried very hard tonight. Lord Carstairs did not seem to have noticed anything amiss during their two dances. He certainly had not said anything. But then, her impression of him was that he was a discreet and polite man; a gentleman rather than a gallant. That suited her. She did not want gallantry. A gallant would expect her to blush and flutter her eyelashes and per-haps swoon. Such a man would at least expect her to feel, and to reciprocate feeling.

No matter how hard she tried, strong feeling for any other person was as far beyond Augusta as the moon. She fingered her brooch, her fingers tracing its familiar, knotted carvings where it hung just above the neckline of her gown. She heard people speak of affection, of familial love and—as she grew older—of passionate love. But Augusta found nothing she could recognize in their words, no answering chord of comprehension within herself. She had read dozens of novels passed to her by other girls, and worked her way through Byron, Keats and Shelley, studying them all carefully for clues as to what love must be. She watched her great cluster of nieces and cousins at the balls and parties she attended. She saw the others gaze into the eyes of their dance partners, saw them leaning together and sighing, and helped them as they schemed for a few minutes alone with their chosen one.

And absolutely none of it touched her. Oh, she could *feel*. She knew frustration, anger, sorrow. But this other emotion, the sympathy that connected one human being to another . . . that was utterly foreign to her. It was as if other people lived in a world of vibrant color and warm light, while she walked through soft gray mists.

It was the same when she looked at Lord Carstairs as when she looked at anyone else. She could see that he was handsome. His hair was a fine shade of chestnut and he wore it in a sailor's queue that looked quite well on him. He was tall and an active life and active service had left him with a finely shaped body.

She found his weathered face to be aesthetically pleasing, especially his bright gray eyes. Added to this, he had a considerable fortune, and unlike some members of the nobility, he took his parliamentary duties seriously, which kept his mind active and engaged.

It was a shame really. Augusta sighed. So much good fortune in a marriage partner should have been given to someone who had the ability to feel it. At the same time, it was those gray eyes that were giving rise to much of the disquiet that had caused her to need to remove herself from their celebration.

When Uncle Gavin and Uncle Morris had called her into the library to inform her of the proposal they had received, they had made it perfectly clear Lord Carstairs was looking for someone to keep his house, to raise any heirs and nothing more. The rush of relief she'd felt in that moment was, for her, intense. *Here,* she thought, *is a man with whom I will not have to pretend I am capable of comprehending love.* She had agreed to the arrangement at once.

Since then, however, the little time she had spent with Lord Carstairs had given her the impression that he was a man who was fully awake to the world around him. Augusta was accustomed to carefully observing those around her. Because it was so difficult for her to understand what they were feeling or what they meant, she needed all the clues she could possibly gather to navigate social situations. She feared his alert gaze, the way he seemed to understand what a person was thinking before they spoke. Such a man could not remain long ignorant of the malformation of her character. What if he decided he did not want to tie himself to a blighted woman and backed out of the marriage?

This, she knew, would bring much unpleasantness down on her and her family, While she might not possess a heart, she did have a conscience. The girls of her family were coming out and court-ing. If Lord Carstairs cried off the marriage, it would make their lives difficult. But she was the beggar in their agreement; his lordship could afford to be the chooser.

The long, low rumble of the pocket doors being drawn open rippled through the conservatory's silence. Augusta froze. Con-trary to what Valeria might fear, Augusta was sensible to the delicacy of her position. She had left her own engagement party and isolated herself in the conservatory. People would, in fact, think she was waiting for someone. There would be talk. Lord Carstairs would be embarrassed, and that could make for diffi-culties. Fortunately, except for the patches of moonlight stream-ing through the arched windows, the chamber was quite dark. Augusta moved to the shelter of a carefully contrived grove of potted orange and lemon trees where her shadow would not be distinguished from those of the plants. Surely it was only some-one looking for a moment's respite from the ballroom's crush, as she had done. They would stroll about the decorative plants for a few minutes, then leave, and she could return to her party. This time she would work harder to put a smile on her face for Lord Carstairs. She had practiced the expression in front of the mirror. She could do it.

Footsteps pattered lightly across the tiled floor. It was not one person who slipped into the conservatory, but two. A young man led a young woman by the hand. The young woman clearly had no trouble putting a smile on her face. Even in the dim moon-light, Augusta could see how the slender, pale flower of a girl gazed raptly at her companion, a dark-haired fellow come fresh to manhood, to judge by his wiry build. To Augusta's dismay, the pair moved directly into the curve of the little citrus grove, so only a thin screen of trees and greenery separated her from them.

But these two did not see her there behind the ferns and orange trees. They only had eyes for each other. The young man wrapped both arms around the girl's waist. As their bodies pressed more tightly together, levity deserted the couple, replaced by a strange intensity.

"Julian . . ." the girl whispered.

"Hush, Melissa. I know."

Julian cupped Melissa's delicate face in both his hands and lowered his mouth to hers. It was an open, heated kiss these two shared, unabashed and unhurried. Augusta stared, clenching her brooch. Julian's hands slid up Melissa's back, slowly, as if he treasured each inch of netted satin that passed under his palms. Then he moved them around to the side, brushing her breasts so that Melissa hummed low in her throat, even as her mouth continued to work against his.

At last they broke the kiss and Augusta thought they would leave, but they stayed, pressed against each other, smiling into one anothers' eyes.

"I need you." Melissa laced her fingers into her lover's dark hair. "Please, Julian."

"Oh, my dear," Julian breathed, and kissed her again, flicking his tongue lightly against her lips. "I want you so. But we should take care . . ."

"Please," whispered Melissa once more.

Julian, it seemed, had no heart to refuse her. Again they kissed, and Melissa's hands wandered freely over her lover's body, touching everywhere: shoulders, chest and muscled thighs, lingering especially over his taut buttocks. Julian sighed and growled and pulled her even close, crushing her soft body against him, rubbing his hips against hers until she gasped.

Augusta knew she should close her eyes. She should back away. But she could not move.

Julian turned Melissa in the circle of his arms so that her back was to him. He ran his hands lightly down her front, pausing at her breasts, stroking them lightly but thoroughly, so that she shivered against him and he smiled wickedly. Then he leaned her forward, keeping one arm wrapped about her waist and his hips pressed firmly against her as he opened the tapes of her dress with his other hand. He was more expert at such work than Augusta would have expected a man to be, for in a matter of moments, he was able to draw Melissa's shining ball gown over her head and lay it carefully aside on the ironwork bench.

Melissa swung her arms up over her head and pivoted on her toes to face her lover. The moonlight turned her chemise translucent, showing up her curved figure in clear silhouette. Julian went down on one knee and held out both hands. Melissa walked gracefully into his arms, fully aware, it seemed, of her own beauty in that moment.

Slowly, Augusta became aware of a strange sensation in her. The soft gray mists that always seemed to cradle her thoughts had thinned. In their place came an awareness of confinement, as if she pressed up against the cold, mullioned windows of the conservatory, watching the lovers from the far side.

Julian wrapped his arms around Melissa, bringing her close so he could rub his face against her belly. It was an intimate gesture, and the sensation of division, of the glass wall inside Augusta's mind strengthened. What was it these two had in them that she did not? What connected them so tightly?. She had searched and searched for answers to such questions, but her inability to comprehend had never seemed to her as monstrously unfair as it did in this moment.

Julian stood, dragging his hands up Melissa's rib cage, holding her gaze with his own as he brought his hands to her sloping shoulders. She was breathing hard, and her eyes were half lidded. She arched her back, and Julian pushed the sleeves of her chemise down to bare her breasts to the moonlight and his flashing gaze.

"Is it not beautiful?" said a man's voice behind her.

Shock caused Augusta to shoot upright.

"Don't worry, Augusta," whispered the man, and now she thought she heard a smile in his deep voice. "It's quite all right."

Now she recognized the voice. Lord Carstairs, her fiancé, stood behind her, and stood very close. She could sense the warmth and solidity of his strong body, and catch his masculine scent of leather, spice and brandy even over the heady aroma of the orange trees.

It was not possible to expire of shock, not really, but in that moment Augusta wished she could. Perhaps she could manage a faint. Her knees felt weak enough to buckle credibly.

On the other side of the screen of trees and greenery, Julian murmured to his Melissa. He closed his hands over both her bared breasts, kneading them firmly, watching the delight on her face. She grasped his forearms, pressing herself toward him.

"I was leaving," Augusta said, to Lord Carstairs, to herself, even as she watched Julian's hands working against Melissa's soft white breasts. His fingertips grasped her ruched nipple and rolled it back and forth. Melissa pressed her hand over her mouth to stifle her moan.

"I was leaving," Augusta said again.

"Shhh . . ." Lord Carstairs reached around and pressed two fingers lightly against Augusta's lips. His other hand closed about her arm, not so much holding in place her as firmly suggesting she should stay where she was. "Be patient a moment. I will get us both away."

Carstairs's hands were warm. Somewhere, distantly, Augusta was aware of that warmth spreading down her arms to pool low in her belly. Her lips felt the callouses on his fingertips, perhaps from the ropes he'd handled as a sailor. It was a gentle touch, but not soft. It would not be right if it was soft, she was oddly sure of that.

Lord Carstairs moved his hand from her mouth, but slowly, drawing those calloused fingers across her lips, leaving trails of light behind.

Julian was murmuring to Melissa. Reflexively, Augusta leaned forward, straining to hear. Her left hand pressed tight against her own belly. Lord Carstairs showed no sign of moving, or of taking his heavy, strong hand from her arm. She should pull away. She should leave on her own. This was wrong of her, of them. What this other couple did—the way they laid down to-gether on the tiled floor so Julian could kiss his way down the curve of Melissa's body as his hands slowly pushed her muslin chemise up over her thighs until he exposed the tangled nest of gleaming curls between them—this was indecent.

But watching it, staring at it, that was worse. Augusta knew she should at the very least turn away. This struggle inside her, this push of her awareness against the glass wall inside her mind, this was dangerous. She felt that instinctively. Glass could break, and once broken could not be made whole again. There was danger here. She must retreat, back into the safe, gray, distant place where she had always existed. The place that separated her from other people, from passions of all sorts, from love. That was the place where she was safe.

*What is this? Where do these thoughts come from?* A shudder ran through Augusta and she clutched her brooch until its figured edges bit into her hand.

Slowly, almost reverently, Julian lowered his head to Melissa's naked thighs. He kissed first one then the other as his hands shifted them apart. Melissa sighed into the palm of one hand while the other tangled in Julian's hair, urging him closer. Despite her urging, despite her sighs, Julian moved slowly, kissing and licking, but at last he pressed his smiling mouth to those dark curls. Melissa's hips lifted, and he tucked his hands beneath her, kneading and squeezing. He began to lick her there as well, hard and firm. Melissa squeezed her eyes shut and pressed her hand more tightly over her mouth to smother her cries. Her other hand she knotted tightly in Julian's hair, holding him in place, demanding that he continue.

"We can go now," breathed Lord Carstairs into Augusta's ear. "If you wish."

A question waited beneath those words. Could Lord Carstairs honestly believe she wanted to stay here and *watch*? She didn't. She couldn't explain this paralysis that had overtaken her, leaving her helpless to so much as turn away from the sight of Julian's hot, wicked actions with mouth and hands, and Melissa's wanton delight in all he did to her body.

And yet, she still couldn't move. Melissa had begun to thrash madly. Julian moaned against her and gripped her thighs as his mouth pressed more tightly against her. Something was happening, some change. Melissa's delight had taken on a fever pitch, and Julian held her hips tightly, squeezing and lifting her to his wicked kisses, taking her further, and further still, into the strange and dangerous world of delight.

"Please," whispered Augusta. "Take me out of here."

"Come then, Augusta." Gently but firmly, Lord Carstairs guided her toward the door.

Printed in the United States
by Baker & Taylor Publisher Services